Yesterday's Rainbow

January 30, 2007
to Koyei Arakaki
With fond memories
John Tanaka

Yesterday's Rainbow

A tall tale

John Tanaka

Xlibris
Philadelphia, Pennsylvania, Publishers

Dedicated to my five Ts especially to Amy and Dwight, and to Catherine Tarleton for holding my hand and not letting go.

Preface

Many Hawaiian words appear in this tall tale. For those who are unfamiliar with the language, please note that they all end in one of five vowels, a, i, e, o, u, each pronounced "a" as in ah, "i" as in is, "e" as in egg, "o" as in old, and "u" as in pull. Each vowel is pronounced even when it is strung together, like 'e'e'e (mischievous).

There is no plural form in the Hawaiian language ending with the letter "s." For example, whether it is one *lei* or many, the noun is still *lei*. A macron, a straight line over a vowel, indicates a plural noun or a long vowel.

I apologize for sprinkling words not found in Webster's. *Kala mai ia'u!* (Excuse!)

Many historical characters like Captain Cook and King Kamehameha live in this tale, but their settings, dialogue and lives are all purely fictional.

JT

The boast of heraldry, the pomp of power,
　　And all that beauty, all that wealth e'er gave,
Awaits alike the inevitable hour.
　　The paths of glory lead but to the grave.

"Elegy . . ."
By Thomas Gray

1

Captain James Cook, the great English explorer of the Pacific Ocean, left Tahiti in 1777 and pointed the nose of his flagship, HMS *Resolution*, to the North Pacific Ocean. His tender HMS *Discovery*, commanded by tubercular Captain Charles Clerke, followed several furlongs behind.

Cook was on a mission to discover for England the storied Northwest Passage linking Europe with the Orient. The expectation of gaining flag rank from the Admiralty and knighthood from King George III as rewards energized him. He fancied being called Admiral Sir James.

Unknown to him, he had another mission, a fateful one, ordained by pagan gods.

After penetrating the equatorial doldrums, Cook's sailing master saw a phantom outline on the horizon. He checked his maps. He looked again.

"Land tharrr!" he shrieked, eyes rolling.

Walking the deck nearby, Cook grabbed his telescope and aimed. *"Yes indeed,"* he mumbled. "Bligh, check the maps." William Bligh, Cook's sailing master, had them in hand.

"I just did, sir. That position shows only water."

"It's a discovery, sire," rejoiced Bligh's assistant, Ensign George Vancouver. They had sighted O'ahu, an island in the Hawaiian Island chain created by the Polynesian god Hawai'iloa million years before.

Proceeding northwest, Bligh again shrieked, "Land tharrr!" he pointed. Cook saw the hazy outline of Mount Wai'ale'ale on the island of Kaua'i. "There's got to be more islands around here," Cook said. "Let's check this one out. Get closer." Bligh took the *Resolution* past Kaua'i's southern shore and anchored off the eastern village of Līhu'e.

Frightened natives, still in the Stone Age, rushed out in their canoes and circled the ships, thought they were monstrous floating islands. Glimpse of a strange breed of people in alien clothes jolted them. "From *lani!* (heaven!)" a chief screamed.

Seeing the place inhabited shocked Cook.

"We're always second, Vancouver. New Zealand, Cook Isles, Tahiti, now this. How in hell did those Neanderthals migrate to this spot in the vast Pacific in those canoes without compass or astrolabe for direction? Did they just sprout from the soil?"

Vancouver said nothing; he knew the questions required no answers.

Cook squeezed his lips, marked an X on the spot of his nautical map with the date, January 23, 1778. "A rediscovery," he uttered with a frown, unaware that native Marquesans from Polynesia had beaten him to the isles a millennium earlier.

The captain thought of naming the isles "James Cook Archipelago." But, ah, he was after flag rank and knighthood, and jotted down the name of his superior, the First Lord of the Admiralty, the Earl of Sandwich. "Sandwich Islands" they became on his map.

With a squad of armed marines, he went ashore to reconnoiter the village. Native women walking the dusty trails, nursing piglets on their breasts, ducked for cover. Men quaked seeing the marines' muskets and shiny fixed bayonets. Metal! They had seen nothing beyond stone clubs and wooden spears. From the Stone Age they stumbled into the Iron Age.

Cook's party returned to shore, boarded their boats and headed back to their ships. They heard chatter from behind. Cook turned and saw a bunch of women, like mermaids, splashing water and chasing them. They followed the marines up the rope ladders and jumped onboard, hoping to get something from *lani*. Nude from waist up, some hinted of Iberian origin. George Vancouver had not seen more desirable women in all Polynesia.

Swarms of frenzied dregs greeted the mermaids. "God's gifts!" some crowed. Cook knew many were syphilitic but did nothing to prevent an impending disaster of cosmic proportion. Aware of his place in history, he logged his concern in the ship's journal, and disappeared into his quarters with a mermaid.

God forbid! The plunder of a virgin race began.

The girls wanted something. In half an hour, the dregs gave to them ejaculations of the devil's potions on deck, in hold below, even up in the crows' nests. In return they gave the girls iron nails.

More mermaids arrived. They all got nails in exchange.

In February 1778, the *Resolution* and *Discovery* pulled anchor and headed northeast behind schedule. They entered the North Pacific Ocean in late spring and saw walls of ice melting along the North American continental shores.

For the next three months, stubborn Cook, driven by the mystique of the Passage and by his ambition, poked *Resolution's* nose into every uncharted channel as far north as Russian America (now Alaska), hoping to find the mouth of the Passage. He failed. After late August, shadows became longer, and snow began to clothe the glaciers.

"Return to Sandwich Islands," Cook shouted. Even Bligh had trouble disguising his glee. The crew let out preorgasmic "Yahoo" from the bare thought of wintering again in paradise.

Reentering Hawaiian waters, Cook bypassed Kaua'i, surveyed the shores of O'ahu and Maui from the deck and, on January 17, 1779, anchored at tranquil Kealakekua Bay on the big island of Hawai'i.

The huge ships frightened the natives who had seen nothing beyond canoes. *"Auwē! Pilikia,* big trouble," they muttered.

Some thought the man dressed in white standing on the quarterdeck was Akua (God) Lono ika Makahiki returning from his spiritual realm to enjoy the Makahiki festivities starting soon in his honor.

Since only their King Kalani'ōpu'u could pronounce him a Lono incarnate, the local *kānaka,* the Hawaiians, wailed for his early return from Maui.

At next half-moon, a husky chief tattooed on his whole left side, arrived at the scene with his entourage.

King Kalani'ōpu'u, taking short steps, approached Cook on shore and stared at his tricorn naval hat. *"Auwē!"* he screamed, believing he had a triangular head. The king glanced halfway up the masts and mistook the crossbars for the image of Lono. *"Auwē!"* he screamed again.

At Cook's prearranged signal, the gunners on the *Resolution* fired two cannon salvos. The earthshaking boom-booms shook the king off his *malo* (loincloth). He saw how thunder and lighting originate in heaven. Convinced now of Cook's divinity, he mumbled something and escorted him to the *Hale o Mana* hut in the inner sanctum of his *heiau* (temple). He anointed Lono Incarnate with oil and fell prostrate at his feet.

Cook knew he was being mistaken for a pagan god, but did nothing to quash the myth. He had practiced playing deity on other South Pacific shores and brought it to a fine art. He even developed a godly gait when receiving a prostrating chief's hospitality, and never stopped wringing him for more.

For the next three weeks in Lono's name, King Kalani'ōpu'u entertained the Incarnate and his crew during the Makahiki Festivals with feasts and orgiastic carousals of the most bestial kind. More maidens received syphilitic ejaculations that would curse the people and Hawai'i for over a century.

The good times for Cook had to end. In early February 1779, he weighed anchor for a final swing of the Arctic. While still tacking in Hawaiian waters, the *Resolution* and *Discovery* rammed into a typhoon. The ships suffered heavy storm damages.

Cold native stares greeted Cook when he limped back to Kealakekua to make ship repairs.

The Makahiki Festivals were over, God Lono had departed for his realm, and the old chapter had closed. The *ali'i* were ready to resume their internecine wars to grab each other's land.

Cook sensed a disturbing change in the *kānaka's* mood. He was unaware that doubt of his divinity had spread on shore.

"He lusted too humanly, and he lied," the *kāhuna* (priests) said. "He promised his sword to our king, but gave him just few nails when he left."

"Would Lono lie?" another *kahuna* asked, shaking his head.

Junior Chief Kamehameha, who would one day become King of Hawai'i, watched the crippled "floating islands" return clumsily to their earlier berths. *How could God Lono's ships be so stricken?* he thought, as doubt of Cook's divinity also welled in his mind.

The captain and his marines were on shore gathering materials for ship repairs when a bloody altercation erupted with the natives. "Watch out, Captain!" a marine yelled from his shoreboat a moment too late. A chief's dagger found Cook's heart. Spurting blood, he staggered and fell on the shore clutching the dagger handle. Embarrassed over his helpless circumstance, Cook reached out for the angels who had come to take him to the netherworld.

Kamehameha's doubt hit target; only mortals bleed and have a death date: February 14, 1779. Cook had returned to fulfill a destiny ordained by pagan gods to end his godly myth.

Kalani'ōpu'u got Cook's sword and his skull, Kamehameha his scalp.

Captain Clerke hurriedly fixed storm damages, took command of the mission, coughed more tubercular germs into the wind and headed for home without Cook's remains on February 22, 1779, skipping the Arctic.

In London he reported to the Admiralty and to the Royal Society what mattered most, the death of Cook, the expedition's failure to find the Passage, and discovery of the Sandwich Islands. He mentioned nothing about the transgressions of his crewmen upon a virgin people.

Clerke's report exposed Hawai'i to a scheming nineteenth-century world, as God Wākea had feared.

The expedition also exposed to the Hawaiian chiefs the awesome power of Western firearms. Kamehameha realized that control of the Isles rested with the chief who could muster them most, quickest.

A race was on.

2

In 1758, a beautiful chiefess of non-sacred *kapu* (taboo) rank, Keku'iapoiwa II, was in labor with a single attendant. She was writhing for days on marshy ground in the bog of Kohala, on the big island of Hawai'i. It was a place where ghostly night marchers frequently filed past their old haunts. At last on the third night she gave birth to a huge bastard boy already half-man, and named him, Kamehameha. Many chiefs had been enjoying her intimate favors, including sacred *Nī'aupi'o kapu* chief Keōua of Ka'ū and King Kalani'ōpu'u. She wondered who might have fathered her son.

The boy inherited his mother's non-sacred *kapu wohi* rank that relegated him to a backup role in Hawaiian affairs. But his fortune changed in 1769. Keōua, seeing future greatness in the youth, claimed Kamehameha, eleven, impulsively as his second son.

But Keōua suddenly died of sickness at twenty-eight. King Kalani'ōpu'u seized the chance, claimed Kamehameha as his second son and made him a chief of his junior line.

A master at warcraft, the king drilled his son on matters a chief should know. "Show reverence, praise your gods often," he said. "Warriors follow a pious chief into battle believing the gods would be on his side.

"Understand the deeper meanings of *pono* and *'Ai kapu*. *Pono* is not just moral goodness, it is a blissful state of cosmic equilibrium in the land when the Ali'i nui is in *pono*. If a chief plans war on you, the equilibrium is upset. The only way you can restore *pono* is to obey God Kūkā'ilimoku's demand, that you go to war against that chief and defeat him.

"'*Ai kapu* is not only our fundamental *kapu* that ritually separates women from polluting men. It empowers any chief to challenge authority to restore *pono*, what King Umi-o-Liloa did centuries earlier."

Challenge authority! That clicked in Kamehameha's young mind.

The king spent his longest time on God Kūkā'ilimoku's esoteric *heana kanaka i'aloa*, the human sacrificial ritual. "The God is hungry for male human offerings," he told Kamehameha. "But he must be fed correctly. You must transfer the spirit of the body on the altar to the God. If you fail, your *mana* (spiritual power) will sink before your *ali'i* witnesses, and Kūkā'ilimoku will disown you. I'll show you the correct way with real bodies on the altar."

The king blundered when he let his young queen Kanekapolei teach Kamehameha the secrets of love. With hands-on coaching, she gave birth to his first child, a son. They named him Ka'oleioku.

When Kamehameha reached manhood at sixteen, the townfolks of St. Andrews, Scotland, were already into a game called golf. The big, unusually quiet young chief preferred eating alone, seldom talked or laughed, approved with a nod and disapproved with silence. He owned a large face, a narrow, hairy forehead, a droopy mouth and a stout nose that separated his round menacing eyes. Without a youthful hint, even stoneagers thought him unhandsome.

As a member of the king's junior line, Kamehameha lacked the *mana* (spiritual power) to become a towering chief. His fortune again changed.

After Cook's apotheosis in 1779, King Kalani'ōpu'u, having fought his last battle and feeling his end, named his sacred senior son Kiwala'ō his heir, and bequeathed to him all his lands except the *moku* of Kona and Kohala. He saved them for Kamehameha. And in an unexpected move, the king also entrusted Kamehameha with his feather war god Kūkā'ilimoku, god Kū's pivotal embodiment. "Guard him with your life, march into battle with him," he told Kamehameha.

He swore he would.

Having Kūkā'ilimoku gave to Kamehameha the *mana* that he lacked and intensified his mystique, made him a legitimate usurper of kingly power, a fact not lost on a jealous, frightened Kiwala'ō.

Kamehameha began to attract unaligned *ali'i*, including Ke'eaumoku, a thoroughbred with blood ties to the great chiefs of Maui, and Chiefs Hoapili and Kalanimoku, also of Maui, who opted to lay in fealty before him, not Kiwala'ō.

King Kalani'ōpu'u died in 1782. Kiwala'ō inherited his lands, but his clever uncle stole some choice lands. When Kamehameha received nothing in *kālai'āina* (land redistribution), his chiefs recommended war to restore cosmic equilibrium in the land, what Kalani'ōpu'u had taught Kamehameha. "Plan the strategy," he told Kalanimoku.

Kiwala'ō caught the mood. He decided to march on Kona and crush his brother Kamehameha before he became a menace.

They converged at Moku'ōhai, a fishing village south of Kealakekua Bay. Kiwala'o, arriving first, took the high ground. He had a simple strategy: with overwhelming force, drive Kamehameha's men towards the sea and slaughter them in water.

He saw Kamehameha enter the village with his commanders, including Ka'iana, the cunning half brother of Maui King Kahekili. Kiwala'ō lined his troops in a *kahului* (crescent) formation and charged. Kalanimoku saw them coming with spears, slings, clubs and daggers. He formed a *kūkulu* line formation of his troops to confront them. They met near the shore. In a pitch battle Kiwala'ō's superior numbers inflicted heavy casualties. His crescent began to close.

Just when the battle seemed hopeless, Chief Ke'eaumoku saw Kiwala'ō at the point of his crescent exhorting his troops. He stealthily approached and pounced, grabbed Kiwala'ō by his throat and sank his thumbs between his clavicles. Blood spouted, his body quivered. Without field command, his crescent crumbled.

Momentum shifted to Kamehameha's side. "Kill everyone!" Ka'iana yelled. The battle of Moku'ōhai was soon over. Kamehameha claimed all of Kiwala'ō's gods, lands, and people and became, at twenty-four, the youngest Ali'i nui (Chief Ali'i) of the island of Hawai'i. With Ke'eaumoku's thumbs, *pono* (righteousness) momentarily returned to the *'āina* (land).

Kamehameha laid his brother on Kūkā'ilimoku's *lele* (sacrificial) altar and performed his first *kapu luakini* ritual without coaching. He succeeded, barely. Although they were never close, an intense compassion for Kiwala'ō seized Kamehameha during the ritual. He wondered why.

It hit him months later. He realized that any body before Kūkā'ilimoku was ritually just short of himself lying on the altar to restore *pono*. His succeeding passionate rituals became storied. His *mana* escalated.

Kiwala'ō's younger brother, High Chief Keōua, retreating from Moku'ōhai to his land of Ka'ū, pledged revenge. "Kamehameha will lie on my *lele* altar," he pledged. The land was again in disequilibrium.

After Moku'ōhai, Ke'eaumoku gave to Kamehameha his beloved daughter Ka'ahumanu, seven, to solidify his position with him.

"Ho'omaika'i" (Beautiful), Kamehameha said, and warmly received the child.

She was born around 1775 inside a cinder-cone cave in Pu'ukau'iki, Hāna, Maui. Her mother, *Kapu* Chiefess Nāmāhana, half sister of Maui's King Kahekili, wondered who was her blood father. Among her lovers, Ke'eaumoku, with his long face and very large mouth, resembled the child most. He clinched the honor and became her husband.

Kamehameha developed an occult love for the child and a fear of her that lasted a lifetime. He married her when she turned nine and brought her into his nine-hut *kauhale*, his compound in 'Upolu, near the Mo'okini *luakini heiau*. His three other queens ignored the child bride at first, but they soon brought her into their fold. They realized she was Kamehameha's favorite.

Ka'ahumanu had a hard core that surfaced early. When Kamehameha denied her from eating pork and banana, foods *kapu* to women, she went into a rage, scratched his face from temple to mouth, but he forgave.

Ka'ahumanu was sex driven. By fourteen she had shifty eyes for boys her junior, often driving them with abandon when the Ali'i nui was away.

She also craved power. She cared little if her husband kept adding wives and ladies-in-waiting, including some commoner girls he spotted, so long as his over a hundred illegitimate children didn't challenge her for power.

None dared.

3

After Captain Clerke exposed Hawai'i, Western ship captains began checking her out, found a one-stop destination for everything they wanted: provisions, fresh water, calm harbors, materials for making ship repairs. And women. Notoriety of the place spread.

The captains learned of the chiefs' craze for western firearms. In exchange for two-dozen rusted muskets of the English-Bengal war vintage, some even older, the harpy captains got all the pleasures they wanted on land and enough provision to go to Canton in style. Both sides in the barter were in a titter.

One February day in 1789, Kamehameha received a stunning gift of arms.

It came about with Simon Metcalfe, forty-eight, gruff, square-jawed English captain of his gunship, *Eleanora*. Needing a deckhand for his coming trip to China, he hired an Englishman, Isaac Davis, thirty-one, a drifter along the holes of Liverpool after the American Revolutionary War. "Put him to work under you," he told *Eleanora's* boatswain, John Young.

Davis quickly impressed Metcalfe with his seafaring savvy. He told no one how he acquired it. "That's my son, Captain Thomas Metcalfe," he said, pointing to him standing alongside Simon's other schooner, the *Fair American*. "He's going to Philadelphia soon to accept delivery of English weaponry. We're meeting at Kealakekua Bay, Sandwich Islands, to gather provision and leaving together for China. Davis, you're his boatswain."

Stunned by his quick promotion, he rushed to shake Thomas's soft hands. "I am pleased to serve you, sir," he said.

After a smooth sail to America. the *Fair American* went up the Delaware River in July 1788.

They called on Colonel Clyde Stensen of the army's Quartermaster Corps, reaching him quickly.

"Sir, I'm Thomas Metcalfe. We came to take delivery of an order of English weapons placed by my father, Simon. Are you familiar with it, sir?"

"Indeed," the colonel said. "They are ready for pickup. I will take you there." They were led into a huge wooden storage shed. "There it is," Stensen said, pointing to a pile of weapons stacked neatly in military posture.

A former English Redcoat at Yorktown, Virginia, Davis instantly recognized the weapons he had used before Marquis General Cornwallis surrendered his army to Washington in 1781. Davis squinted down the whale oil-lined barrels of several muskets and cannons. He found no rust. He picked a musket at random, loaded a round, pointed it at the ground and squeezed the trigger. The flintlock worked fine. The ammunition was dry.

"Accepted, sir," Davis said, beaming. The two went onboard the *Fair American*. Davis dragged out a metal tub filled with gold coins from under his bunk and finished the transaction in ten minutes.

"Can your men rig a cannon on the foredeck? We'll pay," Davis asked.

"We'd be glad to, *gratis,*" the colonel said.

Two mornings later, the *Fair American*, loaded with booty, sailed proudly down the Delaware for destination Kealakekua Bay six months away with a cannon mounted on her foredeck. "Fine work," Thomas congratulated Davis.

A dreadful end awaited Thomas at destination.

Father Simon had arrived earlier in the Sandwich Isles. With time to spare before meeting his son, he entered Kona harbor, north of Kealakekua Bay, to trade for provision, unaware of the natives' compulsive urge to steal anything off a *haole* boat.

Over fifty natives went onboard with baskets of bananas, coconuts, dog meat and sweet potatoes to barter. Simon, on the watch, spotted a *kanaka* slip something into his *malo*. "Cut his loincloth, get it back," he yelled, pointing at him. The crew cut it off, recovered an iron wrench and threw Chief Nalu overboard. His loincloth fluttered down.

Nalu vowed revenge. But before he could, Simon left for Olowalu on the southern coast of Maui to finish restocking with no thought of making history.

That evening, Simon roped down his shore boat with an armed guard onboard. *One less thing to do in the morning*, he figured. When day broke he saw just the rope dangling.

Pointing to it he screamed to the natives coming on board to barter.

Intimidated by Simon's red neck, they brought back a finger and a piece of wood. Simon knew the finger was the guard's and the wood, stripped of metal, was from the boat's keel. In full-blown rage, he ordered his crewmen, "Rake um!" The foredeck became a quagmire of slippery blood. They blew scores more off their canoes in a historic massacre.

Still not satisfied, Simon bombed Olowalu. After washing blood off the deck he left for Kealakekua Bay, dropping anchor in January 1789 near the spot where Cook's *Resolution* had been. He finished restocking and waited for his son to arrive. Weeks went by. His crewmen kept panning the horizon from the crow's nest for the *Fair American*.

A bored John Young left for shore with four armed guards to explore the inland. When they failed to return at dusk, Simon fired a cannon round signaling them to get back. He fired additional rounds next morning. "Damn," Simon blurted. He weighed anchor and left for China, hoping he would meet Thomas in Canton.

After fixing storm damages in Rio, a tired Thomas Metcalfe sailed into Kona Bay weeks later, instead of Kealakekua. He had what Kamehameha wanted most.

At the Bay fishing, Chief Nalu couldn't believe seeing another tall ship arrive with a cannon on her foredeck. *What a present for Kamehameha!* he crowed. Nalu and his men climbed on board the *Fair American* with baskets of fruits for the captain. Seizing a moment of chance they pounced, killed Thomas and his crew except one and dumped their bodies overboard for the delectation of crabs. The group snagged Isaac Davis hiding in the hold and kept him as a prize.

The masterless schooner bobbed in the Bay waiting to be claimed.

A runner rushed to Kealakekua. He told Kamehameha, "Nalu captured tall ship in Kona with a cannon, plenty western weapons and ammunition and a *haole* (white man) hiding in the boat."

Kamehameha screamed, *"'Oia 'ea?"* (Really?) He told Chief Kalanimoku, Ka'ahumanu's cousin, "Watch these *haole*," meaning John Young and his four armed guards.

He rowed hard to the Bay and saw Nalu waving from the deck of a sleek schooner. The Ali'i nui went alongside and climbed on board. "This boat is yours," Nalu said. "The captain and crew except one are dead."

Kamehameha went to the cannon, ran his hands down the big gray barrel and went below. His eyes widened when he saw the cache of muskets, bayonets, cannons, cannon balls, grapeshot and ammunition. *"Maika'i,"* he whispered, and rubbed his nose against Nalu's, his sincerest expression of thanks.

He stepped inside the captain's quarters, saw a metal tub below the bunk. He pulled it out. "Uaa," he yelled seeing a hoard of gold coins.

The stunning unexpected gift of the ship and cargo astounded Kamehameha.

"Prepare a feast for Nalu," he said. Coming from the Ali'i nui, it meant something huge.

That afternoon Kalanimoku dragged John Young and Isaac Davis to the party as Kamehameha's guests.

"John!"

"Isaac!"

The dumbfounded friends greeted each other.

"They got you too?"

"Yes, with four of my men while we were on shore at Kealakekua," Young said.

They laughed at each other in flimsy loincloths.

Kamehameha sat downwind of an *imu*, an underground oven, inhaling the aroma of a reef shark baking. An hour later, the cooks raised it from the *imu* and laid it onto a *koa* board. The meat, hanging off the cartilage, smelled of crab, the favorite food of reef sharks. After the *kāhuna* performed their propitiatory chant to the gods, the cooks placed the fish before a hungry Kamehameha. He tore large chunks off the underbelly and swallowed them whole. In fifteen minutes he was *pau* (finished) eating. He washed his hands in a gourd bowl, drank the murky water, burped and left, forgetting to thank Nalu or welcome his *haole* guests. He spent the rest of the moonlit evening onboard the *Fair American* pacing her deck and playing with gold coins. The reflection of the moon off the oil-lined cannon barrel intoxicated him.

He had gruff, square-jawed Simon Metcalfe to thank.

Eleven years after Cook, Thomas Metcalfe gave to Kamehameha an overwhelming firepower advantage over Kiwala'ō's younger brother, Keōua, if only the captured *haole* would teach his men how to use iron weapons.

Young and Davis often laughed over their plight while planning escape, believing their cunning would be no match for an aborigine. Twice Kamehameha caught them in fetal, stowaway position in holds of visiting ships. He rubbed their heads and forgave.

They were too valuable to punish.

Kamehameha made life comfortable for the two, building for Young and Davis seven-hut compounds, each staffed with male cooks, servants and maidens ready to satisfy their every want. It was a lifestyle more opulent than anything they could have had in the holes of Liverpool.

The *haole* began to settle in. They learned to speak broken Hawaiian, enough to communicate. Two girls in Davis's compound showed early signs of pregnancy. The thought of escape began to fade.

As months passed, Davis and Young found loincloths comfortable, slept soundly on the ground, ate roast dog, raw fish, *poi* (taro paste) with dirty fingers, hardly missing the niceties of English utensils. They learned the secrets of *pono* and *mana*, and began to observe *kapu* days with prescient knowledge of the gods' demands.

The two became *haole* pagans.

Kamehameha brought Young and Davis into the inner sanctum of his War Council, giving to each the chance to share in the spoils of war. It was exciting, heady stuff for the two who possessed nothing of consequence before captivity.

They showed him the way to power.

4

In early March 1789, Kamehameha summoned Davis to his compound. When he arrived he found a motley bunch of thirty-five heavily tattooed young men milling around. *Who they?* he thought.

"I handpicked them," Kamehameha said. "Teach them how to use iron weapons, so they can teach others. I want a mixture of warriors armed with iron weapons, clubs, spears and slings, to fight as a team. You think it's a good idea?"

An integrated unit. Might work, Davis thought, *but can anyone teach those Stone Agers how to fire muskets and cannons?* He saw a young cripple in the bunch with an owl perched on his shoulder. *What is he doing here?* he wondered.

The Ali'i nui read his mind. "I want a miracle," he said.

"When do I start preparing?"

"Now."

That sealed Davis's commitment. He assembled a *kahuna* corps of carpenters, drew sketches on dirt of portable wooden mounts for the cannons and caissons and said, "I want three each by tomorrow."

He conscripted twelve cooks and sixty lithe, quick-footed men to tote the cannons and do heavy labor. After a week's search for a bivouac site, Davis chose Hōlualoa on the western slope of active volcano Hualālai. It was cool there and close to home.

He called the thirty-five and told them, in tolerable Hawaiian, "We go to Hōlualoa next week, stay there for six weeks. I will teach you how to use English weapons and fight like English soldiers. Understand?"

"*Ae,*" they yelled, looking at Kamehameha standing nearby.

On departure morning Davis passed out bandoleers, muskets and bayonets in scabbard to the trainees, and showed them how to wear or carry them. "From this moment you are going to sleep, eat and shit with them next to you. Understand?"

They wondered why, but nodded.

Only the young cripple Alapa'i, just thirteen, had an inkling.

Kamehameha declared, "Hōlualoa *noa*," free of *kapu*. He wanted the *ali'i* and commoners to mix together and train free of ritual constraints.

Davis, wearing a *malo*, glanced foolishly at him and bellowed to his men, "Follow me!"

Kamehameha went to Kealakekua Bay on a canoe with fifteen paddlers. He met Young on board the *Fair American* and asked, "Teach my best canoe paddlers how to handle your ship."

No chance, Young thought.

The trainees arrived at their bivouac site near a brook after a two-hour march over bushy terrain, and dispersed with assigned duties. They cleared a field for close-order drills, found lava caves facing south for sleeping and storing ammunition, and dug latrines and *imu* (underground ovens) for roasting staples like taro, sweet potatoes, breadfruit and green bananas. After a dinner of only staples, Davis gathered his troops and told them, "We begin physical training tomorrow morning. We start easy. Those who quit must go home. Understand?"

They kept quiet. That night, even the toughest-talking *kānaka* avoided sleeping in caves, fearing the cold touch of *'uhane hele*, the wandering spirits. They slept bunched in the open, preferring the comfort of each other's snores.

The cripple Alapa'i slept alone. The trainees thought he did not belong and wondered why Kamehameha had picked him. *He'll soon fail,* they predicted. Owl Lola, Alapa'i's companion, stayed close by and knew better.

Next morning, Davis led the troops on a quick march up the slopes of Hualālai with muskets slung on their shoulders. Some big guys dry heaved. Mālolo, a big guy, would have never made it back to camp if Alapa'i didn't lug his musket in addition to his. *"Mahalo nui"* (Thank you very much), he sheepishly said to Alapa'i when they returned to camp.

Later in the week near day's end, the troops found a stream spilling a smallish waterfall into a hole about twenty feet wide.

"Jump in," Davis said, in the day's first welcomed order. They dove in nude, drank the cool mountain water with hint of ginger and let their exhaustion float downstream.

No one asked Alapa'i to join. He went downstream alone to soak with Lola hovering above. Mālolo appeared, asked Alapa'i, "Can I join you?"

The trainees passed the first week of drills with shoulder aches and blistered feet.

Davis gathered his men and told them, "From this week you are going to learn how to use iron weapons, what you came here for."

They cheered the break from forced marches.

He pulled a bayonet from scabbard, touched its sharp point and said, "We start with this. A Frenchman in the town of Bayonne invented it about the year sixteen hundred."

Bayonne? Sixteen hundred? They meant nothing to them.

"You fix it to the muzzle-end of the musket like this. In combat you try to poke it into the enemy's biggest target, his belly. If you miss, give him the butt. Watch." With a shrill he lunged forward and pierced a dummy's belly, withdrew and swung the butt end into it. The dummy shattered.

Davis's speed astonished the cadremen. The bayonet became a frightening weapon. Some gave it a religious significance. "God Kū is the god of everything straight for female penetration. This bayonet is Kū." Respect for it soared. The cadremen remained on the field poking dummy bellies long after the orchestrating birds had called it a day.

Next morning, Davis had them around the *kanona* (cannon). "At Yorktown, Virginia, in 1781, we used this exact weapon. You will learn to fire it today."

Davis identified the functional parts and passed out some balls. "When you fire, this ball will go through the *palala* (barrel), travel over five hundred feet and smash into the target." Davis paced off five hundred feet. The weight of the ball and distance it went impressed the recruits.

"Three men operate a *kanona*. One swabs the *palala* like this after each firing, another reloads from muzzle end like this, and the leader brackets the target with the *kanona* sight and fires. The team must fire a round in less than twenty seconds," Davis said, stressing his last words.

"How long that?" the cadre men asked. Davis tapped up to twenty. They got the number.

Alapa'i listened, shaking his head.

"Show us," the troops yelled. Davis hoped he remembered. It was at Yorktown eight years earlier where he fired it last. Pointing to a boulder about four hundred feet away he said, "I'll try to smash it in three. Two of you help me."

One trainee swabbed the barrel, the other loaded and Davis aimed. "Cover your ears," he yelled and fired; the ball landed way left of the target, creating a dust storm. The cadremen screamed, beholding the cannon's earth-moving power.

Davis exhaled, pumping his arm.

He fired the second. It landed right of the target.

He stopped to explain. "You see I have bracketed the target with the first two shots? I'll adjust my sight in-between the two and will fire three.

"Understand?"

"*Ae.*" They kind of understood.

"Close your ears." He prayed and fired. With the explosion of powder the target lost its shape. Davis thanked his god, clenching his fist.

The cadremen thought it the work of an angry god.

Thirteen-year-old Alapa'i didn't cheer. Davis caught his negative attitude and asked, "What do you think?"

Without a hint of boast he said, "I was thinking, we must hit target in two, maybe one. Save ammunition, iron balls, and gain speed that way."

"Want to try?" Davis belligerently asked.

Alapa'i nodded.

"Go ahead," Davis said.

Alapa'i asked for no help. He swabbed, loaded and fired four quick practice rounds. His eyes caught each shot's trajectory in slow motion. He thought a cannon was nothing more than a powered sling.

"I am ready," he said.

Davis called his cadremen to watch the deformed in action. Pointing to a sidehill boulder about three hundred feet away, he asked Alapa'i, "Destroy it in two." No one except Mālolo thought he might.

Alapa'i squinted through the sight and fired, intending to strike it in one. He missed high by a whisker. He made a fine adjustment and fired two. The target disappeared as shrapnel of stone.

The cadremen erupted. Mālolo smiled. Davis shrugged. *Just lucky* he thought. He was more impressed with Alapa'i's speed, getting off the second shot by himself in less than ten seconds.

Davis picked a boulder farther away.

Distance didn't matter, Alapa'i already knew a shot's trajectory. He took aim and smashed it in one.

Forgetting his gawky walk and distorted face the recruits yelled, "*Maika'i!*" to the kid who didn't belong. Lola flew down and perched on his right arm, made eye contact as if in praise.

The five-feet-eight Alapa'i humbled Isaac Davis and became an instant giant among his peers. They wanted to sleep next to him, eat with him to get his *mana*. Owl Lola was satisfied.

That night the twinkle of a lone star kept Davis awake. *Who is this freak; how did he do it?* he thought, and half-dozed.

Alapa'i was born a *kaukau ali'i*, the lowest rung of the *ali'i* caste in 1778. His genealogy showed no lineage to a god. At birth, his left leg was longer than his right, and his right eye was noticeably lower than his left. It was common practice among *ali'i* families to take deformed babies out to sea and let go. His parents refused.

Alapa'i's father, Kekaha, died early. He fought with Kamehameha at Moku'ōhai in 1782, where an enemy spear from behind closed his life. In the passion of the moment, his wife joined him in death. Alapa'i, four, became an instant orphan.

No one cared except commoners Waimano and his wife, Ke'enai, who toiled on Kekaha's *kō'ele*, a small land subdivision. They loved Alapa'i, and asked the chief succeeding Kekaha, "Can we *hanai* (adopt) him, please?" Normally, commoners couldn't adopt an *ali'i*. But these were not normal times.

"You sure?" the chief asked, puzzled that anyone would want him. Ke'enai nodded with loving eyes.

"He is yours," he said.

Alapa'i grew up as a loner, not by choice. Other children in the *kō'ele* avoided playing with a deformed, had fun making fun of him. Only his new parents and owl Hina, Lola's older sister stuck close by.

Hina, with brown and white feathers, had a wingspread of about two feet, and a saucer-like facial disk around her large forward eyes that defined her wise-looking face. She had a sharp, hooked beak for hunting preys at night, and yellowish eyes, with intense black pupils that could see in the dark. With her powerful legs and long talons she could squeezekill even a baby mountain pig. Pagan gods gave to

Hina an instinct to look after the deformed Alapa'i and be his companion.

The gods also passed on to Alapa'i uncanny gifts for slinging. He could sense downrange wind velocity and direction by the air passing over his ears, and see his projectiles moving in slow motion. By seven, he could whirl a two-inch rock and whip it with astounding gravity-defying speed to target.

Waimano never suspected Alapa'i's gift until they went hunting. The boy kept knocking unconscious fast-moving boar with a whip of his wrist. Waimano wondered.

It crushed young Alapa'i one day when his dear owl Hina perched on his arm for the last time and died in his hands, perhaps of old age. But her younger sister Lola came to his side. She had Hina's wise look, the facial disk around her intense eyes and the instinct to protect Alapa'i.

At twelve, Alapa'i's fortunes leaped. People in Kona heard of his slinging prowess and pushed him into a contest with the village's perennial slinging champ, the giant Hanawai.

Kamehameha went to watch.

As usual, it was a contest of who could knock three coconuts off lava pedestals about forty, sixty and eighty feet away in fewest attempts.

The confident champion gathered twelve stones before him and said, "You go first." Alapa'i nodded. He sensed the downrange airflow, planted his longer left leg on a rock and began to whirl. With successive quick wrist flicks, his stone missiles blasted all three coconuts off their pedestals—in three.

Hanawai rubbed his eyes and went downrange to see, found the stones had impaled into the tough coconut husks. Shaking his head he walked back and gave his sling to Alapa'i, the ultimate submission of a competitor.

Alapa'i thought it no big thing, but not Kamehameha. Despite the boy's handicaps and young age, he picked Alapa'i in February 1790 to join the cadre corps. It would be the most far-reaching strategic decision of his life.

After seven intensive days on the *kanona* the cadremen found the workings of the thirty-five pound English flintlock musket simple. They were finished with target practice in two days.

The trainees were gathered one evening around a campfire, their minds far away. Davis interrupted their reverie. "Let's give Hawaiian names for the *kanona*, musket and bayonet," he suggested.

The group awoke. "Good idea!" Nalu said.

"Let's start with the *kanona*. It's half-English. How about 'Lopaka?' That's me, my nickname."

They couldn't refuse the captor of the *Fair American*.

"Let's honor Thomas Metcalfe," Naniloe said. "How's 'Koma,' Thomas, for the musket?" *Dull*, they thought but they settled on "Koma."

"The bayonet. No need to honor anybody," Pai'ā said. "Because it's for poking, how's *ule?*" He pointed at his penis. The men convulsed. *Ule* stuck.

Ke'eaumoku smiled at Davis, told him, "Your name 'Isaac' too difficult to pronounce. You also need a Hawaiian name. How's 'Aikake?'"

Hmmm, Aikake. "All right, I'll take it."

On the last training day in April 1790, owl Lola saw a chief and his retinue approaching.

She swooped down, alerted Alapa'i. He went downhill to check. "Ali'i nui!" he shouted when he got closer. Hōlualoa hills reverberated with cadremen's roar. Kamehameha had come. They ran toward him and knelt.

"Rise, rise. I came see how you were doing."

He smoothed the hair of a kneeling Davis. "Training successful?" he asked.

"*Ae*, very. You have thirty-five teachers ready to train *kānaka* recruits."

"How did Alapa'i do?"

"Fine. He is a genius."

"I thought so."

"Watch him."

Davis called his unit to formation. Pointing to a boulder about six hundred feet away he ordered Alapa'i, "Destroy it."

With his Lopaka and caisson haulers Alapa'i moved stealthily forward. At around three hundred feet from target, he stopped, loaded a round and signaled. His men hit the ground and covered their ears. Alapa'i let one go. A quake awakened the gods. His single shot smashed the boulder into smithereens.

"You wanted a miracle, you got it!" he crowed to the Ali'i nui.
Kamehameha wore a rare smile.

His retinue created a bistro on the hill for the trainees, enough to
feast a hundred kings. After six weeks on camp mess the trainees turned
into foraging animals after smelling a blend of roast pork, crabs, lobsters,
salted *'opihi, limu, poi,* and more.

At the end of the party Alapa'i asked the cadremen, "Shall we tell
the Ali'i nui the Hawaiian names we gave to our weapons?"

The crew all yelled, *"Ae!"*

Kamehameha's belly ached when he learned about the *ule*, proving
there was nothing wrong with his facial muscles.

Kānaka love sexual jokes. But Kamehameha was laughing over
something personal. He wished his were eighteen inches long.

Someone asked Davis, "Tell the Ali'i nui your Hawaiian name."

"They named me, 'Aikake.' You like it?"

"Yes! Easier to pronounce! Give John Young a Hawaiian name too."

"'Olohana!" Mālolo suggested. "He shouts 'All Hands' all the time."

"Good, tell that to Young when he shouts next time." Becoming
serious, he told Davis, "English gun merchants busy in Hilo and Lahaina.
We must stop them."

"No, let them sell all kinds of weapons. Our enemies must collect
all kinds of ammunition for them, too. If we stick only to our standard
Koma and Lopaka, we can blow them away with our superior firepower,"
a confident Davis said.

Kamehameha, not *lōlō* (stupid), grasped Davis' advice. He swaggered
back home with his mind fixed on Maui.

He was unaware that his fifteen *kānaka* canoe paddlers at
Kealakekua had surprised Young. They learned to anchor, weigh anchor,
steer, tack, and handle the *Fair American's* sails in just six weeks. For
their final examination, Young let them navigate around the island of
Hawai'i under his close watch. They had earned top marks.

During the next several months at Holualoa, after the cadremen trained
hundreds of recruits how to kill with iron weapons, Aikake drilled them to
fight as a team with club-swinging, spear-throwing regulars, as
Kamehameha wished. Davis created his first integrated team of a thousand
men. He told Kamehameha, "I think Alapa'i can command it."

Kamehameha smiled and nodded.

Kalanimoku was alarmed. "No, not yet, the unit too big for him, and at just fourteen, he's too young to lead big men."

"Give him the chance," Kamehameha said. "Let's test him and his unit against live enemies on Maui. Aikake, are we ready?"

"Ready for war," Davis assured.

5

Maui King Kalanikupule got an early wind of the Ali'i nui's invasion plan. The king guessed that he would land somewhere along the lee shores.

The Ali'i nui's spies returned with exciting news: "King Kalanikupule split his force, one went to Lahaina, another to Olowalu. No troops in Hāna."

Hāna, good omen. Ka'ahumanu's and Kalanimoku's birthplace, Kamehameha thought. "We go to Hāna in two nights," he told his chiefs.

"That's too soon, let's finalize a Maui strategy first," 'Olohana urged.

"No, we go to Hāna first while it's safe," the Ali'i nui said. He told the spies, "Meet us at Hāna in two mornings with fresh enemy news."

One night in July 1790, Kamehameha's smallish army of three thousand men ready for war shoved off from the Kona staging ground for Hāna in their *wa'a kaulua* double-hull and single-hull canoes.

Disaster lurked.

From five hundred yards offshore, through predawn fog clearings, men in lead canoes held Hāna Bay in sight. Suddenly, the outrigger of a canoe jammed with the hull of another canoe. Oncoming canoes riding the waves crunched into them at full speed. Successive loud collisions created a surreal pileup that eventually spread over a quarter of a mile. Panic screams hung over the Bay. If Kalanikupule's forces were waiting in Hāna, they could have decimated Kamehameha's helpless men.

The canoes slowly untangled. Dazed warriors struggling to paddle made it to shore. Alapa'i swam the last hundred yards with a concerned Lola hovering above.

Kamehameha's spies, witnessing the horrifying spectacle, saw their Ali'i nui flag to shore and stumble onto sand. They dragged him to the upper shoreline and reported, "Kalanikupule is still waiting for you at Lahaina and Olowalu. No enemy troops in Kahului."

The news uplifted Kamehameha. He summoned his ruffled commanders and told them, "Kahului is open. Let's regroup and go."

The commanders gave a weak nod.

Chief Lalamilo did a double take when he saw Chief Ka'iana.

He found a moment of privacy with the Ali'i nui and told him, "I see Ka'iana. He earlier left the Isles for the Orient and I heard he returned with iron weapons and disappeared into the hills of Kauai. Watch out. That group of musketeers he is with must be his own. He proved himself at Moku'ohai as a strategist, but be careful."

"Yes, I know. He thinks only about himself."

"That is right," Lalamilo said. "He has no loyalty to you. If he can get more by joining our enemy against you, he will."

"That's why I have my friend Chief Hoapili watching his every move."

The Ali'i nui had taken a risk. He wanted the firepower of Ka'iana's musketeers. Ka'iana obliged. He wanted his share of victory spoils. It was all business for both.

The forces regrouped and left for Kahului in battered canoes. A Hāna resident loyal to Kalanikupule rushed in his canoe to tell his king in Lahaina, "Kamehameha and his army landed in Hāna yesterday morning, now heading for Kahului."

"What?" the king screeched at his *ali'i*. "Why you let him land on my *'āina?*"

The king had no fortunetellers who could have predicted Hāna.

"Kamehameha's goal is Lahaina. Let's destroy him early," Kalanikupule told his chiefs. "Gather your troops, we are going to Wailuku, draw him into 'Īao highland and fight him from a superior position."

Kamehameha landed without entanglement next morning outside of Kahului. His scouts had more news. "Kahului is still free, but Kalanikupule's army is now heading for Wailuku. Someone tipped him off."

"Never mind, let's take Kahului in next hour."

Before noon, the defenseless Kahului village was in Kamehameha's *malo*. A scout arrived at dusk with more news. "King Kalanikupule and his whole army entered Wailuku village this morning and went directly into 'Īao. They left Wailuku undefended."

Unbelievable. Is this a trick? Kamehameha wondered.

Trusting his scout he said, "Let's go, make Wailuku our base."

In August 1790, Wailuku, the gateway village to the highland four miles away, fell. On the go since Hāna, Kamehameha was exhausted. After a simple dinner he told his chiefs, "Let's meet in the morning to discuss strategy."

Early next morning a scout burst in, told Kamehameha, "I went towards 'Īao Valley to check," he said. "I think I found an enemy concentration northwest of here. I came to it by smell of fish cooking."

The news flushed Kamehameha. "Let's go, shock them while they're eating."

Before daybreak the Ali'i nui's forces were already moving westward along the old trail, avoiding the wider 'Īao Stream Trail to guard against meeting enemy patrols.

Alapa'i took his unit far downwind. He did smell food cooking and moved towards it. At daybreak he came to a clearing. His eyes narrowed on a concentration of busy warriors about two hundred yards away. Alapa'i saw Lola circling them.

"Give the Ali'i nui the enemy location," he told a messenger.

While crouched he loaded three Lopaka and waited for Kamehameha. He approached and signaled. Alapa'i raised his arm and let go. "Boom, boom, boom!" His three blasts echoed back from green 'Īao Pinnacle. A thousand birds with feathers bristling scattered from branches.

Alapa'i's iron balls caught Kalanikupule's main force by surprise. In panic, he ordered his troops into a crescent formation to face Kamehameha. Alapa'i moved closer, let go five more aimed at its center. The enemy fell into hopeless disarray. Alapa'i signaled, "Charge!" A senseless massacre began. Enemy groans like the finale of a demon's symphony hovered over the battleground. Those retreating toward the Pinnacle were quickly surrounded. "Kill them all!" Ka'iana yelled.

With Alapa'i's eight precise Lopaka first-strikes, Mauians' blood turned the valley floor into a slop of hemal soup.

But Alapa'i couldn't rejoice. The killings he helped inflict troubled him deeply. He went on one knee and pleaded to the dead, "Please forgive."

Sporadic shootings ceased and 'Īao became all quiet by noon. The last group of warriors under Alapa'i returned to Wailuku leaving behind proof of Man's innate linkage to animals of prey.

King Kalanikupule, unprepared to challenge Kamehameha's integrated force and its speed, deserted his men early. He slid down a *pali* (cliff) to escape, wrenched his hip and reached O'ahu a crippled man stripped of *mana*.

The synergy of an integrated force awed Kamehameha. *I can go to O'ahu and destroy King Kahekili's army twice my size and bring pono to the Island!* he told his gods.

"*Maika'i*," the Ali'i nui praised Alapa'i. He knew he had made it happen. Alapa'i smoothed Lola's head feathers and told her, "*Maika'i*."

He called Kalanimoku and asked, "Is Alapa'i too young?"

He ignored the question and said, "I'll follow him."

The concept of the integrated force forever changed the style of warfare in Hawai'i. Kamehameha found the old *kūkulu* and *kahului* battle formations obsolete against fast-moving integrated units attacking them from all directions with awesome firepower. No other chief in Hawai'i had such units.

Before the Ali'i nui could savor *pono*, two messengers from the big island of Hawai'i arrived and told him, "Keōua and his men, about three hundred, burned Waimea village, damaged the women and destroyed taro patches. We think they are on their way to Kona. "Please come back and stop them."

Kamehameha aborted his march into Lahaina and claim Maui. Keōua, Kiwala'ō's brother, became a higher priority. "Get twenty *wa'a* ready at Kahului," he told Kalanimoku. I'll leave tonight for Honokōhau (the port village north of Kona) and face Keōua in the morning. Have Alapa'i join me with half of his force. Send Hoapili and his troops to Lahaina to guard the lee shores. You, return to Kona after you clean up 'Īao," he told Kalanimoku. He asked scout 'Aikau, "Meet us in the morning with fresh news about Keōua."

'Aikau was waiting next morning with bad news.

"Keōua and his men entered Kona yesterday, burned the village, went wild, and left."

Kamehameha vomited. He couldn't believe that the holder of the sacred *Ni'aupi'o kapu* would plunder a defenseless village just to spite him.

"Which way did he go?" Alapa'i asked.

"In direction of Waimea. Maybe he will take the Hāmākua trail at Honoka'a to Hilo and then the volcano trail to Ka'ū."

The Ali'i nui mounted a chase. He aborted it at Honoka'a, but never mind, Goddess Hi'iaka Pele was roused and waiting for Keōua at the volcano. She had a score to settle for his heinous deeds against women.

When his advance forces were on the Kilauea volcano trail heading for Ka'ū in a jolly mood, Pele erupted, trapped them in a ring of fast-closing molten lava.

Hours later, Keōua arrived at the scene with his main force. Kīlauea was innocently quiet. Just the pungent smell of hot sulfurous gases hinted of her earlier behavior. He was shocked seeing his half-cooked men slumped in ankle-deep lava. He took another trail for Ka'ū, brooding over the meaning of the tragedy.

§

Ha'alou, the sacred wife of High Chief Kekaulike, was waiting for Kamehameha at Kona. Soon after he returned from Honoka'a, she told him, "I have a message for you from a reliable soothsayer."

"What is it?" he asked.

"He told me that if you would build for god Kūkā'ilimoku the biggest *luakini heiau* in the realm and offered to him Keōua as your inaugural sacrifice before the start of the next Makahiki, the *mana* of the *heiau* will carry you to victory over all your enemies without getting a scratch."

Ha'alou was quick to caution him. "Be ware, every soothsay has its reverse side."

"What is it?" he pressed.

"If you tried and failed you must die. A disappointed Kū will kill you."

Kamehameha pondered his options for a month.

On a dreary fall morning in 1790, he summoned his *ali'i* to 'Ahu'ena Heiau. In deep basso, he told them, "I decided last night to build Kūkā'ilimoku's biggest *luakini heiau* and have Keōua on the *lele* altar before the start of the next Makahiki. I must die if I fail. If I fail, I want all of you to join me as my *moepu'u*, my comrades in death."

Horrified, they thought, *Impossible to build heiau in eight months. Must we die with him?*

Olohana caught them in panic. He told them, "We have no choice, we must build the *heiau* and find Keōua before the next Makahiki. There's no other way we can stay alive."

The *ali'i* helplessly agreed, told Kamehameha, "The *heiau* will be standing before the next Makahiki with Keōua on the *lele* altar."

After inspecting several sites, Kamehameha chose a cliffside knoll near the fishing village of Kawaihae. It had the natural grade for rainwater drainage, a panoramic view from Kohala Mountain to active Hualālai Volcano and a hundred-mile stretch of the Pacific Ocean. He walked to the cliff's edge and saw below God Lono's ancient Mailekini Heiau and men fishing in tranquil 'Ōhai'ula Beach.

He named the future *heiau* Pu'ukoholā (Hump of the Whale). Lono hoped it would not cast a morning shadow on his *heiau*.

Work began in mid-February 1791, a day after the close of the Makahiki.

Four sacrificial bodies were ready to sanctify the corners of the *heiau*. Kūkā'ilimoku hungered for a human offering at the beginning and end of every major construction phase of the *heiau*.

A gang of thousands recruited by the Kona chiefs began passing, hand-to-hand, large lava rocks of the same brown shade from distant sources to the *kāhuna* artisans waiting for them at the *heiau* site. With bluerock chisels and rock hammers they began formfitting over nine thousand rocks a day for the foundation, floor and walls. Kamehameha exhorted the weary, "Move faster!"

Work never ceased. By the sixth week, eighteen huge, carved wooden god idols and the *'anu'u* tower, made with materials sacred to a *luakini heiau*, stood on the finished floor. Four inner-sanctum huts neared completion.

The unbroken chants of *kāhuna*, groans of the rock gang and stench of old, maggot-infested sacrificial victims in the *lua* pit, lent to Pu'ukoholā a dire feel.

A *kahuna* laid the last rock just six days before the October start of the Makahiki festival of 1791. After five hundred human sacrifices and two thousand five hundred dead through hunger and sickness, Kamehameha's stubborn *ali'i*, *kāhuna* and *maka'āinana* had the two million-rock Pu'ukoholā standing. The impressive pantheon to Kūkā'ilimoku on the cliff was ready to receive a worthy inaugural sacrifice.

Twins from Kona called on Keōua in Ka'ū.

Kamanawa stood before his cousin, said, "Kamehameha invites you to visit him at Pu'ukoholā to discuss peace," veiling the intent in metaphor.

The other twin nodded.

Keōua had been depressed ever since he saw his half-cooked men on the volcano trail. He wanted to make amends. He had followed the advice of his war council, but swore never more. Fatalistically, he told Kamanawa, "I will go."

Consternation erupted. His *kāhuna* and *ali'i* told him, "Don't go, you will only become the inaugural sacrifice."

Fated to fulfill Kamehameha's destiny, Keōua would not listen. He just wanted to let sleep the anguished spirit of High Chief Keawe whom he had murdered for land, expiate his shameful plunders and prove to his people and *'aumakua* that he was indeed made of divine stuff.

The beach at Ka Lae (South Point) was heavy with wails of thousands when he left next morning with thirty-two companions in death in six *wa'a* bedecked for the occasion. One member of the group resembled Kamehameha up to his sagging mouth.

Keōua paused at Kona. Although he had earlier plundered the village, the innately compassionate Konawainans understood the purpose of his pathetic voyage, and received him and his companions with water.

After Kona, the group paused a mile away from Pu'ukoholā for a final death ritual against the backdrop of stoic *heiau* walls and a foreboding *'anu'u* tower wrapped in black tapa cloth. Keōua removed his *malo* and threw it into the ocean; then with a single stroke he severed the tip of his penis with a shark's-tooth dagger, an ancient allegorical act that he was no longer of the earth. Showing no pain, he dipped into the ocean with his companions to purify his body before death. Demiprincess Puakō swam out and offered him water.

He took a sip and began his final mile on an October day in 1791.

From the bow of his lead canoe he saw Kamehameha's warriors lined in battle formation along the shore below Pu'ukoholā. Resigned to death, Keōua kept going. He recognized Ke'eaumoku standing waist-deep in water, a *halu* spear cocked. A moment later he saw it coming, glad it was being thrown by a *kapu* chief, not a commoner warrior. He had come to die a day before the start of Lono's Makahiki festivals in mid-October 1791, and made no attempt to duck.

Keōua leaned forward and caught the spear with his throat. For a long conscious second he experienced the apotheosis of his soul for the final journey to Kūkā'ilimoku's *lele* altar.

His men persisted to shore. All but one became Keōua's *moepu'u*. Kamehameha recognized Ka'oleioku, son of his youth by Queen Kanekapolei. "Go back home," he said, and gave him a canoe.

Ka'oleioku obeyed, only to become an outcast in Ka'ū for accepting life.

The *kāhuna* cleansed Keōua body of blood and laid him on the *lele* altar for Kamehameha's *luakini* ritual to the War God. After a day on the altar, they took his body to *Hale Umu* (Oven Hut) in the innermost sanctum of the *heiau* to reduce him to skeleton. The people in Pāhala, Ka'ū, swore they smelled Keōua's burning body that ascended as smoke and settled over the village. Keōua wanted to return to his land before leaving for his *'aumakua* realm. Old timers say the smoke now hangs over Wai'ōhinu in Ka'ū as a pink cloud to remind its people of the price of *pono*.

Kamehameha walked to the seaside edge of the *heiau* and puffed his chest. He had just become the uncontested Ali'i nui of the whole island of Hawai'i without getting a scratch. He next vowed to have O'ahu's King Kahekili, probably his blood father, on Kūkā'ilimoku's altar and claim even his wives.

6

Months before the start of the Pu'ukoholā Heiau construction, the Ali'i nui had asked Davis, "We lost too much powder and weapons at Hāna. Go Philadelphia on *Fair American* immediately and bring back more."

"*Ae*, I'm ready," he said.

By June 1791 Davis had rounded Cape Horn for destination Philadelphia. From time to time Kamehameha wondered if he would defect, take his schooner, gold and all. But he guessed not. He felt he had established a special bond with Aikake on that graduation day in Hōlualoa. He was sure Davis would return with the stuffs he needed.

Davis arrived in Philadelphia, passed security, went to the familiar Union Army's Quartermaster Corps building and told a guard, "I came to see Colonel Clyde Stensen."

"Sorry sir, the colonel has retired."

Davis swallowed air.

"Colonel John Potts is our new Yard Chief. I will take you to him."

They met in his office. Potts, tall, stiff and fiftyish, said, "I had hoped you would return. Heard many good things about you from Colonel Stensen before he retired. Had a good trip?"

Davis answered sprightly, "Yes, sir. It took us six months to the day to get here in our small schooner. You have our English weapons in stock?" He got quickly to the point.

"Yes, we do."

Davis sighed, relieved. "Are they ship shape?"

"Like last time. Come, I'll show them to you."

"Not necessary, sir, your word is good. Here's my order."

Potts scanned the short list:

> 6 Cannons, 8-inch, Model ESW-65-8
> 3,000 rounds of 8-inch cannon balls and grapes
> 3,500 rounds ammunition for the ESW-65-B
> 3,000 MRX65 muskets
> 200,000 rounds/musket shots and ammunition
> 3,000 bandoleers
> 1,000 French bayonets with scabbards

"You came all the way here just for that?"

"Yes, I figure I'm close to the forty-ton limit of my seventy footer, sir."

"Have you seen the English eight-barrel rotating guns?" Potts asked. "They're deadly but we don't use foreign weapons. Maybe you can. We have a hundred, with shots and ammunition to go. Want to see one?"

"I'm at weight limit but yes, Colonel, just to see."

They walked to a firing range. "There she is," he said pointing to a weapon resting on its two front legs.

"My god, never saw that before!"

"The English had over five hundred of them in a Baltimore warehouse. Lucky for Washington, Cornwallis surrendered before he took delivery."

"What happened to the rest?"

"Stolen, by bandits and Indian hunters."

"Can you fire it?"

"Of course. Let me explain. It is fired lying prone. The eight barrels inside that cooling cylinder will rotate and fire as fast as you can crank the breech past the firing pin. Shoots half-inch shots pretty accurately over three-hundred feet," Potts said. "The soldier will show you."

"Fire when ready!" Potts ordered. He began cranking at targets over four hundred feet away, firing eight rounds in three seconds, most hitting targets.

One gun has the firepower of fifteen muskets, Davis thought, "I'll take the entire stock and all the shots and ammunition you have, but cut my musket order to one thousand five hundred."

God knew he would need a rotating gun soon.

Walking back from the range he passed a familiar shed. "Can we step inside, sir?"

"Certainly. Your shipment is in there."

Davis entered and his eyes rolled. "Your inventory of English weapons is so huge. Can I return several more times to take delivery?"

"Yes. Just pay the Corps one thousand dollars and the whole thing will be yours, including the rotating guns."

Only one thousand dollars? Davis wanted to scream, "Yahoo!"

"Incidentally, where's Sandwich Islands and why do you need those firearms?" Potts asked.

"Not Sandwich. We call it 'Hawai'i,' an eight-island chain in the middle of the Pacific. My chief wants to unite the islands under his supreme rule. To do that, he needs western arms. That's why I'm here."

"Pretty exciting, Davis."

"Can your men help us load the cannons?"

"Certainly. We'll be at dockside tomorrow at zero eight hundred with your purchase. Hawai, did you say?"

Loading went smoothly the next day.

"Let's conclude this transaction," Davis said. They went into his stateroom stuffed with ammunition and powder. He reached below his bunk and pulled out a tub full of gold coins that came with the *Fair American.* "Please, sir, take one thousand dollars."

Potts examined the gold coins. "Take thirty-nine," he told his clerks.

Davis was astonished. *Only thirty-nine?* He learned that his coins were worth much more than what he had earlier thought.

"Before we leave could you mount a cannon on the foredeck and charge me? We had one there before."

"Gladly, there's no need to pay," Potts said.

Davis grabbed some gold coins and gave them to Potts. "Please accept these as our expression of thanks from home."

Potts flipped one high, accepted it and gave the rest to his men.

The colonel asked, "Have you handled powder on a ship before?"

"Y . . . yes sir," Davis replied wondering why his question.

"I saw you drag that tub from under the bunk. The friction could have ignited a spark and blown this ship and us to Heaven. You should lift when moving anything near powder."

"Thank you for the caution, sir," Davis said.

The army towed the *Fair American* to the middle of the Delaware, pointed her south and let her go with Davis at the wheel. Greedily loaded down to gunwale, she had lost her sleek, majestic form. Like a bloated hippo with just its nostrils above water, she began to move south for the Atlantic.

Nippy November air of 1791 filled the hippo's foresails. Indian Summer leaves had fallen. Bare branches on starboard side pointed to heaven to await spring.

The return voyage would astound the crew.

The *Fair American* was off the Florida coast heading south toward Rio, her nose still above water. From his crow's nest Pāoa took a double take.

"Come up," he yelled to Davis. "Ship coming straight at us from port. Could be pirates!"

Davis went up the mast faster than a monkey, grabbed Pāoa's telescope. "Pirates!" he confirmed. He slid down and called a hasty meeting. "A pirate ship is coming. We look heavy. I think they want to see what we have. I say they must kill us before they take our cargo. What do you say?"

"*Ae*," the crew screamed, ready to die for the Ali'i nui.

"All right, listen."

His orders were brief, concise. Nobody knew his resume included a stint as a pirate deckhand after the War! He knew the value of going on the offensive and creating consternation with a successful first strike.

"Konia, wipe the Lopaka bore clean of whale oil and load the first round. Put five rounds alongside. Pakeo, degrease twenty Koma, fix bayonets and load. I'll have three rotating guns loaded and ready."

Inside of twenty minutes, the bloated hippo became a gunboat.

Davis continued, "Keep Lopaka covered and Koma lying flat on deck. Wave at them. Let them think we are defenseless traders. When we rise together at around three hundred feet from the pirate ship I will yell, 'Fire!' Konia, go for the hull. Pakeo, your target is their Lopaka crew. The pirate captain is mine," Davis said in immaculate Hawaiian. "Any question?"

"*'A'ohe* (No)" they yelled, pumping their fists.

"Pāoa, get back up. We're roping you six loaded Koma at bottom of next swell; shoot somebody on the other side. Good luck!"

Davis turned to the stateroom jammed with powder and prayed, "Kūkā'ilimoku, don't let them hit it." He couldn't believe he didn't say, "Dear God."

The men found pieces of soiled tapa paper they would wave.

"Half mile," Pāoa shouted down. Davis had precious minutes to get three more rotating guns degreased and loaded. From under cover of tapa cloth Konia rehearsed the sequence of aiming and firing the Lopaka at top of a swell. The Koma squad already had the feel. They had fired many imaginary rounds and couldn't wait for the real thing.

"Seven hundred feet," Pāoa yelled. "It's a brig, about a hundred-footer. Two cannons on foredeck and four at starboard aimed at us. Counted about fifteen men. She is trying to overtake."

Davis was proud of his reporting.

Just then two intimidating cannon shots hissed over the *Fair American*, pirate talk to stop for boarding. A third and a fourth went over.

Davis felt, *This is it.* He took a sharp tack to port and pointed his one-cannon battleship straight at the pirate ship, making her a smaller target.

"Pirate boat straight ahead!" Davis yelled. "Fire next!" Konia stripped Lopaka's cover and stared through its sight. He had learned from Alapa'i how to strike a moving target in one. The Koma squad had muskets at their cheeks.

At top of the next crest Davis yelled, "Fire!" Konia let one go at the broadside. Davis and his crew emptied their barrels. A shuddering sound echoed back.

Pirate gunners answered, their cannon rounds swishing harmlessly overhead. Davis knew the firepower of a trader had shocked them into firing in panic. He tacked starboard, reloaded, and prayed for no collision. "Target at port," he yelled.

When they resurfaced, the ships were sailing parallel two hundred feet apart. Konia, Pakeo and Davis again let go as innocent pirate shots skied over. At top of the next crest Davis smelled smoke, and saw the pirate ship listing. With impunity, they emptied their barrels on the distressed ship.

They heard screams from the other side.

"Maika'i!" Davis exclaimed.

The crewmen and Davis joined hands and thanked their gods.

After that Christmas day 1791 distraction, the gunboat *Fair American* with Davis at the wheel resumed her course for destination Kona, her nose proudly above water.

At Hōlualoa, the hills rocked with Lopaka firings deep into the night as recruits prepared for Maui. The supply of ammunition dwindled. "Shall we cut down on our use of powder?" a worried Alapa'i asked Kamehameha.

"No, that won't be training. Use it up. Davis will come back with more."

On Aikake Davis's one hundred and ninety-fifth day after leaving Philadelphia, someone yelled, "Land!" Davis rushed to his side and spotted the distant outline of Mauna Loa. The crewmen screamed with joy and thanked their gods.

Davis slumped to his knees. *Sweet home, the most beautiful sight of my life*, he sighed. After the long trip, the memories of Colonel Potts and the pirate ship had faded into antiquity.

A tumultuous welcome of thousands greeted the bloated hippo on this day in May 1792 when she made a majestic turn into the port of Kona.

Kamehameha climbed onboard the *Fair American* and hugged Davis, who noticed the Ali'i nui's deeper facial lines. *"He mai* (Welcome back)," he said from his heart. "You had good trip?"

"Ae, I have everything you wanted."

"What's that?" Kamehameha asked, pointing to wooden structures tied down on deck.

"Wheels, for moving Lopaka and caissons fast on land," Davis explained.

The Ali'i nui had not seen wheels before. "How they work?"

Davis untied one, sat the Ali'i nui on the connecting shaft and wheeled him around the deck.

"Whee!" he yelled, on the roll.

They went below deck. The stacks of cannons and balls and muskets amazed Kamehameha. "How did you keep the ship afloat?"

"I prayed to Kūkā'ilimoku. We have more Koma and Lopaka in Philadelphia, all paid."

Kamehameha saw a stack of strange weapons. "What's that?"

"Rotating guns. One has more firepower than fifteen Koma. I brought back a hundred with many rounds of ammunition," Davis gloated.

Kamehameha smiled, taking Davis's word.

Next day, in a formal Kona beachside ceremony, he draped yellow-feather capes with red-feathered borders on the shoulders of Aikake Isaac Davis and Olohana John Young. They had just become High Chiefs.

"I have an announcement," Kamehameha said, interrupting the joyous mood. "I need fifty more *wa'a kaulua* and twenty-five additional *peleleu* to take our seven thousand men and supplies to Maui and O'ahu. We only have one hundred-fifty mostly old *wa'a kaulua* (double-hull canoes), fifteen *peleleu* and maybe two hundred single-hull war canoes.

He shocked Alapa'i. "We're getting twenty-five new *peleleu* in two years, but if you want fifty more *kaulua*, you must wait maybe five, six years," Alapa'i said. "We have over three hundred hulls half carved and drying, but we cannot rush wood. Besides, I don't think we need more canoes or seven thousand men for O'ahu. Just three integrated units and two thousand men in support are enough if we can land safely without getting tangled."

"Olohana, you said you have an idea how to prevent pileup?"

"Yes!" Seizing the group's attention, Young pointed at a beached *wa'a kaulua* and said, "Alapa'i and I redesigned and tested it."

They walked over. "I see nothing new," the Ali'i nui scoffed.

"See, the two hulls are not parallel; the front ends are closer together than the rear ends. The slight wedge shape makes handling easier, reduce chance for pileup."

"You think so too?" Kamehameha asked Alapa'i.

"Yes, I made sharper turns at full speed to avoid trouble."

"Ke'eaumoku, change all *wa'a kaulua* and *peleleu* to wedge shape. We are going to O'ahu with five thousand men," the Ali'i nui said.

Alapa'i was glad. "Good, I will leave for Maui tonight to change the twenty five *peleleu* to wedge shape."

A chief yelled, "A group of *haole* coming this way."

Kamehameha turned and saw Captain George Vancouver, the former ensign under Captain Cook. He was now in charge of England's explorations in the Pacific. Vancouver left his marine detail behind and approached the Ali'i nui carrying something.

"*Aloha,*" he said with a crisp salute. "I see you are in a meeting."

"Yes, but we can talk. Nice to see you again."

They strolled to the beach.

"I have a message from my government. We deeply appreciate your offer to cede Hawai'i to England, but we are declining. We have no interest in acquiring islands in the Pacific.

"I also come with a personal message. The continuing depopulation of Hawai'i is shocking. The once-crowded islands are becoming sparse. For Hawai'i's sake, why not settle your differences with King Kalanikupule by negotiation, not by war? Stop killing your healthy *kānaka kāne* in their prime."

The Ali'i nui shot back. "Don't forget, your diseased people started it. But wars are sacred to God Kūkā'ilimoku. I must continue our wars until all my enemies are vanquished and our land is in *pono*."

Vancouver shut up. He didn't come to argue about pagan religion.

"I'm leaving tomorrow and won't be back until next February. I want you to have this," he said, and gave to Kamehameha a cast-iron Dutch oven. The pot measured thirteen inches across and six inches deep. It came with a heavy iron lid and a handle to hang over a fire. "I will be back tonight to cook for you my farewell dinner in this oven," he said.

Vancouver returned with all the ingredients. He prepared for Kamehameha pot-roast pork wrapped in taro leaves, with sweet potatoes on the side. "With this pot you won't need *imu*," he said.

Kamehameha wouldn't eat anything prepared by a *haole*, but he broke his rule. He tasted the roast. *"Kupanaha* (Wonderful)!" he drooled, and thanked Vancouver. The Vancouver oven became his prized possession. He took it everywhere, even into battle.

With it, the Ali'i nui became the first grand chef in Pacific Rim cuisine.

7

Kamehameha's edgy troops, stuck at the Kawaihae staging ground waiting for a launch order, let out a big *"Hulō* (Yea)!" when they saw a fleet of twenty-five *peleleu* canoes sailing in with Alapai'i' in the lead. *"Ho'omaika'i,"* the Ali'i nui screamed, greeting Alapa'i just in from Maui. "Finally," he told his commanders. "Get your five thousand men ready. We must leave for Maui before *kapu-Kāne* (27th), that's in seven nights."

Led by the *Fair American*, his grand fleet left Kawaihae in April 1795 and landed at Lahaina next morning. Maui offered no resistance. She was waiting to be claimed since the 'Īao battle. The chiefs of nearby islands of Moloka'i and Lana'i submitted quickly to avoid being slaughtered.

Ka'iana scanned the vast domain that Kamehameha had just inherited. *This should have been mine*, he bitterly thought. As a grandson of Ali'i nui Keawe, his bloodline was superior to Kamehameha's and wondered why King Kalaniopu'u didn't vest him with the War God Kuka'ilimoku. *I should have been at this point of grabbing absolute power in the Isles, not Kamehameha*, he moaned.

Ka'iana deserved to be an outsider. He enjoyed the excitement of foreign lands, and the high life of serving as a stud to court ladies in Canton, who wanted him at their calling. He never tried to build a power base at home. Kamehameha had been building his since Cook.

After securing Maui, the Ali'i nui landed at Pāpōhaku Beach on the western shores of Moloka'i, his jump-off point for O'ahu. The beach offered expansive ground for staging, close proximity to the strong westerly current of the Kaiwi Channel to O'ahu and proximity to the village of Kaunakakai on the southern shore of Molokai.

Kamehameha had a secret meeting scheduled there with sacred Queen *Ni'aupi'o* Liliha.

She had gone into hiding in the village together with her mother Kalola and sacred infant daughter Keōpūolani after her husband, Kiwala'ō, was killed by Ke'eaumoku during the failed battle at Moku'ōhai. But Kamehameha's stealthy agents had them tracked.

Liliha reluctantly greeted her mortal enemy when he arrived. Kamehameha went on his knees and told her, "After I take O'ahu, please come to Kona with your daughter and live in my safer haven." That was a metaphoric order, not a loving wish.

Kamehameha pushed no further. He bowed and knee-walked away from her sacred presence. He returned to Pāpōhaku Beach and saw Ka'ahumanu and Kaiana in a lovegrip. Like always he pardoned her, but stamped Ka'iana for death.

Across the channel on O'ahu, fear of Kamehameha's imminent invasion spread. Kalanikupule's scouts nabbed two enemy agents, one snooping in 'Ewa, the other in Honolulu, both carrying the trademark of their profession: an expandable English telescope.

"Wring them out separately," King Kalanikupule ordered.

Under extreme torture, they began to sing the same song. "Kamehameha landing at 'Ewa Beach late *Welo* (April) with ten thousand troops." They mumbled minute invasion details before losing consciousness.

The separate spiels matched! 'Ewa Beach. In late April. Ten thousand troops. Kalanikupule had all the intelligence he needed.

"Paki, move your forces to 'Ewa Beach. Kamehameha will be landing there early dawn soon. Have your strongest rowers in their *kioloa* (long, narrow racing canoe) patrol the 'Ewa coast. When they detect enemy coming have them rush to shore to sound alarm."

At Pāpōhaku Beach, a scout brought startling news to Kamehameha and members of the Council. "Kalanikupule making big troop movements to 'Ewa side," he said.

John Young smiled.

Kamehameha clenched his fist. "Gather Council members," he asked.

He told them, "We have good chance to land unopposed if we left tonight. Kalanikupule is moving his troops to 'Ewa."

"Where do we land?" Ke'eaumoku asked.

"Maunalua Bay at Le'ahi. Alapa'i and I will lead."

"*Ae!*" they yelled and scrambled to make preparation.

Nearing midnight, the Ali'i nui wished his decoys, "*pōmaika'i*" (good luck).

Kamehameha tied the idol of Kūkā'ilimoku securely to the foremast of the *Fair American* and yelled, "We go!" Alapa'i smoothed Lola's head feathers and said, "We go."

Five thousand in his fleet of double-hulled *wa'a kaulua, peleleu* and single-hull canoes with many womenfolk onboard were on the way. Their loud battle cries could have carried to O'ahu.

The reflections of the half-moon off their splashing wet paddles energized the night.

But Ka'iana had little to cheer. Ka'ahumanu had warned him before launch, "Head for Kailua on O'ahu." He knew that was a death warning. Not yet ready for the spiritual realm, he told his men, "Be prepared, at my signal we are breaking away for Kailua during the invasion."

At the halfway point to O'ahu, the waters of Kaiwi Channel began to churn and rock Kamehameha's fleet. He knew the Channel was capricious, but not this fickle.

What a perfect weather for making a jailbreak, Ka'iana thought. Another thought, a diabolical scheme, crossed his mind: *Maybe I can use the roiling sea to sneak up on the Fair American, climb on board and surprise Kamehameha with my dagger, then seize command of the invasion force as the new Mō'ī.*

He liked his chance.

With aid of a strong Kona wind he drifted laterally and approached the *Fair American* with his canoe oarsmen. Kamehameha, on the quarterdeck assessing the moment, thought he spotted Ka'iana. He turned away a moment too late.

With the crucial element of surprise lost, he aborted, rejoined his group and signaled his brother. It went from canoe to canoe. They drifted to the right. Ka'iana counted all his canoes, and signaled, 'Now!' and started a furtive dash to O'ahu's windward shore.

Before sunrise, the king's oarsmen patrolling the 'Ewa coast heard screeching, frightening sounds. Squinting toward the horizon, they thought they saw the silhouette of an armada. With hairs standing they dashed to shore and sounded alarm.

Kalanikupule shrieked, *"Nui!* Great! The disclosures of the captured agents matched! The king ordered his commanders, "Remain low until they land, then charge at my signal. Take no prisoners."

When dawn broke, the defenders saw musket-armed warriors in eighteen canoes just sitting offshore. The decoys froze Kalanikupule's entire army. After an hour, with mission accomplished, they abruptly headed east to rejoin their group.

The king screamed to his *'aumakua,* realizing he had been duped. He squinted toward the horizon hoping to see Kamehameha's main invasion force approaching, but he saw just gulls.

8

Kamehameha's five thousand landed unopposed in late April 1795 at Maunalua Bay north of Lē'ahi (Diamond Head), most in wedge-shaped canoes. Young's strategy had worked to perfection.

The Ali'i nui asked Konia, "Go find Ka'iana, give him the *ule*." But the chief was gone. Kamehameha suspected an insider's tip-off, a woman's.

On shore, Alapa'i secured the Maunalua-Lē'ahi beachhead before the birds had their morning feed. Scouts returning to the Lē'ahi base reported, "The immediate coast and inland clear of enemy troops."

The Ali'i nui offered coconuts from Le'ahi on Kūkā'ilimoku's portable altar and thanked the spirits of the two agents who had given their lives to make the unopposed landing possible.

Ka'iana made a successful break. He landed with his force north of Alāla Point in windward Kailua. Without rest, he led his men around the Kawainui swamp and scaled the Pali, going nonstop for sixty-two hours since Moloka'i. He arrived at Nu'uanu Valley and sent two messengers to find and deliver his message to Kalanikupule.

With directional aid of local folks, they staggered into his Ewa headquarters and met the king. One said, "High Chief Ka'iana, with a hundred men and equipment, deserted Kamehameha's invasion fleet, landed this morning at Kailua. He is now in Nu'uanu Valley ready to join you in fighting Kamehameha. Can you visit him to discuss details?"

"It's trickery. Ka'iana is one of Kamehameha's leaders. Don't go," the king's *ali'i* urged.

He agreed. "Go back. Tell Ka'iana to come here if he wants to meet me." The messengers left hurriedly.

Ka'iana shook his head in disgust when he learned of the king's response. But having no choice, he was on the trail again.

"*Pehea 'oe*," the king greeted a weary Ka'iana when he lurched into his 'Ewa camp. They had not seen each other since *keiki* time.

Ka'iana felt the accusing stare of the *ali'i* gathered. He told the king, "Kamehameha landed at Lē'ahi this morning with five thousand troops, half musketeers, ten *kanona* and unlimited ammunition. My men and I deserted him last night. We want to join you in fighting him."

Ka'iana lacked trust. *Is he planted?* some *ali'i* thought.

But he was bright news for a downfallen Kalanikupule. "Thank you, yes, join us," the king replied and rubbed noses tearfully.

"Lē'ahi?" the king asked, without hinting surprise.

"*Ae*, Kamehameha and a cripple boy, Alapa'i, led the landing. The boy is deadly with the *kanona*, goes anywhere like the wind and does impossible things easily."

Chief Pepe'ekeo didn't care about Alapa'i. "We thought Kamehameha was landing at 'Ewa. His spies told us that."

"They are not spies!" Ka'iana said. "They're volunteers trained and planted by John Young to tell lies, to mislead you."

The king's whole body trembled. "Are we going to lose the war because of two liars?" he moaned.

"No, we haven't even started to fight."

"Where shall we meet him for a decisive battle?"

"That depends on what we have. Before we commit can I inspect your equipment and men? We still have time."

"*Ae*, come with me," Pepe'ekeo said. He escorted Ka'iana past the king's artillery brigade and musketeers armed with an assortment of dated equipment.

"How many men have you got?"

"Over ten thousand."

"I saw six *haole*. Who they?" he asked.

"Hired men from off the ships. They're smart with *kanona*."

Ka'iana was disappointed. He had seen soldiers of fortune take off when the going got tough.

Hiding a letdown, Ka'iana returned to the meeting after the brief inspection and told the king, "Let's not fight Alapa'i in the open. Meet him in a place like Nu'uanu Valley where thick forest can neutralize his *kanona* and force Kamehameha into close, hand-to-hand combat. We could overwhelm him with our larger force."

Using a stick, Ka'iana scratched a simple map of Nu'uanu Valley on dirt. "I have a suggestion. Why don't we suck Kamehameha up the main trail to here," he said, marking an X *makai* (oceanside) of the first upside-down waterfall. He told the king, "Let's say you position your main force all along the Kapalama side of the X and lay in wait. I will leave the trail early and take our artillery to a higher position on the 'Ālewa side. I will position my five *kanona* wherever I find an opening to the Niolopa trail, and will wait for Kamehameha to pass. I won't need any *haole* help.

"After he passes my *kanona* sight I will fire to cut off his rear and scare his army. When you hear my *kanona*, let's say you pour out from hiding, and find and kill Kamehameha in hand-to-hand combat," he told the king. "If you succeed, his troops will panic. We can easily slaughter them and the war can end right there. What do you think?"

The king sat riveted. "I follow you!" he said. "We too," his *ali'i* joined, approving the strategy. It seemed simpler killing one man than destroying an entire army. The elated king promised Ka'iana the island of Maui after victory.

Kalanikupule's spies returned from Lē'ahi with the latest intelligence. "Kamehameha not moving out, maybe camping overnight."

"Good. Let's move to Nu'uanu now," the king said.

With his ten thousand troops Kalanikupule arrived before dusk at X, joined by Ka'iana's men along the way.

A trio of stealthy Kamehameha scouts followed Kalanikupule's troops into the valley. They returned to base after dark and reported, "The king's entire army went into Nu'uanu Valley leaving Honolulu undefended! We saw Ka'iana. He left the trail early, about half mile from the first upside-down waterfall and disappeared into the 'Ālewa-side forest with a *kanona* brigade."

Kamehameha's strategy for Day Two jelled with that intelligence.

He headed for Honolulu early next morning taking the safer route around Lē'ahi crater to Mānoa and onto the upper Pūowaina (Punchbowl) trail at Kapa'akea, avoiding the shorter route to the village over mud flats of Ala Wai and Kewalo. At daybreak, he stood below the summit of Pūowaina breathing down on Honolulu. A trail bald from thirst led into the village of three thousand people.

Emboldened by the *mana* of Pu'ukoholā, Kamehameha marched down and secured the village and harbor without getting a scratch. Frightened villagers greeted the invaders with water, but the Ali'i nui had a strict *kapu* against accepting anything from the people on enemy land.

He could see from Honolulu the still adolescent, verdant Nu'uanu Valley between 'Ālewa ridge to the east and Kapalama heights to the west. He knew of its twenty-foot ferns and giant trees clothed in vines, and of cool streams alive with *'ōpae* (freshwater shrimps) and fish that had migrated from the ocean eons earlier. He regretted that for sake of *pono* god Wākea's landscape must soon be painted in red of enemy's blood.

His commanders met for a strategy session. They had six battle plans on the floor, discussed each way into the night without reaching a conclusion on any. The Ali'i nui said, "We know where he is, his strength and all about Ka'iana. Let's rest, sleep on the information and continue our session tomorrow morning."

Kamehameha returned early and found Young and others still arguing strategy. He told them, "We cannot use Lopaka inside Nu'uanu forests. We must pull Kalanikupule out and let him fight our kind of war along the open trails."

A long silence followed.

"Olohana, you told me many times about how William the Conqueror won the Battle of Hastings in 1066. I think some of his ideas are suited for Nu'uanu."

Hmm, Hastings, Olohana pondered.

"What's William strategy?" Council members blurted.

Young explained the ploy in detail. After days of discussion, a modified William stratagem fit for Nu'uanu jelled. "That's it!" Kamehameha rejoiced. "Let's rehearse it. Olohana, you know the ploy best. Lead the drills."

Maneuvers and rehearsals went deep into the night.

Kalanikupule's spies watched and shook their heads.

After ten days Kamehameha asked Olohana, "Are we ready?"

"Yes, we can go tomorrow morning. Tako and our chiefs now know exactly what to do at the decisive, exact moment."

"Gather the commanders for a final meeting," Kamehameha asked.

They arrived ready for war. "You know your part," he said. "Timing is crucial. Let's review. Like we rehearsed, we are going up the Nu'uanu trails in three columns. Olohana will take the main Niolopa trail and lead. Tako will follow and Alapa'i's thousand men will follow them. On our left flank Ke'eaumoku will take his thousand men up the Wo'olani trail on Kapalama side, and on our right flank Hoapili will take his men up the Pauoa trail on Ālewa side. Our formations can change, like we rehearsed, depending on what Ka'iana and Kalanikupule do. I will be in the rear of the Niolopa trail with my two thousand backup troops."

Many chiefs still thought it strange that a *haole* would lead the march, especially into a battle this crucial. But Young took complete charge and everything fell into place.

Came the morning of this fifteenth day of the month of *Iki'iki* (May), 1795. With the march up the valley just hours away, the troops had a snack of baked *'ulu* and dried *'ōpelu*. For many it would be their last. "Fall in," the Ali'i nui ordered at predawn, Kūkā'ilimoku's favorite time.

The dark, cold winds swishing down from the Pali fibrillated the tempo of war. Kamehameha's frenzied troops, with their faces and bodies painted for war assured him they were ready for pitch battle.

The Ali'i nui walked over to John Young, wished him, *"Pōmaika'i."*

Young fit an imitation *haka*, a feathered helmet, on Tako's head, draped an *'ahu'ula* cloak of tapa, dyed yellow, over his shoulders, and handed him a spear. "Tako, turn completely around," Young said. He inspected and saw a stunning Kamehameha fake.

Young thrust his right fist forward. The grand march was on for the most decisive battle ever fought in Hawai'i. Twelve *kāhili* bearers and six *kāhuna* beseeching Kūkā'ilimoku's help, led the march. Hewahewa joined them holding a *hau* branch upright. Alapa'i smoothed Lola's head feathers and let her go.

Conch blares, obviously blown by Kalanikupule's spies, went up the valley to signal the start of Kamehameha's march. The secret was out. The antagonists avoided pre-battle skirmishes.

With each step into the valley, Young and his troops mentally rehearsed the Hastings retreat, knowing a slight timing miscue would mean certain death. Young passed the ridge at Niolopa at dawn and came to a clearing approaching the first upside-down waterfall. His sharp blue eyes caught movement at Pu'uka'ani, a high ground on the 'Ālewa side. He sent a runner alerting the troops behind.

When the news reached Alapa'i, he suspected Ka'iana. Slipping from rank with a company of men, he headed for the rear of Pu'uka'ani. In the distance he saw Lola circling, a telltale signal. They zigged and zagged around boulders and through thick underbrush and came to a small clearing. Way below Alapa'i saw men hustling behind an ancient lava-rock wall.

They inched down without moving a blade of grass. Alapa'i recognized Ka'iana. *That's him! Poor soul, he left his rear exposed, maybe thinking the steep terrain was impassable.* Alapa'i felt sorry for what must happen to him.

Alapa'i loaded three Lopaka and set his sights along the wall.

"Hulō!" Ka'iana yelped when he saw John Young and "Kamehameha" pass his cannon sights. He was stunned seeing three columns moving up, but he had no way of alerting the king. After they went farther up the valley, Ka'iana aimed.

Lola swooped down. *Quickly,* she seemed to say, her head feathers bristling.

Alapa'i motioned his troops and fired his epochal three salvos a moment before Ka'iana would have. The valley recoiled; the shock busted Alapa'i's right eardrum. He watched his volleys speed in slow motion through tall grass beneath *kukui* branches and smash into the wall. A large section vanished as lava shrapnel.

His musketeers, with fixed bayonets, charged, but froze at the impact area when they saw pieces of humanity bleeding.

Lola fluttered down, struggling. Alapa'i lifted her off the slope and held her in his hands. "Lola!" he yelled. She lifted her bloody head, then went still, her wise eyes shut for the ages. Her last mission was over, a combat casualty fell by a shrapnel. Shattered, Alapa'i dug a hole with his bayonet and buried Lola wet with his tears. He bid her a difficult, *"Aloha 'oe, Aloha auia 'oe* (Farewell, I love you).

Alapa'i rushed downhill after the service and found Ka'iana still conscious, his stomach open. Alapa'i bent down, said, "I am sorry." Ka'iana returned a faint smile before it froze. "Lay their bodies on the trail, let our enemies see them," Alapai'i yelled.

Meanwhile, believing the cannon blasts were Ka'iana's, O'ahu's king ordered, *"Ho'ouka* (Charge)!" His troops poured out of the rain forest possessed. Young, with an instant headstart, ordered, "Retreat!" With decoy Tako he turned and ran just ahead of flying spears. Kamehameha saw them running. "Clear the trail, take assigned positions along the flanks. Nalu, setup your rotating guns," he yelled.

As Young hoped, the defenders mounted a full-scale, wild chase of "Kamehameha." They soon became ensnarled in a replay of the Englishmen who fell into William the Conqueror's trap at Hastings, England, over seven hundred years earlier.

Ke'eaumoku and Hoapili 's thousands rose from both flanks with spears, clubs and fixed bayonets and decimated the shocked pursuers over a quarter-mile stretch. Swift enemy replacements kept coming, many falling to rotating gunfires. But with superior numbers Kalanikupule slowly reversed Kamehameha's initial momentum and inflicted heavy casualties. Trampling over fallen bodies of retreating invaders they began to break out of the trap. Nalu and Paoa lay quivering with their skulls smashed. Kamehameha threw in his reserves. A pitch battle extended deep into the thick valley now soaked in blood, as Alapa'i watched, helplessly.

Momentum swung to Kalanikupule's side.

Someone yelled in panic, "Pepe'ekeo *ma—ke* (dead), Ka'iana and his men, too, along the Niolopa!" The news spread. The defenders fell in disarray.

Sensing a dramatic turn, Kalanikupule fled into the forest to escape Kūkā'ilimoku's altar, like he did at 'Iao. Some O'ahuans, retreating to the Pali just ahead of their pursuers, jumped over the cliff to avoid capture and torture. Without field command, the defenders along the trails were slaughtered, became victims of a massive carnage.

Battles in Hawai'i seldom last more than a day. This one for O'ahu was over by noon. In those few hours, piles of *kānaka* in their prime littered pristine Nu'uanu Valley. Residents along the old Niolopa trail could still hear their groans on half-moon nights even when the Pali winds are howling.

Pono as defined by Kūkā'ilimoku returned to the land.

But only briefly.

Gods Wākea, Lono, Kanaloa and Kāne, in despair after witnessing the carnage, closed ranks. They implored the war god, "No more bloodletting of our people."

Kūkā'ilimoku turned belligerent, said, "Kaua'i not yet conquered. Only war can unite the isles and bring lasting *pono*."

A confrontation became inevitable. The opposing gods clashed in an epic struggle for dominance on a supernatural battleground. The majority soundly beat Kūkā'ilimoku and plucked clean his symbolic feathers. The god quivered and died.

Thus ended the life of the God Kū's paramount embodiment among his seventy-six others, dead on a supernatural battlefield.

"Bring me Kalanikupule and Ka'iana," Kamehameha asked Alapa'i. His aides brought Ka'iana and laid him at his feet. But the search for Kalanikupule failed.

The king was deep in the forest of Nu'uanu with Mamo, son of the king's trusted Ali'i Kalāheo of Kaneohe. They roamed the interior eating mountain apples, guavas and occasional *'ōpae* (shrimps) and thought of escaping—to Kaua'i. But, in a first brave act, the king decided to surrender. He wanted to spare his people of torture by Kamehameha, so long as he was at large.

On a chilly seventh night the two sat on a boulder still warm from afternoon sun and talked about the morrow. "Go to Kaneohe tonight to your people," the king ordered Mamo. "I will go alone in the morning to face Kamehameha."

Mamo refused. "I am going with you," he said, closing further debate. The king's eyelids quivered.

That night Mamo fell a young *kauwila* tree about eight feet tall, cut off its lower branches and trimmed the upper into a cylindrical shape, creating a giant *kāhili*, a symbol of Hawaiian royalty that he would carry when approaching Kamehameha. He wanted to give to his master a dignified end.

They tried to doze for the last time but the king couldn't, too distressed of being abandoned by his gods. Mamo awoke early, trimmed the top into a more perfect cylindrical shape and tied a ribbon just below the cylinder. Its majesty gripped the king.

At daybreak the king cut off the tip of his penis and waded into a nearby stream to purify his body. In his last words to Mamo he said, "I am ready."

Mamo held the *kāhili* upright and led their descent to the valley floor. In the distance he sighted Kamehameha's camp. Mamo turned and told the king, "I am also ready." He raised the *kāhili* higher and swaggered toward the camp.

The Ali'i nui saw the two approaching. He recognized a naked Kalanikupule by his limp.

The old king stopped before the new and knelt to await his word. Behind him Mamo was challenging the strong mystical Pali winds to hold the *kāhili* upright.

"Identify yourself," Kamehameha said, looking down on a pitiable human. Godly *Ni'aupi'o* Kalanikupule, the vanquished King of Maui, Moloka'i, Lana'i and O'ahu, knee-walked three more steps before a man of far lower *kapu* and chanted his genealogy in kingly fashion. He recognized Ka'iana lying nearby.

After the old king positively identified himself, a spear pierced his body at pointblank from behind. He clutched the protruding tip, turned to Mamo as if to say goodbye, and collapsed.

It was Mamo's turn to get the spear.

"Identify yourself," the Ali'i nui asked the *moepu'u*.

Mamo planted the *kāhili* on the ground, knelt beside his gory king and chanted his noble genealogy. Kamehameha learned that his father, of higher *kapu* rank than he, happened to be a childhood acquaintance.

Fascinated by the *kāhili* he asked, "You created it?"

"*Ae.*"

"How did you get the ribbon?"

"Ripped my *malo*," he said, facing down.

Kamehameha had never seen a *kāhili* created by divine hands. Mamo's spiritual devotion, his strength, his manners and dignity, impressed Kamehameha. They were qualities he wished of his *ali'i*.

He decided to save Mamo.

"Come closer. Touch tip of my spear," Kamehameha ordered.

"Please, no, let me join my king!" Mamo begged, aware of the consequence of touching.

Alapa'i went to Mamo's side, said something.

On the Ali'i nui's next attempt, Mamo gently touched the tip with trembling hand.

A roar of approval echoed through the valley. By touching his sacred spear, Mamo instantly became one of Kamehameha's new *kāpi'i* (personal attendants). Alapa'i was ecstatic.

"Help the defeated people on O'ahu, nurse them," Kamehameha told Mamo. "They are now my people." And he asked Alapa'i, "Take Mamo under your personal care."

Even with his right eardrum punctured at Pu'uka'ani, Alapa'i heard every word.

Mamo vowed to serve his new masters faithfully for the remainder of his borrowed time on earth.

9

Kamehameha's five greatest years had just ended. He succeeded in everything he tried, as if ordained by Kūkā'ilimoku to bring *pono* to the land. Only the harmless king Kaumuali'i of Kaua'i was not yet at his warty feet.

"Take Kalanikupule back for Kūkā'ilimoku, destroy all of their weapons, we don't need any, and clean up the place," Kamehameha told Kalanimoku. "Clean up" meant burying the dead, taking the wounded back to base, ritually consecrating the battleground, and restoring Nu'uanu to its earlier innocence.

Kamehameha was striding back to the Kaimana Hila Lē'ahi base when a warrior went alongside him with Ka'iana's cutoff head mounted on his bayonet. Although ashen, he still wore his last smile.

The sight was too much even for Kamehameha. "Take it to Ka'ahumanu," he said, waving the warrior away.

Walking with Peleuli farther behind, Ka'ahumanu fainted when she saw the head. Convinced it was her husband's doing, her hate for him became indelible in her soul.

Soon after returning to Le'ahi, he gathered the members of his War Council to his *heiau* where Kalanikupule, his body cleansed of blood, was already on god Kūkā'ilimoku's, *lele* altar. Kamehameha was unaware that he would be passing Kalanikupule's spirit to an inanimate, dead War God.

The Ali'i nui and his chiefs harbored colliding thoughts while marching back to Lē'ahi. After the ritual he told the Council members, "I say we go to Kaua'i in one week as a continuation of Nu'uanu."

Ke'eaumoku dropped his dagger. "No, we are too close to Makahiki."

"That's five months away," Kamehameha snapped, believing he could take Kaua'i and Ni'ihau by merely showing up.

He turned to Olohana for support.

"Even against a weak Kaua'i we cannot just go," Young said. "We took O'ahu in a day, but we prepared for years."

He looked at Alapa'i.

"Kaumuali'i will someday submit to you," Alapa'i said. "Why don't we stop further killings and put our whole energy into increasing the food supply for our people and curing our sickly?"

Taken aback by their negative responses Kamehameha mumbled something guttural and said, "We go to Kauai after end of Makahiki next February. Close camp and return to Kona."

The *ali'i* rejoiced. They wanted their share of land spoils now, not war. Since olden days, a victorious king in a war shared conquered lands in *mālama 'āina* with his chiefs who had helped him win them. But they were too scared to ask Kamehameha for their share.

Ka'ahumanu seized their mood. After they returned to Kona, she told her husband, "With no war until next spring, now is a good time for you to *kālai'āina*, divide and share conquered lands with your chiefs."

"They told you? Tell them they will get lands after I take Kaua'i," he erupted, wanting to use Kaua'i as bait to keep his chiefs committed.

All the powerful Maui *ali'i* were now aligned behind Ka'ahumanu. Land spoils lifted her power to rival the Ali'i nui's.

Kamehameha, in angst, feared a dagger by one of his disgruntled *ali'i* to restore *pono*.

Anxious to mend his *mana* that Ka'ahumanu had wounded,

Kamehameha thought of Keōpūolani. He called Olohana and Hewahewa and told them, "Go to Kaunakakai on the *Fair American* tonight and bring Liliha and her daughter to Kona."

"*Ae.* They may be guarded. Shall we go with a force?"

"No, go peacefully. Tell Liliha I still want her and Keōpūolani to come to my haven in Kona on the big island and be under my protection. Be ware they may try to escape or commit suicide."

On a June morning in 1795, the people of Kaunakakai saw the *Fair American* offshore. Her presence shocked Liliha.

Olohana and Hewahewa went to shore and waited. No formal announcement of their arrival was needed.

Liliha appeared and greeted Kamehameha's prostrating emissaries. "Please rise. What brings you two here?" she asked, as if she didn't know.

The emissaries related Kamehameha's wish.

"I told him last time that I will go to Kona if Keōpūolani goes. She wasn't ready last time. I will ask her again. Give her seven days to decide."

"*Ae*, we wait here," Hewahewa said with the Ali'i nui's caution lingering. *Escape? Suicide?*

The arrival of the emissaries distressed Keōpūolani, now eighteen. She knew why they came. *How can I be near that lowly enemy of my family?* she lamented.

On the sixth day Keōpūolani told mother, "I thought long, and came to the conclusion that we have no choice. My life is spoiled. I will go to Kona and be near our archenemy only to take father's revenge one day," she said, with her fist clenched.

Revenge! Hate! They merged in Keōpūolani's soul. Liliha understood.

They went to the beach next morning to submit to the emissaries. The saddened people of Moloka'i were there at *kapu moe*. "You may rise," Keōpūolani said. "My *kapu* is lifted. We go now, may never see you again. Thank you for letting us spend our happiest times in Moloka'i."

"*Aloha 'oe,*" Liliha added and chanted a farewell she had composed. But her choking words became lost on a people overcome with grief, and the winds blew her last stanza to the sea.

When they stepped onboard the *Fair American*, Young flashed a signal to the oarsmen waiting in a racing canoe. They sped off to inform Kamehameha. He had earlier instructed Young, "Don't sail immediately for Kona after they board, cruise around Maui leisurely. I need four days to cool Ka'ahumanu and prepare for their arrival."

As expected, Ka'ahumanu erupted when he told her of their coming. She did expect this moment and feared his future sacred child might challenge her for power. She slowly cooled. Ka'ahumanu lacked the *kapu* to bear a sacred male progeny or any progeny since she was barren. She decided to let the coming events passively unfold.

On the fifth morning after leaving Kaunakakai, the *Fair American* sailed into Kona and anchored offshore. Liliha stood tall on the deck and saw a mass of enemy *kāhili* blanketing the beach. She followed

Hewahewa, her *kāhili* bearers and entourage down a new gangplank and onto a bedecked *wa'a.*

With the oarsmen's five deep digs, the canoe glided to shore. Liliha lifted her skirt and stepped onto shallow sands. She wore a yellow *pā'ū* with green fern-leaf design dyed by her Moloka'i people. Its formfitting style accentuated her unusually slim body for a Hawaiian *wahine.* A *lei niho* separated her breasts.

Sacred drums of *Hale Pahu* began to beat to awaken the gods and goddesses to witness the spectacle.

No one in Kona except Kamehameha and Hoapili, his friend and comrade, had seen the stunningly beautiful Liliha, thirty-two, over six feet tall, her dimpled childhood smile still remaining. She married her brother Kiwala'ō when only thirteen, and had Keōpūolani at fourteen.

Kamehameha and Ka'ahumanu led prostrating chiefs from as far away as O'ahu and Maui in full regalia to welcome her. She stood erect, gave to both a perfunctory bow and followed Hewahewa to a shade beneath a tree. She felt Ka'ahumanu's stare from behind.

Keōpūolani was still ensconced in her upper-deck stateroom treasuring her last moment of freedom.

The stateroom door slowly opened. A chubby goddess emerged with mournful eyes wearing a beige *pā'ū* skirt with green taro-leaf design created by her Moloka'i people. She wore nothing above the skirt, not even a *lei niho,* to express her disdain for Kamehameha.

She followed Hewahewa, her standard bearers and entourage down the gangplank and boarded the same canoe. After it glided to shore Keōpūolani went to the foredeck and greeted the prostrating chiefs and chiefesses. *"Aloha,"* she said, with outstretched arms. "Rise, this beach is *noa,* free of *kapu.* Thank you for your welcome." She then stepped onto the beach without lifting her skirt.

They were shocked, awed hearing the voice of a goddess. Women choked and big men cried seeing a sacred chiefess on a pathetic journey.

Kamehameha and Ka'ahumanu knee-walked towards her. Neither had met Keōpūolani before. Hewahewa formally presented Ka'ahumanu to her while Kamehameha chanted a welcome. *"Mahalo,"* she said, disguising hate. Her soft, clear one word captivated the people of Kona again.

Hewahewa escorted her past a long row of kneeling *ali'i*. Seeing Hoapili surprised her. She gave to him a faint smile.

When she arrived in the shade where mother was waiting, a conch-shell call announced the start of a royal procession to Kamehameha's *kauhale* a short distance away. The deep, sonorous sound resonated in Keōpūolani's heart.

The procession arrived at a large hut built by Kamehameha in four days for this occasion. Layers of wall-to-wall *lau hala* mats covered the floor. Just the open door let light into a spacious blind interior. The air inside smelled of fresh *pili* grass.

Kahuna nui Hewahewa escorted the goddesses to their places at the rear facing the entry. He sat Kamehameha at the entry facing them. The rest found their places.

Hundreds of lit *ipu kukui* candles burned around a central square. Keōpūolani was ready to endure a ritual of exchanging valuable gifts with Kamehameha. Acceptance of each other's gift would create an *'ohana*, a familial relationship between them, a relationship she and her mother dreaded.

Naumu, representing Kamehameha, commenced the rare proceedings. In a long chant, he paid homage to Liliha and Keōpūolani going back to their ancestral deities. He thanked, by name, fifty gods and goddesses for bringing them safely to Kona, and asked the deities to bless this moment.

Keōpūolani didn't hear a word. Her deep-set eyes, remindful of Kiwala'ō's, often wandered to Hoapili.

When Naumu finished, it was Liliha's turn to give praise to Kamehameha. With so little to praise, she ended her chant early after thanking him, his queens and ali'i for their welcome. She took a long pause and reluctantly passed to her daughter the gift she would give to him.

With that cue, Kamehameha removed his *malo* and crawled stark naked towards her to receive it. Nudity was the attire when approaching a living goddess.

The people in the hut bit their lips, held back a laugh seeing his awkward, unpracticed style. His *ule*, going to-and-fro, seemed more threatening on this day than his face.

He arrived before the goddess, reached out and received from her a large, light brown gourd calabash over two feet in diameter, three feet tall. "It belonged to my father, King Kalaniopu'u, who gave it to his son, my brother-husband," Liliha said. "I took it with me to Moloka'i."

Its symmetrical lines and calcified grain impressed Kamehameha. *Kalaniopu'u's. Must be ancient* he thought.

Kamehameha chanted his acceptance, crawled back and passed it to Naumu, who handed Kamehameha a heavy, tapa-wrapped object.

It was now his turn to present a gift to Keōpūolani. Cradling it between his arms, he went towards her with his buttocks high and swaying, his penis hanging like entrails. Those already with stomach cramps could watch no more. Liliha thought of captivity to hold her scream.

He arrived before the goddess, leaned forward and laid his offering before her. She removed the wrapping and held a conch shell about eighteen inches long with fifty-two short-spaced whorls.

A *kahuna* informed the goddess, "The earlier call you heard was from this conch. No other exists. It is said the first Marquesans who settled in Hawai'i a thousand years ago found it awash on our beach. A call from this *mana*-laden conch can be heard from here to the top of Hualālai."

Keōpūolani held it in awe. She had been earlier beguiled by its haunting call, but dreaded the consequence of acceptance.

Having no choice, she whispered, "*Maika'i* (Wonderful)," and bowed to Kamehameha, sealing her *'ohana* relationship with him.

Not all in the *hale* were happy. Many sympathetic *ali'i* shuddered seeing a goddess bowing to a nonsacred chief and joining him in *'ohana.*

Kamehameha crawled back, retied his loincloth and returned proudly to his eating hut with calabash in hand. The others left early, leaving just mother and daughter to their caged *'ohana* world.

Keōpūolani cried until morning, blaming her sacred *Pi'o kapu* for her incarceration. But the thought of revenge relieved her crimson sorrow.

With Keōpūolani nearby, Kamehameha's *mana* soared. He lost less sleep over Ka'ahumanu's silence.

10

The prospect of a more joyous event brightened the mood of the people in Kona. In early December 1795, Kamehameha matched Alapa'i, now seventeen, to marry Pualaninoe, sixteen, daughter of High Chief Kahelanui, he of doubtful loyalty to Kamehameha.

The match elated Kahelanui. Alapa'i's deformities and lowest *kaukau ali'i* rank didn't matter. He thanked Kamehameha and said, "I will take Alapa'i as my son."

But his wife Kahelanuiwahine worried. "What would Pualani think?"

"That is not a problem. Our problem is breaking her engagement to Nāpali. We must find a nice way. Alapa'i is hero of the kingdom and close to Kamehameha. We gain big by that. I will go to Hilo, tell Nāpali's parents."

The trip was canceled. Young Nāpali had gone berserk a week earlier with a mouthful of syphilitic chancre sores and drowned at sea.

Urged on by the Ali'i nui, Pualani and Alapa'i became betrothed.

Alapa'i worried, told Mother Ke'enai, "I have nothing to support a wife."

The Ali'i nui learned of his concern, told the hero of 'Īao and Nu'uanu, "I give you an *'ili* of my Kona *moku*. It is now yours. It comes with a thousand *maka'āinana* working the land and eighteen *ali'i* overlords."

The imposing gift stunned Alapa'i. He couldn't believe that a land so close to his heart since childhood was now his.

Under Hawai'i's strict *kapu* system, no lowly *kaukau ali'i* like Alapa'i could own an *'ili*, or have superior *ali'i* subserve him. But the Ali'i nui made a rare exception for hero Alapa'i. This had happened only once three centuries earlier, when half-commoner 'Umi-a-Liloa, through conquest, rose to become king and made every *ali'i* in his domain subserve him.

Kamehameha chose 'umi (tenth) of the lunar month of *Kaulua* (February) for their wedding day, a day free of any god's *kapu*.

But Alapa'i, conscious of his deformities, worried that Pualaninoe might not accept him. They still had not met.

Pualani and family arrived early for the wedding. Guests gawked seeing a stunning bride in a white *pā'ū* tapa skirt with dyed designs of *kalo* (taro) and *'ulu* (breadfruit) leaves, both symbols of plenty. She wore a *lei* made of twisted vines that half-hid her breasts.

Guests besieged Alapa'i when he arrived with his entourage. They reached out to touch him, deformities and all, to get some of his *mana*. He wore a reddish *makaloa malo*, one of many wedding gifts from Kamehameha. *Makaloa* sedge, known for its soft, strong fiber, was *kapu* only to Kamehameha but he made an exception on this day for Alapa'i, who felt undressed wearing something so soft around the crotch.

The couple met for the first time on this wedding day, and exchanged shy bows. She didn't notice his deformities. Her beauty slammed Alapa'i.

After the wedding ritual, a conch blare summoned the deities to witness their consummation ceremony. The *kāhuna* led the couple to a small center square surrounded by ti plants and told them, "Lie down, face up, bodies touching." They started to roll a thick, black tapa cloth over them to the loud drumbeats and propitiatory chants wishing the couple fertility. The sound peaked, then it died when they became fully covered. Just coconut fronds swishing with the breeze disturbed the nuptial site. In silence the *kāhuna* rolled back the cloth and exposed the two whose union had just been spiritually consummated before their gods.

The Ali'i nui in attendance wished he had such a formal ceremony when young Ka'ahumanu became his.

That evening he staged a lavish wedding party. At the height of the festivities, Kamehameha handed a lit torch to Alapa'i and told the couple, "Enjoy your new *kauhale*." He reminded Alapa'i, "Return at dawn. Go back to 'Ewa and begin preparation for Kaua'i."

Home was twenty minutes away, running. Holding hands they ran ignited. Pualani didn't notice his gimpy stride. They arrived at their *hale moe* lit with candles by their help.

Alapa'i was a virgin, rare for a youth his age. He had only dreamt of coitus. The thought of being intimate inflamed his soul.

"Pualani," he called by her name for the first time. They exchanged nervous, tentative smiles and embraced, the first time ever for Alapa'i with any girl. By then neither cared if the gods were watching a couple soaked in passion.

Came dawn, Alapaʻi bid his sad bride *aloha* and returned to Kona. During the long canoe ride to the ʻEwa staging ground on Oʻahu, Alapaʻi sat, watched the oarsmen dig while he grieved over the haunting thought that he must soon kill fellow Hawaiians on Kauaʻi, or be killed.

In Kona, Kamehameha spent his days ensconced inside the ʻAhuʻena Heiau beseeching dead Kūkāʻilimoku for a favorable omen to launch. Frustrated, he tied the inanimate idol of his War God to the *Fair American's* foremast and sailed for Oʻahu in March 1796. Approaching Ewa, the sight of his long row of beached war canoes pointing to Kauaʻi energized him.

After landing, Kamehameha told his War Council members, "I was trying to get Kūkāʻilimoku's favorable omen to launch. I gave up. We are going to Kauaʻi at midnight in a week."

"Without his favorable omen?" Keʻeaumoku asked.

"Yes, but he will support us if we offer to him befitting sacrifices before launch. Return in the morning to finalize landing site."

The council members dispersed to gather their thoughts. *Befitting sacrifices? Maybe us?*

They returned next morning after tossing all night.

Kamehameha told them, "I thought last night that Kaumualiʻi would have his defense stretched thin because he doesn't know where we would land. That means we can land anywhere safely."

"Where best?" Davis asked.

"Poʻipū."

A long silence followed. Kalanimoku had no fresh idea, but he told the Aliʻi nui in a hushed tone, "Keep Poʻipū secret only with us."

"Why?"

"Some council members like Mamalakaha and Puowaina talk too much. Information can leak." Puowaina happened to be one of the Aliʻi nui's many half brothers.

The men prepared to dive overboard for shore. Kamehameha stopped Kalanimoku in time and ordered, "Have Mamalakaha and Puowaina prepared for sacrifice before launch."

Before midnight in late March 1796, two befitting bodies cleansed of blood were at rest on Kūkāʻilimoku's *lele* altar.

The push-off after the sacrificial ritual lacked the warriors' usual screams and drum beating. The prevailing somber mood bothered Kamehameha.

Three hours into the launch the night exploded. Crackling lightning bolts zigzagged down and singed the waves of Kaua'i Channel. Gale winds snapped the *Fair American*'s foremast and dumped it into a wild sea. Kamehameha yelled, "Lower sails! Return 'Ewa!" But no one heard. It was Lono's way of stopping a war and preventing more slaughter of his people.

The *Fair American* made it back to 'Ewa next morning dragging her foremast. The Ali'i nui went to the mast, found the idol of Kūkā'ilimoku gone. In panic he searched the deck. Gone, lost to the waves!

Kamehameha sat devastated at the beach watching his battered forces stagger back.

At his lowest moment a scout from Kona arrived with hostile news. "Ka'iana's brother, Namakea, and about six hundred of his men devastated Hilo two days ago. They entered Waimea yesterday, raped the women, busted taro patches and burned many huts," he said. "We think he is going to Kona next to do same thing, to take his brother's revenge".

Namakea? That coward! he cursed. "Gather the remains from last night, I am going back to Kona to face Namakea in the morning," he told Ke'eaumoku. He asked the scout, "Meet us at the Bay with fresh news."

Kamehameha saved his last painful instruction for Kalanimoku. "I will not be returning to 'Ewa. After we leave, repair the *Fair American*, consecrate Ewa Beach, gather the troops and return to Kona."

The scout was waiting in Kona when Kamehameha arrived next morning with Davis, Alapa'i and three hundred members of his integrated force. "Namakea troops spent another night looting Waimea," he said. "They may be on the Māmalahoa trail now heading for Kona."

"Good, not yet here!" Kamehameha drew a familiar strategy on sand and left for the hills and deployed. They heard voices around mid morning. A jolly Namakea and his men were approaching, unaware that they had just seconds more to live. Alapa'i squinted through the tall grass and let go when they came into his sight. His blasts created a dust storm. Namakea and his troops disappeared in the storm.

Kamehameha was wrenched. *I should have gone to Kaua'i immediately after Nu'uanu without listening to my chiefs. I could have crushed Kaumuali'i just as easily as Namakea*, he muttered, pounding his fist.

With his *mana* lying mangled at 'Ewa by Lono's will, he again felt exposed like he did during the *mālama 'āina* crisis. He imagined seeing his *ali'i*, who were denied lands, following him with daggers in hands.

Unable to function normally the Ali'i nui summoned his top *ali'i* to Ahu'ena Heiau in Kona in early April 1796. No one including Ka'ahumanu knew why.

She came with a different look, heavier, her face rounder, newly tattooed on her left side from armpit to toes, and on her tongue. Harboring disdain for her husband, she had been overeating and punishing herself. Kamehameha found her sexier when new fat stretched her old tattoos.

"*Heahea*. Welcome," he greeted his chiefs with an uncommon smile. No woman was permitted to step into a *luakini heiau*, but he excused Ka'ahumanu. "I promised you land after Kaua'i. But the gods stalled our victory. While we wait for the next chance, I will make some appointments and share lands with you now," he said, making eye contact with each.

The visitors stared at each other in joyous disbelief after hearing, "Now."

"Ka'ahumanu, my gods say you are a *Pu'uhonua*, a sanctuary, a goddess. From this moment, only the gods and you can grant pardon and amnesty to a person seeking your mercy. Use your power wisely. In addition, I give you the Waikīkī *ahupua'a* from the *Ko'olau* to shore."

They were his pivotal grants.

Her ugly feelings toward him took momentary flight. Kamehameha knew he could now sleep better after seeing her shed thankful tears.

The *ali'i* closest to him, even those powerful Maui *ali'i* of doubtful loyalty, received major land grants and appointments.

"Boki Kama'ule'ule, I appoint you governor of O'ahu." The brother of Kalanimoku flashed a puzzled smile.

"Kalanimoku, you are the *'Alihikaua* (Commander) of the army."

Shocked, he asked, "What are my duties?"

Kamehameha didn't know.

No matter, Kalanimoku was happy. *'Alihikaua* sounded big.

The control of Hawai'i's four major seaports and surrounding lands went to Kamehameha's favorites. "Hoapili, take Lahaina. Aikake, you have Fair Haven (Honolulu Harbor). Olohana, Kawaihae is yours." The

Ali'i nui surprised everyone when he told Liliha, an occasional sexual mate, "You have Hilo harbor."

The port chiefs got one order: "Impound any arms shipment and report it to me." Preventing a *coup* ranked highest among Kamehameha's priorities.

When Kamehameha awarded *kaukau ali'i* Alapa'i an additional *'ili* of his Makiki *ahupua'a,* and an adjoining *'ili* to Kainoa's father, Kahemoku, the top *ali'i* raised no objection this time.

"I have a condition for the gifts and appointments I just made," the Ali'i nui told his sixty new landowners.

Jubilation ceased. He felt their stare.

"Help me bring our army to original strength so I can please Kūkā'ilimoku," he said with a second Kaua'i invasion attempt in mind.

The meeting adjourned awkwardly. "Do not go yet," the Ali'i nui told Kalanimoku and waited for the others to clear. To his new Commander he asked, "How will you get three thousand more men to bring our army to original size?"

"I'll give new landowners a quota. Ask them to fill it."

"What if they fail?"

"They won't. They want to keep their lands."

"I also need more *wa'a* to cover what we lost at 'Ewa."

"How many more?"

"Forty *kaulua.*"

"By when?"

"Soonest."

"That would be in eight years."

Kamehameha frowned and walked away. He had no choice but to wait.

11

With the next Kaua'i invasion attempt stalled, Kamehameha decided to fulfill a long cherished wish for a sacred male heir.

On a dreary *Makali'i* morning in December 1796, the Ali'i nui called on Portmaster Liliha in Hilo and told her bluntly, "I came to tell you I want to marry your daughter."

Liliha was offended. *Tell me? Not ask me?* She had been dreading this moment, fearing her daughter's choice was life or death—life, by bearing for him a godly heir, or death, to deny her from having a sacred child by another father.

"I will speak to her today," she said in a whisper.

Kamehameha walked away like an animal denied an instant kill.

Keōpūolani's mind was already made at Kaunakakai, Moloka'i, years earlier. She told her mother, "We have no choice. I will marry him, be near him, just to take father's revenge one day."

Revenge! The thought made marriage tolerable.

A stricken Liliha accepted her daughter's decision. She told the Ali'i nui, "Keōpūolani will marry you. When?"

He rubbed his eyes and said, "I will send someone to tell you."

A messenger arrived the next day at Liliha's compound. At *kapu moe* he said, "The Ali'i nui set wedding day a week from today. He wants a small wedding. You be her only attendant."

Week from today! Cold, from a third party. Liliha was in fury.

On wedding day, all of Kamehameha's wives were elsewhere. Ka'ahumanu was in Hāna, Maui, contemplating her future.

After a brief wedding ritual, the *kāhuna* escorted Keōpūolani to a compound *kapu* to men except Kamehameha. After his frequent nocturnal visits, she began to show early signs of pregnancy. The *kāhuna* rejoiced and stopped Kamehameha from further entry into her compound. She wished her pregnancy would last forever.

In late December 1797, Keōpūolani gave birth to a boy prematurely at grandmother Kalola's old compound in Hilo. Liliha buried his umbilical cord where no sorceress would find it.

The infant, already with his father's features, survived. Kamehameha at last had a *Nī'aup'io* godly heir. He named him Liholiho 'Iolani and knelt in fealty at his feet.

Months later Ka'ahumanu told Keōpūolani, "I love Liholiho. Can I *hānai* him?"

The practice of adoption was common among *ali'i*. "You may," she said, unaware that Ka'ahumanu wanted to turn him into clay in her hands.

Keōpūolani had delivered to Kamehameha his fervent wish. Now it was her turn to ask, "Can I visit my friend Hoapili on Maui?"

"You know him? How?" a surprised Kamehameha asked, more curious than jealous.

"Hoapili often visited my mother in Moloka'i. I met him there and we became good friends."

"You can go any time, just tell me in advance so I can have the *Fair American* take you there," Kamehameha said.

Hoapili? He smiled, shook his head.

Alapa'i returned to his *'ili* in Kona one March morning in 1800 after nearly a year on Maui supervising *peleleu* construction crews.

"Paipai!" Mother Ke'enai screamed when she saw him enter the compound. "Welcome back. Long time!"

"Yes, too long. How is Pualani?"

"Fine, she is in *hale moe*," Ke'enai said, suppressing a smile. Alapa'i hurried over. He heard a loud cry. He peeked inside.

"Pualani!" Alapa'i yelled. Ke'enai excused herself.

"Paipai, you're back! Come, meet Mākaha, your son!"

"What? I'm a father?" He rushed to her side and touched the baby's soft nose. He scanned for his deformities, found none. "Pualani, he's beautiful!" he exclaimed. "When Mākaha born?"

"Two months ago. You like his name?

"Yes, you make me so proud," he said. They were soon rolling on *lau hala* floor as only lovers would and thanked their *'aumakua* for this moment.

Two more Alapa'i *keiki* arrived two years apart, both girls, 'Eme in 1802, and Lani in 1804. Each time Alapa'i looked for deformities, found none and thanked his gods. Waimano and Ke'enai, Alapa'i's aging commoner parents, were ecstatic that they had a new generation of Alapa'i to care.

12

Preparation for the second Kaua'i invasion attempt began in late 1802. The long dormant hills of Holualoa again shook with Lopaka blasts. Unable to cover their ears, the neighbor dogs and roosters begged with outstretched necks, "Cease fire!"

By March 1803, mobilization reached full scale. Under Kalanimoku's watch, fuzzy-cheeked recruits were ready to kill with aging Philadelphia iron weapons.

Alapa'i reported to Kamehameha, "Delivery of forty *kaulua* (double-hull canoes) next year is on schedule, but our ammunition is low. We lost too much at 'Ewa."

"Davis!" he yelled. "Go back to Philadelphia arsenal and bring back more of everything." He needed an overkill of ammunition and weapons for his style of power warfare.

Hope this is my last, and I won't meet pirates, Davis prayed.

In February 1804, Alapa'i's canoemen gave to the Ali'i nui a sight to behold. They arrived from Maui in forty *kaulua* with sails up. After tarrying offshore, they glided to shore. "Here they are, as promised," Alapa'i said, with a hint of boast.

The majestic sight awed Kamehameha. He felt the war for Kaua'i was already won.

Kamehameha walked from one end of the beached canoes to the other, a very long line, touched the bows, stepped into many and praised his gods each time.

A sacrificial offering to god Kūkā'ilimoku closed the evening.

"Are you now ready for Kaua'i?" he asked Kalanimoku.

"*Ae*, with the additional *kaulua* we can go anytime after Davis returns."

"Good, let's go tonight to Waianae and wait for him. I want to catch the wave and go to shore on a new wedge-shaped *kaulua*. "

On this day Aikake was just two hundred miles off Kona. In April 1804 at sundown he made a majestic turn into Kona Bay with the *Fair American's* hold jammed with weaponry. He had encountered no pirates this time.

Chief Kalanimoku climbed onboard. "Welcome back," he told Aikake and crew. Had good trip?"

"*Ae*, got everything the Ali'i nui wanted. Where is he? Where's everybody?"

"They're all at the Waianae staging ground waiting for you and getting ready for Kauai. Let's go."

Aikake made a smooth turnaround with Kalanimoku onboard and headed for Waianae on the lee shores of O'ahu.

Kamehameha was pacing the shores when he saw his schooner heading his way. *"Hulo!"* he screamed again. He rushed out, climbed the ropes and grabbed Aikake and his sores. *"Aloha,* we were waiting for you. Trip successful?"

"Yes, come below, I want to show you. I brought back everything, we have nothing left at Philadelphia."

"Wheee!" the Ali'i nui hollered seeing the stuffs jammed in the hold.

He told his aides, "Go to shore, start beating the drums, raise the war tempo." He kept the launch time in two weeks a deep secret, except to Kalanimoku, Alapa'i and Ke'eaumoku.

"You got God Kūkā'ilimoku's omen this time?" Ke'eaumoku asked.

Kamehameha sheepishly said, "No, but he will support us because he wants *pono*."

God Lono heard. He shook his head and asked, *When will he realize that his War God is dead?*

In May 1804, two nights before the launch, an eerie silence awoke Kamehameha. The war drums had stopped beating. He rushed outside, heard ghostly cries floating in salt air over Waianae sands. The drummers lay face down near their last vomit. He saw Ke'eaumoku gasp for air, his neck swollen twice-normal size before he fell dead at his feet. Scores of warriors were into their last agony.

They had all turned purple.

Pandemic swept the staging area. Kamehameha went prostrate, "Punish me no more," he begged his gods. But gods Wakea, Lono, Kāne and Kanaloa refused. They wanted to render Kamehameha incapable of ever waging war again.

Foreigners in Hawai'i called the pandemic "bubonic plague," transmitted by fleas off infected rats. More rats than people called Hawai'i home.

The number of deaths overwhelmed Kamehameha. With his back hunched, he let the devastation run its course.

Kamehameha's closest *ali'i* began to wonder, *First 'Ewa, now Wai'anae. Has he lost his mana to rule?*

The remains of the second invasion attempt littered the purple sands of Wai'anae. The Ali'i nui hustled at the beach, helped his troops bury the dead, beach the canoes, store weaponry and powder inside lava tubes, things he would never do, to bring early closure to this debacle.

He returned to Kona with his remnants brooding over his bruised *mana*.

Alapa'i trudged back to his Kona *'ili*. "Paipai!" Waimano yelled, seeing him just standing at the entry to the *kauhale*. "We heard bad things happened in Wai'anae and prayed for you."

"*Mahalo*, I prayed for all of you too. How is Pualani?"

"She and your children are just waiting for you."

"I go surprise her," he said, forcing a smile.

With the next Kaua'i launch off his mind, Kamehameha had to do something different. *I'll get away from Kona*, he thought. He gathered his family and retinue and left for his large Honolulu *kauhale* to be near the harbor, a gathering place of his favorite friends.

"Come with us, too," he asked Alapa'i.

He nodded and moved to the O'ahu *'ili* that he recently received from the Ali'i nui. Pualani loved the cooler temperature of Makiki and hoped the move would be permanent.

Ali'i Kahemoku, who owned the adjoining Makiki *'ili*, paid an early call on his friend with his wife, Chiefess Kahua and son Kainoa, now seven. "Kahemoku!" Alapa'i yelled when he saw his old wartime comrade, and embraced him. "I came to introduce my family," Kahemoku said.

"Good, stay for dinner."

§

Already forty-six in 1804 and his army in shambles, Kamehameha's facial lines deepened, his back hunched. He let his two Kaua'i debacles shape his middle age.

Without wars to plan or fight, Alapa'i begged Kamehameha, "Let's use our time and energy to save our sickly. Nothing in our 'āina is more challenging, sacred."

His pleas failed to stir Kamehameha. The thought of Kaumuali'i rejoicing was eating his soul. In frustration he threatened all sea captains banishment from Hawaiian waters if they were caught trading in Kauai.

The threat worked! Kauai's contact with the outside world ceased. The island returned to its isolated pre-Cook days.

In June 1806, Captain Dooley McGowan of Portsmouth, Maine, a trader and a frequent Honolulu visitor, called on Kamehameha with exciting news. "I just returned from Canton. I found an expensive, fragrant wood the Chinese call sandalwood. I see your womenfolks soak tapa cloth in water floating with 'iliahi chips, to give the cloth a nice fragrance. The chips smell like sandalwood. If your 'iliahi is sandalwood, your forests are full of it and you may be worth millions in gold."

"Millions? How much is that?"

"Enough to buy the world," McGowan joked.

"I'd like to own the world, that is exciting!" Kamehameha said, wanting to hear more. "My English friend, Captain George Jardine, is in port. He can take a sample log to China to test the market if you promise to give him the exclusive trading rights to it in China—if he finds a market."

"Of course exclusive," Kamehameha said. "I'll deliver a log to him."

Jardine's *Butterfield* left the Isles one summer day in 1806 with an 'iliahi log tied down on her deck. McGowan would have gone, but he was not registered with a *taikun* (Chinese official appointed by the Manchu Emperor to prevent unauthorized foreigners from landing in China).

An "Old China Hand," Jardine was registered with a *taikun*. Upon arrival in Canton he called on an old friend, *taikun* Ling Chow Yee. "I brought sandalwood from an island in the Pacific Ocean," he said. "Come with me, tell me what you think of it."

"Let's go," he said. He boarded the *Butterfield* with Jardine, scraped off one end of the log, and sniffed. He looked up and smiled. The captain was disappointed. He knew that when a Chinese trader smiles, it was his polite way to say, "No."

"The smell too weak. Ones from Burma stronga," Ling Chow said. "Don't waste time on this."

Jardine dropped a brief note to McGowan and never returned to Hawai'i.

In mid 1808, American sea captain Nathan Winship revived the *'iliahi* mystique. He had a suspicion. He found the perfume of larger, older logs more intense. He purchased a log around a century old, loaded it onboard his *O'Cain* and left for Canton with Kamehameha's blessing.

Upon his arrival, a *taikun* learned from Customs that the *O'Cain* carried sandalwood. His emissaries, Wu Peifu and Li Hung boarded the ship, gave Winship a perfunctory bow. Wu bent down and sniffed the sap of a perfume aged a hundred years. The other noticed the log's oversized central heartwood. Neither smiled. With raised eyebrows, they spoke to each other in Cantonese.

"Here, three hundred twenty dollars in Spanish silver," Wu said.

"Five hundred fifty," Winship countered. "An additional two hundred dollars for shipping."

The other emissary nodded.

Winship veiled his smile with a somber front.

The emissaries went to shore wide eyed. They soon returned with a certificate with a big red-wax seal, and seven hundred fifty-dollars in Spanish silver. "Here is your silver for the log, and this is your pass to enter Gwangzhu next time. *Taikun* Chinn Fu's name on it. And bling back many more same kind log, allight?"

"Allight, I mean all right."

Winship asked the emissaries, "I want to buy some curios. You have?"

"Yes, all kinds, come with me to warehouses." With that certificate Winship passed inspection and stepped onto Canton. He followed Wu. The variety of curios he saw in three warehouses astounded him.

"Choose what you want, we help you load."

"Don't load until you tell me the price," Winship said, smiling.

"No wolly," the price is free, allight?"

Back in Honolulu, Alapa'i's agents caught the popular Kanihonui, seventeen, Ka'ahumanu's nephew, having sex with her. Alapa'i had to report it. The villagers cringed when Kamehameha signaled to his *kāhuna* with a finger across his neck.

They dragged the youth to Diamond Head, scooped out his eyes to placate the Ali'i nui's angry gods and cleansed his body of blood. The *kāhuna* took him inside the Lē'ahi *luakini heiau* to become Kamehameha's and the kingdom's final sacrificial offering to dead Kūkā'ilimoku.

Enraged, Ka'ahumanu cursed her husband. "Why didn't you let him receive my pardon? Remember, I am a *Pu'uhonua.*"

"You could have prevented it," he said.

Not satisfied with the reply, Ka'ahumanu gathered her faithful chiefs and told them, "I will not pardon the Ali'i nui even if he begged. We must end his *kapu* over us, by revolution if necessary."

Surprisingly, Commander Kalanimoku agreed to discuss revolution if heir-apparent Liholiho would join.

Next morning she had Liholiho at her side. Only twelve years old, he wondered why Kalanimoku and other top *ali'i* were sitting before him with long, unsmiling faces.

"Son, thank you for joining us. Your chiefs and I need your help. We think your father has lost his *mana* to rule our *'āina*. We want you to become King of our Kingdom," she said in a motherly tone.

Liholiho panicked, asked, "What will happen to father?"

Ignoring the question she said, "We just want you to become Ali'i nui."

He began to cry. "I don't want change. Stop talking about it," he said, and walked out.

With that, the plot of February 1809 failed, but the *ali'i* got an intimate peek into Ka'ahumanu's mind.

13

One day in June 1809, an 'Ewa lookout yelled, *"O'Cain!"* Captain Winship was in a hurry. After docking, he ignored the welcoming folks and went looking for the Ali'i nui. He found him swimming in his fishpond.

"Aloha! I just returned from China," Winship said with outstretched arms. Kamehameha climbed the fishpond wall and greeted him. The Captain saw the Ali'i nui's deepening facial lines and hunching back. He said, "I sold the *'iliahi* and got this certificate from *taikun* Chinn Fu Shian Sun. With it I can enter Canton any time and sell *'iliahi* logs directly to him."

The king was impressed with the big red-wax seal on the certificate.

"Here are silver coins worth a hundred dollars. They're yours for the *'iliahi* trunk I took to Canton." He tried to whet the king's appetite.

"Ho'omaika'i, mahalo," Kamehameha said, and dropped the coins into a can. He swished them around as if he wished for more to cover the bottom. *I need much more to buy the world,* he thought.

Winship saw his frown and decided to hit him now. With a forward chin he asked, "Give me the exclusive right to market *'iliahi*. I can sell thousands of logs in China and pay you big," keeping it a secret that maybe only century-old trees had value in China.

Thousands? I better put all the 'iliahi under my kapu, he thought.

"Come back tomorrow morning to discuss it."

Winship gaped. He expected a quick "Yes."

The captain spent a long night twisting and turning.

"Aloha, kakahiaka, good morning," Kamehameha greeted him next morning with news he least expected. "I sent my *kāhuna* to all the Islands last night to put every *'iliahi* tree under my *kapu*."

Winship blinked.

"Now, about the exclusive, you said you can sell thousands of trees. How much you pay me to get it?"

"One thousand dollars in Spanish silver now, and a hundred dollars for each log I take to Canton."

The king's jaw sagged. He expected something big. "Let me think about it," he said.

Alarmed, Winship raised the offer. "Make that two thousand dollars."

The king repeated, "Let me think about it."

The king's answer dashed the Captain's hope of striking gold with sandalwood.

Next morning he brought to shore the stuffs that Chinn had crammed into *O'Cain's* hold and offered them for sale, expecting little in return.

He created a buying frenzy! The *ali'i* grabbed items like trifold mirrors, oil landscape paintings and German military uniforms, paying sinful prices for them with gold that they had saved providing provision to sea captains. Winship sold out by noon.

He was amazed. *Curios more profitable than 'iliahi. I'll ask Chinn Fu for more. Kamehameha can think about my request forever,* he gloated, and stashed the gold into his safe.

A messenger from Kauai arrived in December with hot news. "There is rumor on Kauai that Kaumuali'i wants to discuss peace with you and end Kaua'i's isolation," he reported.

"Davis!" Kamehameha yelled. People two hundred yards away heard him. "I hear Kaumuali'i is eager to discuss peace with me. Go Kaua'i tonight with Alapa'i and Kīhei. Meet Kaumuali'i, confirm if it's true."

They were soon off on the *Fair American.*

Next morning at Līhu'e Beach on Kaua'i, a surprised Kaumuali'i greeted his first outside visitors in over three years and escorted them inland through a huge, curious crowd to his compound.

One of his attendants was the tall, exotic, thin-lipped Nā'ālehu, sixteen, Kaumuali'i's younger half sister. Her good looks and intense brown eyes, like an Iberian's, distracted Davis.

Alapa'i went to *kapu moe* before Kaumuali'i and said, "We hear on O'ahu that you want to discuss peace with the Ali'i nui. Yes? No? We came to find out." It was their first meeting.

"Please rise. We can talk," he said, staring at Alapa'i's distorted face. "Yes, that can happen. Strange you know!"

"Peace means ceding Kaua'i and Ni'ihau to the Ali'i nui. Are you ready to do it?" Alapa'i bluntly asked.

"I might, if he accepts my three conditions."

"Tell me," Alapa'i said.

"After ceding, I must remain Ali'i moku (island chief) of Kaua'i and Ni'ihau, retain control over my people, and have right to name my successor."

"If Kamehameha accepts, are you willing to pay him annual tributes in exchange for the protection and benefits you and your people will get from a united Hawai'i?" Alapa'i asked.

"Benefits? What kind?"

"You can open Kaua'i for trading. You can also let your people go anywhere in the Isles under Kamehameha's protection."

Kaumuali'i lit up.

"About tributes. With what? How much?"

"You can settle that with the Ali'i nui. Can you meet him soon?"

"Yes, if the meeting place is safe, like onboard a ship."

"That can happen," Alapa'i said. "I'll ask Captain Winship. I'll let you know. Kīhei, go find Davis, tell him we are leaving."

Isaac Davis had gone for a walk with Nā'ālehu. After a search, Kīhei found him in her *hale moe* in a compromising mode.

"Davis, we are leaving," he said, looking away.

With a grunt, Davis left Nā'ālehu, his *malo* in hand.

The *Fair American* sailed into Honolulu harbor with an unsatisfied Davis at the wheel. Kamehameha climbed her ropes and jumped onboard. With wide eyes he asked, "Rumor true?"

"*Ae*. We met Kaumuali'i," Alapa'i said. "He is willing to cede Kaua'i and Ni'ihau to you under three conditions, all not difficult. He can meet you onboard a safe ship to discuss cession. Can I ask Captain Winship if we could use the *O'Cain?*"

"*Huloo!* Kamehameha yelled. "Yes, go with Winship to Kaua'i and get Kaumuali'i here before he changes mind. By the way, what are his three conditions?"

Alapa'i gave him a quick rundown.

§

Fifteen years after Kamehameha's greatest triumph at Nu'uanu, Ali'i moku Kaumuali'i and his party of sixteen, including Nā'ālehu, were off Waikīkī on board the *O'Cain*. Alapa'i had predicted this day would come.

The pain of losing sovereignty showed on the Ali'i moku's face. Only Nā'ālehu seemed happy in a red *pā'ū* skirt fragrant with sandalwood. Deckhands lowered the gangplank for Kamehameha's four wives. Three made it up with members of the crew pushing from behind.

Ka'ahumanu never tried. The ship's crew sat her down on a shoreboat and cranked her up on a winch. She thought it was fun dangling in midair. She stepped onboard wearing a pā'ū skirt with orange-colored peony design on silk from Canton, China.

After Kaumuali'i greeted all the queens, he whispered to Alapa'i, "Is Keōpūolani coming?"

"No. She was afraid someone might cast his shadow on her and must die for it."

His lips sagged. Kaumuali'i had been secretly in love with her since she last visited Kaua'i years earlier.

The Ali'i nui stepped onboard last and went on his knees before Kaumuali'i, respecting his superior *kapu*.

"Welcome! Please stand, this boat is *noa*. It's free of *kapu*."

Kamehameha rose slowly and said, "Identify yourself," establishing his superiority early.

Kaumuali'i chanted his noble genealogy. Satisfied, Kamehameha asked for all to hear, "Why you come here?"

"To discuss passing sovereignty of Kaua'i and Ni'ihau to you under my four conditions," Kaumuali'i answered more loudly.

"Your conditions?" Kamehameha asked.

"I must remain Ali'i moku of my two Isles for life, have complete control under you of my land and people, have the right to name my successor, and I must agree to your *ho'okupu* . . ."

"Don't worry about *ho'okupu*, I am very reasonable."

The words, "passing sovereignty," uplifted Kamehameha. He gave to Kaumuali'i no chance to change his mind. "I accept your first three conditions," he quickly replied.

"Tell me about *ho'okupu*," Kaumuali'i pressed.

"It's a separate matter. Let's meet in the morning to discuss it," he told Kaumuali'i and left for shore after whispering to Alapa'i, "Watch Ka'ahumanu." He had earlier caught her seductive eyes on Kaumuali'i.

The Ali'i nui returned to his *hale moe* to ponder. *I can settle for a symbolic tribute of just one 'iliahi tree a year in order to get Kaua'i and Ni'ihau.* He thought of another scenario and dozed off.

With his mind made, Kamehameha returned to the *O'Cain* in the morning. He saw a fully clothed Ka'ahumanu in pain, with the Ali'i moku and Alapa'i comforting her.

"Take me to see Kauili," she begged to her husband, clutching her abdomen. Unable to hurry even in a fire, she was cranked down by the crew. This time she thought it no fun. Four men at the shore lifted Ka'ahumanu on a litter and took her home. She kept asking along the way, "Get Kauili."

Kamehameha, Kalanimoku and Kaumuali'i walked to *O'Cain's* aft and sat down. "I decided about *ho'okupu,*" the Ali'i nui said and paused.

"Yes?" Kaumuali'i asked, taking a deep breath.

"Give me the *kapu* of every *'iliahi* on Kaua'i and Ni'ihau. Nothing more."

No yearly gifts? Kaumuali'i was pleasantly surprised. Faking alarm, he motioned Kapena over and went for a walk to the other end of the deck.

"We have no need for *'iliahi.* Give him the *kapu,*" Kapena whispered. Kaumuali'i's eyes smiled. Being isolated for years, neither knew of its value.

He returned to the meeting and told Kamehameha, as if shaken, "As my *ho'okupu,* you can have the *kapu* of every *'iliahi* on Kaua'i and Ni'ihau. Nothing more."

"We have complete agreement!" Kamehameha yelled to his gods on February 16, 1810.

Hawai'i, united in peace after a century of civil wars! Kamehameha reached the pinnacle of his life on this day,

"Let's go to my Waikīkī *kauhale* and thank our gods," he told the Ali'i moku. "I'll have Naumu stage a celebration."

The Ali'i moku hesitated, *I don't want to go*, he prayed. He wanted the safety onboard the *O'Cain*. But being owned by Kamehameha, he had no choice.

In a pre-feast ritual, the *kāhuna* thanked the gods and Kaumuali'i for making this historic day happen, blessed the birth of a new nation, 'Aupuni Mō'ī o Hawai'i, the Kingdom of Hawai'i, and its Mō'ī (King), Kamehameha.

§

A messenger interrupted Alapa'i. "Ka'ahumanu in pain. She asked for you," he said.

Alapa'i told Naumu, "Take charge," and rushed to her *kauhale*. He found her writhing with the *kahuna kaukakaha* (priest-surgeon) Kauili and six of his swarthy male assistants at her side. "Aaaa!" she screamed each time he gently pressed her lower abdomen.

"Maybe *na'aumoa*," he told Alapa'i. Kauili was one of the kingdom's top surgeons. He learned his trade by dissecting countless enemy men and women, alive and dead. He diagnosed appendicitis.

"Here, drink this *'awa*. I am going to see your inside."

"See inside? *Auwe!*" she yelled and gulped the potent kava-root spirit.

Kauili's assistants removed her *pā'ū* and wiped her lower abdomen with tapa cloth moist with ocean water. With no wasted motion he made a four-inch vertical incision on her blubbery abdomen. She squirmed and screamed. The assistants held her down and absorbed blood with tapa cloth.

Kauili stretched open her peritoneal cavity. With direct overhead noontime sun, the cavity was free of shadows. He cut through a membrane and saw a plump red appendix, confirming his diagnosis. With a fine *olonā* string, he tied a bowknot at the cecum of the large intestine, leaving one end of the string outside her body. He then tied a regular knot immediately below, grabbed his knife and cut off the appendix between the knots.

The operation took only fifteen minutes. Surgeon Kauili had to work fast to shorten the pain time of his patients.

Now came the most difficult procedure, joining the cut muscles of an obese. It required force and delicate touch.

Kauili wiped clean the cut end of the appendix and the cavity of stool and blood, rubbed *kukui*-nut oil around the incision and wrapped a foot-wide roll of white tapa cloth around her body. He took another roll and coated canoe-lamination glue on one side, creating a long, foot-wide plaster. "Inhale deeply, make belly small and hold breath," he ordered. While his men squeeze-closed the incision, Kauili wrapped the plaster around her body many times and wound *olonā* cord tightly around it from edge to edge.

The surgery was *pau* (done) in twenty-five minutes.

"It went good, Your Majesty. Look what I took out," he said, dangling a fat, red finger. She smiled, reached for it, said "*kūkae* (shit), and flung the blubbery stuff. He retrieved it, cut it open and saw what he suspected, guava seeds inside resisting digestion.

"Move around slowly, let cut join. Eat only soft food for one week. Do toilet lying down and no sex! I will return in eighteen days to remove the plaster."

Relieved, Alapa'i smiled and returned to the party. The opening ritual had closed and he found a sullen Kaumuali'i and his son sitting next to the Mō'ī nibbling his leftovers.

Not all of Kamehameha's *ali'i* were pleased with the day's events. Some thought he could have gotten Kaua'i and Ni'ihau unconditionally. Before Kaumuali'i could become a factor, Naihe and Kamo decided to rid him.

Aikake Davis got an early wind of the plot. He whispered to Nā'ālehu, "Tell your father beware."

She went quickly to her father's side. Kaumuali'i kept his calm, gathered his entourage and headed for the *O'Cain*. Nā'ālehu chose to stay behind to be near Aikake.

His sudden departure shocked the Mō'ī and killed the party. It also upset the plotting *ali'i* for missing their target. They suspected Davis for tipping him off. He was getting too close to Kaumuali'i because of Nā'ālehu.

Naihe and Kamo targeted Davis. While one had him distracted, the other slipped poison drops into his cup of *'ōkolehao* (ti-root spirit). Aikake thought it tasted bitter, but guzzled it. The great hero of Hawai'i staggered back home next morning and collapsed. The drops intended for Kaumuali'i had taken hold.

"*'A'ole!* No! No!" Kamehameha yelled when he learned of Aikake's death.

The one-time pirate, hero of the kingdom and owner of extensive croplands around Honolulu harbor, died in his prime. As Portmaster of Honolulu Harbor, he was the sole collector of import duties in gold or silver for Kamehameha and Boki, the governor of O'ahu. No one asked him to account for every dollar.

Davis was within reach of wealth when he died.

His family joined Kamehameha next morning in a farewell to Aikake befitting a Polynesian royalty.

Aikake and Olohana had talked about death from time to time and about the kind of burial they each wanted. Young, the survivor, was ready to fulfill Aikake's wish.

After his family bid him a final farewell at Honolulu harbor, Young and Alapa'i laid Aikake on deck of a *wa'a peleleu* and sailed out before sunset. A rainbow hung over misty Nu'uanu Valley, scene of his earlier triumph. They knew Aikake liked that.

Young, the captain of the canoe, Alapa'i the crew and Davis the lone passenger, arrived beyond the reef. Alapa'i clipped a batch of mixed blond and white hair for his wives. They wrapped his body in tapa, crisscrossed the wrap with heavy cord as only old salts know how and tied a large stone from his land to his feet. They eased his body leg first into the blue water, bid him farewell and let go. They saw Aikake zig and zag down and disappear into eternity as Young recited the Lord's Prayer.

"*Maika'i*," the two heard Aikake say.

Captain Young and Alapa'i returned to shore with a passenger overboard.

The burial on that wrenching day in February 1810 brought closure to the sanguine century of conquest. The Isles were united in peace under one monarch. Davis played a key role in the closure, and became its last victim.

Surgeon Kauili made his promised hut call on the eighteenth day. "On your back, Your Majesty," he said, and cut through the thick plaster and the first layer of tapa. The glue, hardened stiff, formed a corset cast. Kauili held both its ends and bent it open. "*Kamaha'o* (Wonderful)!" he yelled. The incision had joined without any indication of secondary infection. The glue had kept the incision area sterile.

He held the end of the bowknot lying outside her body and jerked. Like magic, it untied at the cecum as intended. Kauili pulled it out and covered the tiny hole and the old incision with new plaster. "I will return in two weeks to remove plaster. No bathing or sex until then."

Ka'ahumanu gave him a nasty stare. Kauili returned the stare with a fat bill of two live pigs. Commoners had a standard charge, a mound of taro or sweet potatoes, but *ali'i* had to pay more. Since

Kauili made about twenty operations a month, he and his *'ohana* never knew famine.

Winship took a shaken Kaumuali'i back to Kaua'i and returned to Honolulu. He purchased an old *'iliahi* from the Mō'ī, gathered his provision and sailed quietly for Canton.

14

The lives of many top *ali'i* were turned topsy-turvy after the unification of Hawai'i. Traditional pagan morals tied to the *'ohana* loosened. "We" progressively became "I" in a permissive peacetime society. With time to spare, many *ali'i* were drawn to immorality, like Kainoa's father, Kahemoku. He discovered sin, reveled with two teenage girls, gambled, lost heavily, and went into hiding from his creditors, forcing his family to live in shame. Kainoa, fourteen, vowed to pay off his father's debts one day.

Kainoa frequently visited the Alapa'i *'ili* to play and work with Mākaha. Their friendship hardened. After his father went into hiding, Alapa'i and Pualani brought him into their family. He became like big brother to Mākaha and his sisters, 'Eme and Lani.

An English ship *Greenwich* sailed into Honolulu harbor in March 1810. Her captain, Dean Triggs, forty-three, strolled into Kamehameha's *kauhale* with a sack of plum sweets from China, what Kamehameha had ordered over two years earlier. Friends since Kona days, he met the king at his fishpond.

"Aloha," they greeted each other.

"You came just in time, come early this evening, I want to talk to you," Kamehameha said, putting two plums in his mouth.

Triggs wondered, *Why just in time?*

He arrived early evening and inhaled the smell rising from Vancouver's pot. The Mō'ī confided, "You know we are at peace. My best advisors are running my *aupuni*. I have so much free time and want something exciting to do. Give me some *haole* ideas."

"Attend to your sickly people, help get them well, establish the kingdom's economy, and mass educate your people, prepare them for tomorrow. There is nothing more important, exciting that you can do," Triggs said.

He had heard that before from Alapa'i. "Anything more exciting?"

Triggs shook his head, then thought of Winship, his competitor.

"You know Winship is off again to China. He had a big success recently selling old 'iliahi in China and curios in Hawai'i. With your 'iliahi kapu you can cut him off and take his business. Is getting rich exciting?"

"Yes! I still want to buy the world! How can I get started?"

"You got to have a big workforce to cut down trees, drag the trunks to port, pile them onto ship decks and deliver them to Canton."

"How do I gather a big workforce?"

"You just said you're at peace. You don't need an army. Discharge the warriors and let them work for you."

The advice titillated Kamehameha. He thought, *I have given to my people endless good to enjoy. Now it's my turn to do what I want.*

After ten days of mulling, he told Triggs, "I will become a sandalwood trader," unaware how devastating that decision would be on his people.

The Mō'ī summoned members of his War Council to his *heiau* and told them, "We are at peace. We don't need an army. I want to disband our entire army and send our brave warriors home," quoting Triggs almost verbatim.

"You want total disbandment?" Kalanimoku asked.

Kamehameha stood for emphasis and said, "Yes, total."

Alapa'i, in panic, pleaded, "We must always have an army for just in case. Who will defend us otherwise?"

"In case of what? We are at peace."

"But many sharks outside," Alapa'i countered.

The Mō'ī lost his patience even for Alapa'i. "After we disband, what should we do with our Koma, Lopaka, and ammunition?" he asked.

"Store them same place, inside Waianae caves," Hoapili said.

"Please, leave at least a pocket defensive force," Alapa'i begged.

The Ali'i nui shook his head. "If any army is needed, I will reestablish it so no worry."

He then tersely announced, "Our army is officially disbanded. Kalanimoku, store arms inside Wai'anae caves. When *pau*, send all our brave warriors home."

The troops marched in formation for the last time on that April day in 1810, and the War Council ceased to exist. They arrived at Wai'anae where old memories still lingered on the sands. The men stored the weaponry in moist caves as ordered and scattered for home on foot or by canoes, wondering what to do next.

Alapa'i lurched back home to Makiki and got the shocking news. His stepparents, Waimano and Ke'enai had recently passed away just days apart, of unknown causes. He later learned from *kāhuna* doctors that they were claimed by typhoid fever.

Evanescence had hit the Alapa'i family.

§

One morning next Spring an excited servant awoke the Mō'ī at his Honolulu *kauhale*. "Look outside!" he said, "the *O'Cain* is sailing in from China."

The news elated Kamehameha. *I will stay in the shadow and watch and learn from what he does,* he thought.

After docking, Winship gathered his *ali'i* friends, including Ka'ahumanu, and staged an all-night presale party to soften them for tomorrow. Kamehameha took mental note. Alapa'i spotted him in the shadow. *My king must be learning how to further debauch the soul of his Kingdom,* he wailed.

Next morning the captain spread his goods on the pier and created another buying frenzy. The last item sold in an hour, a black Derby *pāpale* (hat). The proud buyer put it on his head, paid steeply and walked off, believing it matched his loincloth.

Winship staged a shocker finale. Three Chinese "princesses" left the *O'Cain* and arrived on shore. Winship had saved them for last. Wearing embroidered silk dresses that hugged their bodies, *Ali'i* men gawked seeing oriental beauties. The unexpected astounded Kamehameha.

The most popular, Ling Mei, fourteen, roused the two hundred-fifty pound Hawaiian ladies from indifference. They wished to be as slender, but no one told them they'd add fat by overeating *poi*, or lose it by the reverse.

The chiefs beamed when they learned that the girls had private time to sell. They fought for their moment. A bunch of jealous *ali'i wāhine* had seen enough. They cornered Winship and gave him an ultimatum. "Captain, put girls on next ship to China or we no buy anything from you again."

He caved, paid someone a huge sum for their passage back.

The frivolity of his king and of the kingdom's top *ali'i* crushed Alapa'i.

But illiterate Kamehameha had no ulterior intent. He was just finding satisfaction pursuing instinctive desires. Unschooled, he had no inkling of the needs of an infant kingdom to keep it viable against foreign designs.

§

After the furor over Chinese princesses settled, Kamehameha told Olohana, "I want to get started. Go to Canton with an old *'iliahi* log and come back with gold and curios."

"Princesses, too?" Olohana asked in jest.

Young arrived in Canton six months later in November 1811. *Taikun* Chin Fu learned of a ship's arrival from Hawai'i and hoped she had a cargo of "priceless" *'iliahi*. He climbed onboard, met Olohana and saw the logs. He knelt, sniffed, frowned and said, "Here, seven hundred fifty dollars in gold."

Olohana poorly masked a smile.

"Come with me to the shore," Chin said. "I will give you a certificate with my seal so you can enter Canton next time and see me."

"Thank you, sir," Olohana said. "You have curios I can buy?"

You, too? he thought. "We have warehouses full. You can take what you can carry at no charge, under one condition."

"Yes?" Young asked.

"You return soon in bigga ships with more logs, allight?"

"Yes, sir, allight."

With coolie help, Young spent the next two days stuffing his hold with curios and spices that he chose. Chin Fu appeared, told Young, "Don't forget, come back soon with more logs in bigga ships."

"Yes, sir," Young said, and pulled anchor.

In early May 1812, after six months at sea, Young finally had the Waianae Range in sight. A lookout rushed to see the Mō'ī. "Olohana! He is coming back from China!" he said.

Kamehameha jumped into a canoe and met the ship offshore. "Welcome back," he said with outstretched arms. "I see you have so many sores. You sold log?"

"*Ae*, it's easy to do business in China. I got seven hundred fifty dollars for the *'iliahi* and the curios and spices for free!"

Young took him below.

He looked around. "Where you hiding princesses?" he asked.

Young laughed. "Next time," he said.

After an all-night party, Winship style, Kamehameha spread the goods on the pier. They vanished at Young's steep prices. The Mō'ī never realized his *ali'i* had so much money. Winship, watching in the shadow, felt betrayed.

With unlimited resources of old *'iliahi* trees and discharged warriors to harvest them, Kamehameha lacked only ships to haul them to Canton for control of the trade.

Following Dean Triggs' advice, he purchased three schooners including his *Greenwich* on sandalwood futures. He even approached Nathan Winship and said, "I like buy your *O'Cain*."

Winship glared at him and said, "I'll exchange her for all the *'iliahi* on your *'āina.*" He stunned the Mō'ī and left the Isles for good wearing a grin.

With success assured, Kamehameha launched his Winship-style career.

Pity Hawai'i nei. Pity the sickly, Alapa'i cried.

Pono left the Isles forever.

§

Kamehameha's vessels flew foreign flags.

He called his wife. "We need a Hawaiian flag for our ships. Design one."

"You design it," Ka'ahumanu said, still short on words for him.

The king disappeared into his eating hut where he kept several American and English flags leaning in a corner. He had an idea. He replaced the seventeen stars on the American flag with the English Union Jack, and reduced the number of stripes from thirteen to eight, for the eight Hawaiian Islands, in red, white and blue sequence starting from the bottom.

"What you think?" he asked Ka'ahumanu of his patchwork. She didn't expect to see a masterpiece. In late summer 1812, he hoisted a huge Hawaiian flag on the *Fair American's* main mast and watched it flutter. "Nice!" he yelled. Ka'ahumanu for once agreed.

The Hawaiian flag symbolically launched the kingdom's sandalwood decade. The unfolding Anglo-American troubles assured its success.

After years of bickering, England and America went to war. They agreed on one thing, called it the War of 1812. It spread to the Pacific. British gunboats forced American ships to remain in their last neutral ports of entry for the duration of the war, or be sunk. American gunboats countered, forced English ships into their last ports of entry.

"You are so lucky," a stranded American captain drooled.

"Why?" the Ali'i nui asked.

"Since you fly a neutral Hawaiian flag, you can sail anywhere."

"You mean only I can ship sandalwood to China?"

"No American or English ship will dare."

"Wela ka hao! (Hurray!). Can I buy your ship?" Kamehameha asked.

"I'm ready," the captain said.

Kamehameha promptly purchased her and four other brigs tied down for the duration in various Hawaiian ports, all at distress prices. Overnight, with his large transport fleet, he became the new admiral of the Pacific and cornered the sandalwood market.

But his warrior-slaves (people) grieved. With more deck spaces, the admiral drove them harder to fill them.

15

Distracted by sandalwood, Kamehameha paid little attention to Keōpūolani on Maui. She was spending more time with Hoapili and enjoying her emancipation. But her sacred *Pi'o kapu* still separated her from the rest of humanity. She hated being a Living Goddess.

Her friendship with Hoapili ripened—became intimate. On March 17, 1814, Keōpūolani gave birth to a boy. He inherited Hoapili's features, his round face, deep-set eyes, a wide forehead and thin lips.

She named him Kauikeaouli. Kamehameha welcomed the child-prince as his own.

§

'Eme Alapa'i, thirteen, paid no attention to the arrival of Prince Kauikeaouli. She was in her pubescent world excited with her deepening feeling for "big brother," Kainoa.

Tallest among her barefooted girlfriends, 'Eme wore nothing above the skirt to cover her erupting breasts. Her foreign friends noted her deep-set haunting eyes, upwardly curling thin lips and tall narrow nose. They knew she would soon be physically devastating.

Carrying a lunch pail she frequently went to the wharves of Honolulu to meet sailor friends and talk stories. They waited for her with sweets from around the world. 'Eme tried to share her lunch, often of salted dried *'ōpelu* (mackerel) and baked *'ulu* (breadfruit). Most declined except Alan Rowe, thirty-nine, the serious, blond-haired captain of the *Nantucket Star*. He loved *'ulu*.

They met one morning onboard the *Nantucket*. He took 'Eme to the rail and shocked her. "Do you want to go to Boston, live in my house and go to school there for two years?" he asked. "I have four children, two around your age. I know they and my wife Gail will welcome you."

Go to Boston? Will Kainoa miss me? I would, she thought.

"Captain Rowe, shall we go ask my mother?"

"Let's go, I'll change my clothes."

He emerged from his stateroom. "You look so nice in blue!" 'Eme said.

The captain smiled, disembarked with her and began walking up the trail to her compound talking stories.

"How many are living on your land and what do they do?"

"Over a thousand on our *ili*. Men used to farm, raise pigs and exchange some with our *'ohana* folks living near the ocean for seafood. But many are now working in sandalwood forests. Women make such things as tapa cloths, bowls and *lau hala* mats, but I am told their main job is to give birth.

"My father is chief of our *'ili*. He opens each month with offerings to God Kū, and closes the month with offerings to God Lono. He tries to keep our gods happy so they won't bring famine to our land."

"How many huts in your compound? Where do you eat and sleep?"

"We have eight huts, three main ones separated by *kapu*. Our god Kū believes all women are polluted because they bleed monthly. To prevent women from polluting men, Kū made sure they ate separately. That's why I must eat in a hut *kapu* to men.

"Mother must go to a special hut, *hale pea,* to hide from start to end of her bleeding so she won't pollute men." Rowe had heard about a chiefess who was drowned by the *kahuna* when she made herself accidentally visible to a man during her period.

"*Hale moe,* free of *kapu,* is where our family gather, talk stories and sleep, but we cannot eat or drink in there. Death awaits anyone who does.

"And we have *hale li"ili'i,* our toilet, located down wind. It has just a roof over a deep *puka* (hole) in the ground and a board over it with a hole where we sit. We throw lots of flowers and vines inside so it smells fresh."

"You wipe with what?" Rowe asked, wanting to know just in case.

"Most people use dry banana leaves. But we use raw tapa cloth that my mother makes only for that purpose," she said, giggling.

They approached 'Eme's compound. She ran inside and yelled, "We have a guest!" Mother Pualani and Mākaha peeked out, saw a ship's officer. They rushed to greet him.

"Captain, meet my mother Pualani and my brother Mākaha. This is Captain Alan Rowe of the *Nantucket Star*, now in port. He is my friend, teaches me English."

"So nice to meet you," Pualani said.

Rowe bowed to Pualani and Mākaha. "Pualani, I came to ask you a question." 'Eme began to giggle, so Pualani thought it couldn't be a shocker. She was wrong. "You have a brilliant daughter," he said. "I can arrange for her to go to Boston to study while she lives in our home with my wife and four children. I know 'Eme can return as a teacher, someone Hawai'i needs."

A dream chance for 'Eme, she first thought. But doubts quickly surfaced. *Is he trying to steal her? What will Kainoa say?*

Catching her mood, Rowe said, "You don't have to answer now."

"Please wait," Pualani said, and left with 'Eme and Mākaha.

They returned shortly. "Captain, I think 'Eme is too young to leave us," Pualani said.

The quick decision stunned Rowe.

"I understand," he said, hiding his disappointment. "Maybe next year? Please know that my offer has no time limit. And when you are near the wharf during the next two weeks please come for a visit."

"I will, captain. We are grateful."

It was mostly 'Eme's decision not to go because of Kainoa.

Rowe bowed and started downhill.

"Captain Rowe, I'm going with you."

"Thank you, 'Eme, you don't have to, I know my way back."

"I am going with you!" 'Eme said, and that was that.

He shrugged, smiled, and walked down the trail holding her hand.

§

In the 1815s, the world of 'Eme, Kainoa, and other kids was changing under *ali'i* and *haole* pressure. Many "modern" *ali'i* were beginning to feel uncivilized giving daily offerings to scary-faced god idols who brought them no luck. Stone Age customs of first fruits, the agrarian economy in kind, and the system of *kapu* that had bound the people for a millennium, were fading. So was the power of the once-feared *kāhuna*. Without human sacrificial and other esoteric rituals to conduct, they were becoming common folks.

Even the enthusiasm for the pivotal agrarian Makahiki Festival, honoring God Lono ika Makahiki, waned. Kuakini, Ka'ahumanu's younger brother, like Boki and other *ali'i*, thought the Festival lasted too long. "Let's cut it from five uninterrupted months to about ten days to include only key rituals like the one held on the twenty-third day," Kuakini said.

On that day, starting at sundown, *ali'i* and commoner men and women commingled free of *kapu*, ate *kapu* foods together, and accepted each other's sexual advances. Their salacious ways, symbolizing the sacrosanct union of God Lono with his people to reproduce life in his cosmos, ended at dawn.

The ongoing societal changes failed to hinder Nature's Law. A stupendous god-given passionate force was transforming Kainoa's feelings for a ripening 'Eme. She also felt that force. They became more than close friends, found excitement staring into each other's eyes. Kainoa timidly fondled her breast during a swim. 'Eme teasingly touched his stiff *ule* and swam away.

They nearly became man and wife.

Wild chickens used to roam the hills of Pūowaina (Punchbowl) crater overlooking Honolulu village. Kainoa and 'Eme often went chicken-egg hunting, at times with Alapa'i's brown pup Kāna'e tagging along. On some days, they found more than twelve hens incubating their eggs in tall weeds. They stole a few, and thanked the birds. One afternoon, Kainoa did a double take. He saw behind some branches a small opening on the western slope of the crater.

"I never saw it before. Let's go see!" he told 'Eme. Using dead branches he scratched a path to it

Dog Kāna'e didn't follow, she preferred sniffing for eggs.

"Uiiiii!" Kainoa yelled when he stepped inside a cave. It felt like a place that Time forgot since creation. Kainoa looked for bones, artifacts, found nothing worldly. 'Eme grabbed some yellowish powder off the raw interior floor and brought it to her nose. She thought it smelled of ancient earth.

"Kainoa, this place can be our secret home!" 'Eme said, her face and body pressing against his.

Kainoa was thrilled. He measured the cave. Seven steps wide at the front, twelve deep and the ceiling a foot higher than him, curving downward towards the rear. From the cave's edge they could see Wai'anae Range all the way to Lē'ahi (Diamond Head), and Honolulu below.

The two returned the next day, smoothed the bumps on the cave floor and covered it with layers of *lau hala* mats from home. It became their very private place to fantasize, make love.

"Let's give this place a name," 'Eme said. "How's *Hale'ano'i* (House built on love)?"

That's perfect, Kainoa thought and nodded with his eyes closed.

He took out his knife and scratched the wall. It was hard, but not like rock. "'Eme, we can make engravings on the wall."

"Good, why don't you start with your *aumakua*," she said. "Have your ancestral gecko bless and protect *Hale'ano'i*."

The two kids would remember this exciting day in 1815 for the remainder of their young lives.

§

Months later, Kainoa spotted from *Hale'ano'i* an unfamiliar vessel entering Honolulu harbor.

"Let's go see," 'Eme yelled.

They arrived just after American captain William Tanner dropped anchor of his brig, *Flying Cloud*. They saw four Oriental passengers, three pigtailed men in strange black clothes, and a young woman, walk down the gangplank, men first, and board a canoe. They stepped on shore and a man with a long mustache told a curious Hawaiian, "We from Canton, China, want meet your king."

Kainoa was standing nearby. "We can take you, follow us," he said.

They found Kamehameha at his fishpond repairing the *mākāhā* (sluice gate).

Kainoa bowed deeply and said, "They just arrived. This man wanted to see you."

"My name is Chinn Sun," he told the king. "I am the emissary of the *taikuns* of Canton. He is Ah Fat Shian Sun and he Chun Ji Shian Sun my assistants. And she is Nijun who will care for us. We come to buy your sandalwood," Chinn Sun said. "Can we sit down and talk?"

Sandalwood! The Mōʻī's aggressive stance softened.

"Sit down," he said. "You are all Shian Sun. You folks related?"

"No, Shian Sun is title. You can forget it."

"How long are you staying?" Kamehameha asked, opening Chinn's trunk cover.

"Maybe a long time," he said and slammed the cover.

The Mōʻī opened another. "What is that?" he asked, pointing to something fermenting in a thick glass bottle.

Chinn Sun slammed it down. "You have busy hand," he said.

"How do you intend to buy and pay for sandalwood?"

"I tell you in five days, but first give me fifty big men and tools to dig big hole."

"Big hole? Why?"

"You will know in five days."

A frustrated Mōʻī told Kainoa, "Get him fifty men and the tools they need to dig big *puka* (hole). Stay close and watch."

The emissaries picked a spot on the upper shoreline of the harbor. Carrying a *yec mar*, a measuring stick about two feet long, they told the fifty, "dig." Alapaʻi arrived to watch.

In five intensive days, they had excavated a trench ten *yec mar* wide, twenty long and three deep through lava, sand and cinder.

Chinn told Kamehameha, "Cut old sandalwood trunks, fill hole to the top, then ship them on your boat to China. At Canton we pay you four thousand dollars in Spanish gold for whole thing including freight, allight?"

Chinn's precision impressed Kamehameha.

"I give you answer in a week," Kamehameha said, and left.

He gathered his *aliʻi* and asked them a stupendous question. "How many trees will fill that *puka?*"

After rechecking *puka* size and figuring a whole week, they triumphantly reported, "Four trees."

Kamehameha began to count. *At seven hundred fifty dollars a tree I can get three thousand dollars for the four. So why are they offering me four thousand?* He shrugged, told the emissaries, "Your offer accepted." The Mōʻī hated to dicker when he had the advantage.

The *puka* sent the sandalwood boom to a new high.

"Have the crew dig *puka* in every port," the Mōʻī asked Alapaʻi, who painfully followed the order.

The Mōʻī created more *ʻiliahi* slave corps to fill more *puka*. While the kingdom groaned, his pile of gold got higher to buy the world. He shared a bit in *mālama ʻāina* with his *aliʻi*, but spent nothing on his sickly.

16

Admiral Kamehameha, Hawai'i's richest man, crossed paths with an unlikely character, Russian Baron Alexi Baranov, who wanted a chunk of his sandalwood business.

Baranov headed Czar Nicholas II's otter-pelts business on Kodiak Island in Russian America, later known as Alaska. He taught the native Aleuts how to trap otters, slit their whole underside and peel off their furry skins in seconds, before the animals realized what was happening. The pelts were favored in Canton, China, for their thick, brown underfur free of spear marks.

Baranov's agents were telling him, "We see Hawaiians doing big business in Canton selling sandalwood to the *taikuns*. But they don't know the worth of their variety. Why don't we get involved as their China agent? We can triple what they're getting!"

Alexi Baranov leaked vodka saliva.

He summoned Anton Schaefer, the Prussian medical doctor in his employ. "Go on my boat to Honolulu, Sandwich Islands, check on the inventory of sandalwood in the islands and hurry back to report." Baranov picked Schaefer because only he on his staff spoke English, the lone foreign language, he heard, that the Hawaiian chiefs knew.

The Doktor checked the nautical map for Sandwich Islands and clicked his heels in assent. He was eager to taste the tropics.

In spring 1815, Schaefer, 38, arrived in Honolulu on board the *Ural*. The large number of ravaged people he saw along the trailways shocked him. With help of village folks he found his way to Kamehameha's nearby *kauhale* and met Ka'ahumanu and Alapa'i nursing him. "Sorry to interrupt. I just arrived. I am Anton Schaefer, a doctor and a naturalist serving the Russian Czar," he said, changing his identity. "I am studying the kind of plants and trees in your forests for my book. Can I visit your islands?"

His arrival on the *Ural* gave to him instant credibility. But the Mo'i was too ill to respond.

The Doktor knelt beside Kamehameha lying in a fetal position. He felt his high temperature and rapid pulse rate, and saw his pussy watery stool in a nearby bowl. He suspected cholera, and caught his sweetish body odor of impending death.

I better work fast, he thought.

Schaefer reached into his bag for some herbs from China, boiled them in the Dutch oven and forced the bitter tea on Kamehameha. He fed him a meal a day of fish and taro boiled in tea, nothing more or raw, and cared for him with Alapa'i's help.

On the fifth morning Kamehameha straightened from a fetal position, his abdominal pain bearable. "Make me pot-roast reef shark," he asked.

Herr Doktor Schaefer smiled. He knew he could now get anything he wished for saving the Mō'ī's life.

He repeated, "I am a naturalist." It meant nothing to him. "I am making a study of the kind of plants and trees in your forests. Can I visit the Islands on my boat and go inland to see?"

He heard 'study.'

"Yes you can." Kamehameha asked Alapa'i, "Have Kainoa teach him trees."

The Doktor went to Kealakekua Bay. He saw at the shore a weary bunch cutting a trunk into shorter lengths for loading onto a ketch. He bent down, grabbed some sawdust and brought it to his nose. Its intense perfume stunned him. *So this is 'iliahi!* he thought.

Wherever he went, to Ka'ū, Hilo, Mauna Kea, he saw Kamehameha's emaciated *'iliahi* warrior-slaves struggling not to die.

He left for O'ahu on the *Ural* and docked off Wai'anae. He saw a long stretch of war canoes beached along its shore. "What for?" he asked Kainoa.

"For Kaua'i invasion. Now peace so we no need them."

He went inland, saw vast sandalwood forests in the Wai'anae and the Ko'olau ranges. Corrupt ideas began swirling in his mind. He dumped any thought of returning soon to Kodiak to report on sandalwood inventory.

"Can I visit Kaua'i next?" he asked Boki, holding a map of Hawai'i.

"Ka'ahumanu said you can go anytime. The Ali'i moku is waiting."

Kaumuali'i greeted the red-haired Doktor when he stepped on shore at Līhu'e with Kainoa. "Welcome, I heard you were coming." He introduced a hefty guy: "This is Kanahele. He knows Kaua'i, and will be your guide. Go anywhere, and eat and rest at my compounds. Kanahele knows where."

"*Mahalo, danke sehr,*" the Doktor said with a sharp heel click. Over the next few weeks,

Schaefer found more *'iliahi* forests deep inside Mount Wai'ale'ale and in the Wainiha and Hanakāpī'ai Valleys close to the port of Hanalei.

Overcome with greed, the Prussian began working himself into a position of trust with Kaumuali'i.

Half teasingly, he asked, "You want Imperial Russia to help you take Hawai'i from Kamehameha?"

Kaumuali'i stopped smiling. He looked around to check if anyone was nearby.

"Imperial Russia? How?" he asked.

"Russian navy will transport your men to the island of Hawai'i, and give you artillery support. Kamehameha has no army to defend. If you invade, his sick, hungry people will rise, join you. You capture and sacrifice him to your god and become the Mō'ī of all the islands," Schaefer confidently said.

Becoming Mō'ī! The thought uplifted Kaumuali'i. He looked around again, making sure they were talking privately. *The Russian navy against the Ali'i nui? No contest,* he thought.

"What does Russia want if we win?"

Schaefer saw he had the Ali'i moku hooked. He began pulling him in.

"First, let's talk about me. I want Hanalei Valley and half of O'ahu, from Honolulu east. The rest of Hawai'i is all yours."

"Maui and Hawai'i too?"

"Yes, all of Kaua'i also, except Hanalei. I am not greedy."

"What Russia wants?"

"Just the exclusive right to sell your lumber," meaning *'iliahi.*

Kaumuali'i became serious. He thought, *My people gained nothing after I ceded Kaua'i and Ni'ihau to Kamehameha. And I made a big mistake giving him the kapu to all the sandalwood on my islands as tribute.* He was anxious to recoup.

After a sleepless night, Kaumuali'i committed to treason. "We follow you," he whispered to the Doktor next morning. To show his good faith, he added, "You wanted Hanalei Valley. I give it to you now."

It was the most idyllic spot Schaefer had ever seen. "*Mahalo, danke sehr!*" he exclaimed. It boggled his mind comparing Hanalei to his igloo in Russian America.

"Let's prepare for war," he told Kaumuali'i. "Here are my priorities."

Kainoa rushed home to tell Alapa'i, "Strange things happening on Kauai. Kaumuali'i gave to Schaefer the entire Hanalei valley. Unemployed *kāhuna* are now building his limestone house. The *'āina* is not his, only the Mō'ī can give land away.

"The Doktor is also building limestone bunkers along southern shores. I don't know why, maybe he fears a third Kauai landing. He must be thinking war against us with Russian help," Kainoa said.

Kamehameha became concerned when he heard the news from Alapa'i.

In January 1816, Baranov received Schaefer's winded letter of his "No fail" scheme requesting the Russian navy's help to execute it. He screamed "shit" in Eskimo speak; he wanted from Schaefer just an inventory of sandalwood, not a war plan.

By coincidence, Lt. Otto von Kotzebue, commander of an Imperial Russian warship sailed into Honolulu. Startled, Kamehameha confronted him. "I hear your Czar's emissary, Doktor Anton Schaefer, now on Kaua'i, is planning war on me with Russian navy's support. True? False?"

This is incredible, Kotzebue thought. "False! We never heard of this man Doktor Schaefer. His name is not even Russian. The Czar is your friend. He will never agree to such a scheme," Kotzebue assured.

As proof, he weighed anchor and bypassed Kaua'i altogether. With that snub, the Doktor's invasion plan crumbled.

A humiliated Kaumuali'i asked for Schaefer's head. But the clever Doktor slipped off to Honolulu a moment earlier and left for China, leaving behind the *Ural,* limestone bunkers attesting to his delusion, and his white limestone home with a Russian flag over it in idyllic Hanalei.

17

In earlier times, Kamehameha watched Winship enviously. Now the kingdom's top *ali'i* were on him, figuring how they could grab a chunk of his *kapu 'iliahi* business.

Ka'ahumanu caught their mood. She gathered her trusted *ali'i* and told them, "*'Ai kapu* gives to the Mō'ī divine right to own everything on our *'āina*, including sandalwood, you and me. We must strike down *'Ai kapu*. *Haole* don't have *kapu*, only we have them to serve the king."

"That takes a revolution!" Kalanimoku exclaimed.

"I'm ready."

Hoapili nodded and said, "*'Ai kapu* made sense during conflict times, but not now. We don't have to support the one thousand idle *kāhuna*, who lost their *mana* when peace came. We better follow the *haole* example. They eat with women, enjoy it and no god punishes them."

Other *ali'i* sat silently listening to treasonous talk. But no one opposed. Ka'ahumanu heard, "*Ae*."

She kept quiet about her other reason for wanting *'Ai kapu* crushed.

The former army Commander Kalanimoku cautioned Ka'ahumanu, "If the Mō'ī learns that we are thinking of striking down *'Ai kapu*, he will kill us."

"I know. That's why he must first be dead," she said.

Kalanimoku continued, "We must also show the people that we have strong spiritual support. That is why Queen Keōpūolani and Kahuna nui Hewahewa must join us if we are going to do it."

"I agree. Leave all those things to me," she said. With that the first treasonous meeting ended upbeat.

Getting rid of the Mō'ī is easy, Ka'ahumanu thought, *but getting Keōpūolani to smash 'Ai kapu and her sacred P'io kapu?* She knew the goddess loathed Kamehameha. *But will she give up her sacred kapu?*

Ka'ahumanu gambled she would. She went to Lahaina.

"Yes?" Keōpūolani said, surprised to see her.

Ka'ahumanu scattered the attendants and whispered, "All of us, the queens and ruling chiefs on the island of Hawai'i are wondering if we should end 'Ai kapu. What do you think?"

"Why?" she asked.

Ka'ahumanu divulged her other reason.

"'Ai kapu encourages any ali'i to raise an army and challenge us for power in the name of pono. We can prevent our downfall by making the position of the Mō'ī hereditary, reserved only for our heirs. Besides, we think 'Ai kapu has lost its mana. It won't help our sickly, only gives the Mō'ī the right to get personally rich at our expense."

"He will kill you if you tried to abolish 'Ai kapu," Keōpūolani warned.

"Yes, I know. That's why he must first be dead."

Revenge! My chance! Keōpūolani thought. She wanted 'Aikapu crushed so she can live without her overbearing sacred P'io kapu. Not fully trusting Ka'ahumanu she negatively promised her, "I will not stop you."

Ka'ahumanu heard, "Yes!"

Hewahewa was different. Although his fortunes had sunk with peace, he was still the Mō'ī's personal Kahuna nui. She feared he might squeal on her. But again she gambled, invited him to her hut and asked, "You think we still need 'Ai kapu?"

"No, our society has changed."

His quick reply energized Ka'ahumanu. She said, "Without 'Ai kapu, the Mō'ī will cease to be Akua and own everything, including you, me and the sandalwood on your land. You can sell your 'iliahi and keep the gold."

"True. But more importantly, the political power of a king is still vested too deeply in ritual like in conflict times. It's time we become free of kapu in a new world we are entering."

His response erased her fears. She asked, "Can you join the queens, other ali'i and me in abolishing 'Ai kapu?"

"Not while the Mō'ī is still alive. After he is dead, the new King Liholiho must stamp out 'Ai kapu. Only he can, by eating with ladies."

"Can you join us after our Mō'ī is dead?"

Hewahewa gave to her a painful traitor's nod.

A crucial matter surfaced. Hoapili confided with Ka'ahumanu, "I hear the king is taking back all the lands he gave to us and giving them to Liholiho. Only you can prevent it," Hoapili said. "Please visit the Mō'ī and ask him to let us keep our lands in perpetuity as reward for our lifetime of service to him."

Ka'ahumanu, who also had a vested interest in her lands, agreed. She paid her husband a rare visit.

"*He mai*. Welcome," he said. "It's been long time."

"I came to ask you something," she whispered, cuddling to him. *My last time*, she vowed.

"Yes, what?"

"Your *ali'i* are anxious to keep forever the lands you gave to them. I ask you, reward your *ali'i*, let them keep the lands for their lifetime of service to you. Plenty of lands left for Liholiho."

His aging mind heard a veiled threat, of murder by her *ali'i* if he refused. The memory of Kiwala'ō at Moku'ōhai in 1782 flashed back.

Alapa'i learned of Ka'ahumanu's visit. He frantically urged Kamehameha, "Hurry, reclaim the lands you gave to your *ali'i* and give them to Liholiho now, so he can one day share them with his *ali'i* to gain their loyalty."

It was a centuries-old custom of kingly perpetuation.

Alapa'i is right. I must give my son his chance to rule with kingly power, Kamehameha thought. Then he recalled the diligence of his *ali'i* at Pu'ukoholā, their bravery at 'Īao, Nu'uanu, and their continued loyalty after the failed Kauai attempts. *She is also right.*

He became confused.

"Gather the Ali'i Council," he asked Alapa'i.

An unseasonable chill settled over Honolulu in mid February 1819.

Gaunt Kamehameha, sixty-two, wearing an *'ahu'ula* (red feather cloak) for warmth, welcomed the aging members of the Council to his *heiau* with a raspy, *"Aloha."*

They were eager to hear what he had to say.

For the last time he posed as the undisputed Mō'ī and said, "I am grateful for your long, faithful service to me through all the wars and good and bad times. To thank you, I am not taking back the lands I gave you." Exuding love for those premeditating his death, he repeated what Ka'ahumanu had whispered, then concluded, "Your lands are no longer mine."

Liholiho ashened. He looked around, saw just Alapa'i and Kahemoku, Kainoa's father, distressed. By choosing life over death, the

Mōʻī had just terminated the ancient practice of *mālama ʻāina*, forcing his son Liholiho to rule and live as a land-poor monarch lacking *mana*.

In former times, an heir receiving such a treatment would be compelled by God Kūkāʻilimoku to wage war to correct the injustice. But Liholiho, the first Hawaiian king untrained in war and without an army, had no sting.

The chiefs attending the meeting, including Hoapili, Naihe, Kalanimoku, Keʻeaumoku and the governors of every island, were ready to kiss Kaʻahumanu's feet for turning the Mōʻī around. As a payback, they vowed to subserve her for life.

The old allies of the king and Liholiho began to distance themselves from them. They had so little left to *mālama ʻāina*. Alapaʻi wanted nothing.

The king told Alapai, "I want to return to Kona and swim in my fishpond. Why don't you and your family join me?"

"*Ae,*" he said, and they left together.

A late spring storm soaked Kamehameha's grass rooftops. "I have a difficult time breathing, first time, and I'm cold," he told Keōpūolani sitting at his bedside. She wouldn't go for a blanket.

Kamehameha breathed harder.

He asked her, "Call Hewahewa."

He promptly came. After coughing several times he said, "If I die please hide . . . my bones," he told him, though he was still confident that death would never triumph over his life.

"*Ae,*" Hewahewa replied to please the Mōʻī. In earlier times he had to disappear forever with his bones to keep their hiding place a secret. But old values in Hawaiʻi were crumbling.

On this day, Kamehameha was sinking like a mortal. Keōpūolani sat nearby and offered him no water or sympathy. *My revenge!* she whispered to her *aumakua* with malicious pleasure.

Aliʻis from Kingdom-wide converged on Kona to bid him, *aloha.* They loved the Mōʻī.

Kānaʻe, Alapaʻi's brown dog, smelled Kaʻahumanu's telltale underarm secretion, a different kind of anxious sweat. With teeth peeled she wailed. Alapaʻi kept Kānae under control.

On May 8, 1819, *a bright, iridescent sun was setting off Kona.* Kamehameha, breathing deeply, became motionless with a bite of banana in his mouth. A frustrated Kāna'e, with tongue hanging, went to a corner to lay chin on hand and wailed.

Kamehameha's *'uhane* (soul) spirited from his body, soared over Kona and Pu'ukoholā, and descended on the bog of Kohala, the place of his birth. It touched the hidden gold coins, tarried around nearby hills and shores to recollect old times, then left for the *'aumakua* realm.

Captain Dean Triggs, in Kona village for a fortnight, found Alapa'i walking the harbor in a blank. The old friends sat down to talk.

He saw a distraught Alapa'i and tried to console him with words. "You must be bitter that the Mō'ī didn't do more for your sickly. I am, too. He had the power and gold to do it. He could have educated and prepared you folks better. But he never understood the demands of a world he was entering. He was always looking back at the good old days, not forward. He struggled in a changing world to make changes that would keep the past unchanged. Forgive the Mō'ī. Remember him by his great achievement. He brought peace after over a century of civil wars, and united the eight islands. No other *ali'i* had his *mana* to do it. That is a lot."

"Yes, captain, I love him, I will gladly die for him, but his peace is dooming us."

On the tenth evening after the Mō'ī's death, his friend Hoapili, with Hewahewa and his delegation of *kāhuna*, called on Alapa'i at his Kona *'ili* and placed a *kā'ai* (woven casket) respectfully before him. Alapa'i knew it contained Kamehameha's skeleton in its traditional fetal mode.

"Hide the Mō'ī's bones tonight," Hoapili asked, knowing he would accept and discharge his final duty.

"The Mō'ī asked Hewahewa to hide his bones, so why our father?" Mākaha grieved. His family members knew what must happen if he agreed.

"*Ae*," Alapa'i whispered. At that instant he knew he was no longer of the earth. His life flashed across his mind. Only the flickers of two candles moved as members of his family lay prostrate in respect for the Mō'ī.

The visitors left the hut and disappeared into the night of a young crescent moon.

Alapa'i asked for a coconut from his yard. Pualani brought it. He imbibed its juice and tied the *kā'ai* humbly on his back. After a long final eye contact with each member of his family, Pualani the longest, he also disappeared into the night without turning back. No one knew to where. Kāna'e howled softly and followed.

Alapa'i arrived at Keauhou and walked down a long trail seldom trod to a pebble beach bordered by a cliff that went straight down to the shore. He remembered walking near the edge when he was small, too scared to look down.

"Kāna'e," he called. She was lagging with her mind full. After walking a mile, Alapa'i came to an inlet below the cliff. He heard ominous guttural sounds bellowing from the interior with incoming tides. "We are going in," he told Kāna'e and waded inland with the *kā'ai* tied to his back.

The mighty sounds of captive waves striking the walls echoed doom. Alapa'i knew he was close to the end of a deep cave. Feeling his way in pitch darkness, he found a small flat surface above the tide and decided to rest, too overwhelmed by the moment to be scared or to sleep. Kāna'e, who could see in the dark, went to his side and whined.

Morning came. Sunlight peeping through a hole from above and the tides conducting daylight illuminated Alapa'i's final destination. He found himself in a jagged volcanic cavern with waves striking the sides. Just beyond he saw a wall. He was aware that high incoming tides would fill and pressurize the cavern and send geysers skyward through that hole. Alapa'i had occasionally seen them, but never guessed he would be at the source one day with the truth of imminent death upon him.

Me, a kaukau ali'i, a cripple with my king as companion, he proudly felt. He saw a lava-tube opening on the cave wall. He went in and crawled inland dragging his belly over a floor of lava rocks teeming with *'alamihi* (black scavenger crabs) feasting on hundreds of fish washed in. Kāna'e obediently followed, crying softly. Alapa'i took a brief rest with crabs at his belly, *kā'ai* on his back, blissful that no one would ever find the Mō'ī's bones here.

Without warning, an incoming tide of untamed fury choked the cavern. It whammed Alapa'i and Kāna'e forward. He heard a pop like a ripe gourd bursting on impact. He reached for his head, then his body to check if he was bleeding, but felt nothing. A limp body with a *kā'ai* on its back and a motionless dog were awash in a lava tube.

'Au-eee! That's me and that's Kāna'e! I don't feel any pain. Am I dead? Alapa'i asked

Strangers to Paradise are momentarily stunned seeing their lifeless bodies.

Yes, Alapa'i, stepmother Ke'enai said. *At that instant of pop, when your head slammed against the jagged lava wall, your soul entered a serene New World to spend eternity with the Almighty and us, leaving your mortal body to the crabs.*

Aloha, dear Pualani. I had to serve my Mō'ī. Just the stars and Wākea know where I hid his bones. Be proud of that, dear Pualani, it was my final duty.

Alapa'i asked no one in particular, *Am I in my 'aumakua realm? Am I now a family deity?* He still hoped he was dreaming.

Ke'eaumoku heard his lament. *No, you are in Lani e, the spiritual world of all Hawaiians, my home since 1804,* he replied. *The only deity here is the Almighty. There are no 'aumakua deities in Lani e. All the things you heard on earth—the 'aumakua realm, gods like Kū and Lono, Po, 'Ai kapu and Pi'o and Nī'aup'io kapu ranks, and such things as the ali'i caste—are all inventions of kāhuna to control the people. The ali'i and kauā slaves are commoners. Hawaiians are all one people. Not even the sacred chiefs and chiefesses had genealogical ties to gods.*

A shocked Alapa'i just listened.

With his mind sprinting, he asked mother Ke'enai, *You said my soul left me at that moment of impact. How did it enter into my body originally?*

It came to you at birth as a gift of the Almighty, she said, *to give you the power to think, do, love and create.*

Do spirits die? Alapa'i asked.

Never. The human soul, once gifted, is immortal, Ke'enai said.

I like that; I would hate to keep on dying. Once is enough. Sad that earth people won't know for sure it's immortal until after they die.

Nalu told Alapa'i, *I learned after I came here that spirits are immortal but Lani e is not. It disappears if Hawai'i nei disappears.*

Ahuh, Alapa'i said, not quite getting it.

Where is Lani e?

Waimano, Alapa'i's stepfather, got his chance. *It is not a fixed place somewhere high above, but is of the earth. It surrounds those we love, a skin away. People on Earth breathe the air of Lani e.*

No wonder I just saw Mākaha pounding poi, Alapa'i said. *And I held Pualani close to me. She cannot feel me, but I did, like I had never left the 'āina.*

Isaac Davis rushed over and hugged Alapa'i. *Nice to see you again!* he said. *I thank you for the way you buried me in the ocean.*

Nice to see you too but not here with all you ghosts, Alapa'i said. *I would rather be with Pualani.*

We're no ghosts. A spirit is the ultimate form of our Almighty's creation, Davis replied.

You're an Englishman. How come you are here?

I am a Hawaiian at heart. Spirits go where they belong. I belong forever in Lani e, not somewhere over Liverpool.

Can we spirits help the sickly on Earth? Alapa'i asked. He was concerned about them even after death.

No, Davis said. *Spirits are powerless to make anything happen. Whatever happens on Earth happens naturally, by chance or by the will of the people. Death by old age happens naturally. Death from sickness, by accident or in a war happens by chance, and war itself happens by the will of some people. The Almighty, even with his awesome power of creation cannot change fate. Chance had me fated to die of poison. The Almighty had no power to stop Naihe, save me.*

No wonder, I prayed hard to Lono to help our dying, but he never lifted a finger.

Waimano added, *The Almighty could not answer even someone's simple prayer, like to catch a fish. You catch it by chance.*

Alapa'i's mind turned faster. *Do bad people enter Lani e?*

Yes, we have no other realm, Waimano continued. *There is no such place as hell. But even bad spirits have conscience. After entering Lani e they ask forgiveness of those they had harmed. Souls forgive, don't hold grudges. After receiving forgiveness spirits do penance, seek atonement to restore their original purity gifted by the Almighty. Only then can spirits roam Lani e freely. Kamehameha is now asking forgiveness in Lani e of every 'iliahi slave who labored for him, and is waiting for the last slave to arrive.*

Alapa'i thought some more. *Nalu, you earlier said Lani e disappears if Hawai'i nei disappears. Why?*

Because Lani e is inseparable with our 'āina. Neither can exist without the other. Should our 'āina vanish, or be taken from us, Lani e will also vanish.

What happens to all the spirits in Lani e?

They wander as aliens on their former 'āina. But not to worry, Hawai'i nei is too young and beautiful to die.

Thank you, Nalu, I am relieved. Father Waimano, you earlier said spirits have no power to answer someone's simple prayer. Then what is our purpose in Lani e? I always wondered what I would be doing after death.

We spirits can freely enter into the souls of our loved ones, give to them hope that we are looking after them in their constant struggles, Mother Ke'enai said. *Yours is in Pualani's soul this instant. She is thinking of you and feels you are a part of her and watching over her. That thought keeps her moving forward until she comes to you.*

Yes! Alapa'i exclaimed. *Dear Pualani, feel my touch! Hear my chant. It's me, Paipai,* he pleaded deep from inside her soul.

18

The death of Kamehameha in Kona spiritually defiled the village for his kinfolk, who had to leave for somewhere until it was ritually purified by the *kāhuna*.

"We're going to Kawaihae to escape defilement," the king told Kainoa. "Please join us and take my brother surfing and fishing."

"My pleasure, Your Majesty. We'll go for *'opihi*, too."

Kauikeaouli, six, hugged Kainoa and yelled, "Let's go now!"

Liholiho, Queen Kamehamalu and their entourage left for Kawaihae thirty miles north of Kona, but Ka'ahumanu decided she wasn't going. She knew her husband kept his gold in Kona. Her desire to open his warehouses and grab his gold while Liholiho was away overrode personal defilement.

Ignoring the night in *kapu moe*, she asked her hefty male servants to open the heavy *kapu* door of the Mō'ī's main warehouse. She stepped inside with a lit *ipu kukui* candle. Several rats brushed her feet. *"Wā!"* she screamed. She looked about, found only litter, not even a coin on the floor.

Dismayed, Ka'ahumanu rushed to open other warehouses. More rats and litter.

Only Kamehameha's gods saw where he and Alapa'i hid his gold in Kohala deep inside lava tubes near the shore.

Twenty days after the Mō'ī's death, Ka'ahumanu sent a messenger to Kawaihae. He told Liholiho, "Your Highness, the queen wants you back. She says Kona has been purified."

"What for?" Liholiho asked.

"I don't know. She asked me to tell you it was urgent."

"Go back. Tell her I'm going sailing so don't bother me. Ask her why she didn't join me here. I want to know."

"I cannot leave without you. That was my order," the messenger said.

"Please Your Highness, don't go!" Kainoa exclaimed. "She wants you to abolish 'Ai kapu and strip you of your divine rights."

The messenger made camp—waited.

Four days later Liholiho surprised everyone. "I will go see," he impulsively said. He brushed off everybody and boarded the messenger's canoe.

He returned to find Ka'ahumanu upbeat. "Son, I just called a meeting of the Council of Chiefs. We will meet shortly in father's heiau."

"What for?" he asked.

"To name you King."

"What else?"

"Just wear your best," she said, ignoring the question.

He returned in a redcoat uniform of an English Major General with rows of "campaign" ribbons splashed on the left chest.

Ka'ahumanu knelt before her sacred Ni'aupi'o stepson, asked, "Can we convene the meeting?"

"Begin," he said. It was the first Council meeting in twenty-five years without Alapa'i.

"Thank you, Your Highness." After an intended pause she said, "We meet to inform you that your people and your chiefs pronounce you King of the Kingdom of Hawai'i to succeed our late father."

"You said that before. What else?" he prophetically asked.

In a well-fermented answer she said, "Your Majesty, I must co-rule with you as Kuhina nui (Prime Minister). It was your father's last wish."

"He never hinted that to me!"

"Don't doubt me, son," Ka'ahumanu scolded.

Just back from Kawaihae, Kainoa whispered to Mākaha, "What a lie." Without an army to stage an uprising, Liholiho had no relief. He had to accept whatever order she thrust upon him.

The Council meeting became her coronation, not his.

This is the end of kingship, Mākaha muttered. God Lono overheard. "No, this Kuhina nui thing is the beginning of the end of Hawai'i," he guaranteed.

Only Ka'ahumanu knew she had appointed herself Prime Minister to orchestrate a revolution.

In mid October, the Makahiki festival of 1819 commenced ominously. There was no joyous commingling of the *ali'i* and *maka'āinana* in the annual collection of tributes to the king. It alarmed Liholiho when only lowly *ali'i* joined him in the ritual welcoming God Lono ika Makahiki from his realm. It was an affront by his top *ali'i* punishable by death in earlier times.

His psychic sister Queen Kamehamalu, just back from Kawaihae, warned him, "Ka'ahumanu is planning to trick you into breaking *'Ai kapu. Mālama pono*, watch out!"

Liholiho sauntered to the festival ground in the afternoon. He asked Mākaha to join him. What the king saw froze him in his steps. Ka'ahumanu and a group of ladies were seated on grass enjoying a snack with his sacred mother, not caring if their shadows were cast on her.

Outrage! The offenders must die! he swore. But there were no *kāhuna* around to punish them.

"Sit here son, next to me," Keōpūolani said.

"Don't," Mākaha panicked. "You'll break *'Ai kapu*."

Ka'ahumanu dangled a banana, a *kapu* food to women. "Come have this," she urged.

They're breaking more kapu! This must be the trickery my sister warned me of, Liholiho thought. "Sorry," he told his mother, "I am going sailing," and walked away.

Kalanimoku and Hewahewa, watching from the shadows, stepped out and blocked his way. "Good day, Your Majesty," Kalanimoku mouthed, as if surprised. He pointed to the ladies and said, "We are going there to join the queens. Let's pay them a visit."

"We're going sailing," Mākaha said, pulling the king away.

"Wait," Liholiho told Mākaha. "I'll just pay them a short visit. I'll be right back after I wish them *aloha*." He walked over, sat down with the ladies and did the unthinkable. He pinched something from a gourd cup and put it impulsively into his mouth.

Mākaha screamed. Hewahewa jumped seeing Liholiho expunge *'Ai kapu*, the most sacred taboo against man and woman eating together. For a millennium, that system of *kapu* had ensured a king's omniscience and bound the people as "Hawaiians." That pinch into his mouth stripped the Hawaiians of their identity, turned them into a group of Polynesians residing north of the equator in a place called Hawai'i. *Kumulipo,* the sacred account of Hawai'i's creation in the chant of *Kūali'i,* became smoke. The king sobbed in public and braced himself against what must happen.

That evening, an order went from Ka'ahumanu to her *ali'i,* and to Hewahewa and his three hundred *kāhuna.* They scattered possessed to their assigned destinations and began the destruction of the Kingdom's *heiau* and god idols.

The populace gaped, felt doom seeing their gods topple.

Their deeds came to haunt the *ali'i.* In every ravaged *heiau,* the god idols that the perpetrators left for dead rose from the rubble, confronted the plunderers with red, disbelieving eyes and promised them merciless retribution in *po* for their atrocities. The chiefs dropped their clubs. Their minds snapped from fright and turned soft.

At 'Ahu'ena Heiau, a battered God Kū, father of dead God Kūkā'ilimoku, confronted Ka'ahumanu and asked, "Why?" Her eyelids curled seeing an unforgiving Kū. "For this you will spend eternity without food in *po*," he promised.

"Not *po*," Ka'ahumanu panicked. Her mind also snapped and turned soft.

19

Another revolution, this one of the spirit, would hit Hawai'i nine months later. The American Board of Commissioners for Foreign Missions, a New England evangelical group supported by Southern slave owners, had handpicked a group of young American Calvinist believers in Jesus as the Christ, to go forth to pagan Hawai'i and spread the Gospel to the heathens.

They reached Kona on the big island in March 1820 after a hard trip in their tub, *Thaddeus,* designed more for floating than speed.

Riding the wave of the Second Great Awakening sweeping New England, they came with a mission: destroy Kamehameha's gods and religion and convert the native heathens into Bible-reading, God-fearing puritans of the Bostonian kind, or die trying.

Upon arrival, the missionaries learned that the king was dead, and that his *ali'i* had crushed their gods and religion. But they found the *ali'i* in seizure—in fear of going to *po* for the atrocities they had committed against their gods.

The mission leader, Kahu (Reverend) Hiram Bingham, gloated, "Jehovah preordained the destruction of the king's evil gods for our arrival. Let us begin filling their vacuum with the everlasting blessings of our Lord," the Kahu said, and began soothing the godless chiefs with hope of salvation of their souls in Christ.

The *ali'i* grabbed Jehovah as their savior.

The missionaries dispersed, some remained on the big island, others scattered to the outlying islands in canoes to establish their missions. The Kahu went to Honolulu in the tub.

Bingham visited a dysfunctional Ka'ahumanu in Waikiki and told her, "Jehovah will save you from *po*. But Jehovah is a jealous God. There can be no other god before Him. Christianity and paganism cannot coexist. Either you seek salvation of your soul in Christ, or you go to *po*, to spend eternity with Milu."

"No, no, not *po*," she pleaded.

"The Kahu frightens me," Kainoa said. "He already speaks Hawaiian. And look at his penetrating pupils. He can scare our chiefs into doing anything he wants."

The Kahu had a captive *ali'i* audience obsessed with *po*. He would shake a finger to heaven and cried in a trained, quivering voice, "Your old pagan gods are evil gods, Jehovah is the on . . . ly truuue god. Let Himm enlighten your dark pagan hearts with His Holy Spirit. Gaining salvation in Himmm, through meee, must be your only goal. Do you hear?"

The captive chiefs would mumble, "Yes, yes." Even Ka'ahumanu begged, "I want to join your church now."

The Kahu knew she just wanted to escape *po*. But he wanted to exploit her temporal power to help his cause. "Welcome to our church," he told her. "We will teach you English so you can study the Bible and attend our Bible classes. You will learn Christian values so you can lead a Christian life and, one day, help us bring your people into our church."

"Yes I will," she cried, and became his pawn for life for fear of *po*.

20

Liholiho 'Iolani, King Kamehameha II, skipped the rituals marking the first anniversary of his father's death and sailed for Maui in April 1820 on the *Fair American*. He had difficulty paying respect to his father who had left him land-destitute. Approaching Lahaina, Liholiho's drunken eyes caught a sleek ship sailing in just ahead. Louis Smith, his English drinking partner said, "Look at her elaborate hull design and the cannons at broadside. She seems fit for a king,"

"Fix me a ride. I may want to buy her," the king said, lifting an unopened bottle into his mouth.

Smith arranged one, quickly.

Before Liholiho boarded, he noted her name, *Cleopatra's Barge. What a crazy name*, he thought.

He walked the *Barge's* deck from stem to stern. One hundred-ten feet, about the size of Cook's *Resolution*, he noted. He saw a brass plaque on the wheel pedestal with the inscription, "Built at Kincaid Shipyards, Boston."

Liholiho sauntered below, saw her big, clean galley, a beautiful dining room, rooms for the crew and guest staterooms. He went on a fast exhilarating ride, leaning more than twenty degrees. The thrill clinched Liholiho. The land-poor monarch, with little *mana* and few friends, puffed his ego kinglike and told Captain Stanley Harlow, her third owner, "Sell me the *Barge.*"

"Make me an offer, Your Majesty," Harlow asked, showing no eagerness to sell his haunted ship.

She had a history. On her maiden voyage, a strong early-evening gust blew two lady guests overboard. Their bodies were never found. Just their anguished cries remained on deck. Her two previous owners saw apparitions dancing on deck in the early evening hours. They shuddered, couldn't wait to sell the *Barge*. Harlow, too, had seen ladies float by in party clothes. His hair stood each time.

"I pay you ten *'iliahi* logs for the boat," Liholiho said.

"*'iliahi*? I hear its demand had fallen in China. Just pay me five thousand dollars cash."

"I have so little cash," Liholiho replied.

Harlow let him fidget for a day. Next morning he told Liholiho, "I will settle for four thousand dollars cash, two thousand dollars in two weeks, the balance next month. If you agree you can have the *Barge* now."

After hearing "now," the purchase became irresistible. He wanted to replace the smallish *Fair American* with the larger *Barge* to inflate his ego.

"I accept your offer," he said with a stiff alcoholic breath, and paid the first installment.

"She's yours," Harlow told a beaming Liholiho, and mused, *apparitions and all.*

Liholiho sailed in the evening for 'Oahu. Next morning he anchored off Waikīkī and sent a messenger to call on his stepmother. Ka'ahumanu was at her beachside *kauhale* staring into space. Pointing to the *Barge* the messenger said, "She is His Majesty's new ship. He wants you to join him for a party."

She glanced at the boat and waved him off with a flick of her fingers.

Liholiho smiled when he learned of her silent response. He just wanted to harass her.

The name *Barge* bothered Liholiho. "Not fit for a king," he told his sister-wife Queen Kamehamalu. "She needs a Hawaiian name. You like, *Ha'aheo o Hawai'i*, Pride of Hawai'i?"

"No, Lani (her nickname for him). Never change a ship's name. Bad luck," the mystic queen counseled.

He shot back, "No *haole* name!"

That was final. Next day his crew scraped off the old and painted the new name in bright red, the only paint color on board.

"Get rid of the silver utensils and crystal stemware, too. I rather eat with my fingers and drink from bottles," he told the crew.

Liholiho thought of visiting Kaumuali'i on Kaua'i. Doubt of his loyalty lingered after Doctor Schaefer fled Kaua'i five years earlier. "I want to test him. Send a messenger to Līhu'e," he told Mahi, a former canoe paddler trained by Young, and now his new ship's captain, "Inform Kaumuali'i I will be visiting him soon. He may be closely guarded so get the Lopaka onboard ready to fire if we are attacked," Liholiho said.

"Sorry, Your Majesty, the cannons onboard are just decoration," Mahi said. "Not one works."

The king gaped. *I am cutting the price of the Barge to three thousand dollars*, he vowed.

Flying an outsized Hawaiian flag on *Ha'aheo's* stern, Liholiho arrived off Līhu'e village on Kaua'i.

Kaumuali'i, the one-time traitor, climbed onboard the *Ha'aheo* with his son, went on his knees and bowed before Liholiho, exposing himself to whatever the king wished. "Welcome to Kaua'i," he said, head down.

Liholiho thought it was the highest honor yet bestowed since he became king.

On shore, over a hundred *ali'i*, all carriers of Schaefer's stigma, were waiting in full regalia at *kapu moe* to welcome the king. Although Ka'ahumanu had quashed *kapu* in 1820, the old pagan ways lingered in isolated Kaua'i. The people's show of warmth sent Liholiho's spirit flying above nearby Mount Wai'ale'ale.

During a lavish evening party, Kaumuali'i whispered to Liholiho, "I have put Kaua'i, all my gods, and my people at your disposal. They are yours."

The enormity of the gift startled Liholiho. "Thank you, I accept," he said, then quickly added, "The land of Kaua'i and its people are yours. I give them back to you," in his first major *mālama 'āina*.

Liholiho's doubt of Kaumuali'i's loyalty vanished.

The party got louder. "Let's go to Lahaina where I can return your hospitality," Liholiho said. "Bring your son Keali'i'ahonui along."

Kaumuali'i shuddered. He wanted the security of Kaua'i. But he realized a traitor had no option.

Ha'aheo arrived two mornings later off Lahaina. Liholiho asked Mākaha, "Tell Hoapili I am here with Kaumuali'i and his son. Send a big welcome. I expect a feast this evening for my guests."

Mākaha understood.

Lahaina shore was soon crowded with chiefs in a galaxy of canoes greeting the king and his guests. Liholiho forgot it was a fabricated welcome.

Ka'ahumanu, resting in her *haole* Christian friend's guest cottage in Kahului, Maui, heard of Liholiho's triumphal visit to Kaua'i and of his arrival in Lahaina with Kaumuali'i and son. She decided to ruin his visit.

A runner arrived in Lahaina to see Liholiho. He told the king, "Queen Ka'ahumanu wants to invite Ali'i moku Kaumuali'i and his son for a party in Kahului two nights from now. She is inviting you too. What shall I tell her?"

How did she know we're here? he wondered. "Tell her I went fishing."

But to Kaumuali'i, Liholiho said, "You two better go to keep peace. I will wait here until you return to take you back to Kauai."

They nodded reluctantly and followed the runner on an uphill trek over several deep drop-offs and streams toward Kahului village.

They arrived limp at her cottage next morning.

Ka'ahumanu saw the two, yelled, "Mabo (her personal nickname for Kaumuali'i), Keali'i'ahonui. Welcome! Thank you for coming. I heard you two were in Lahaina so I thought I should at least welcome you. I have a party planned for this evening. Please come."

"Thank you, Your Majesty," Mabo said, cursing her hospitality.

"Don't Your Majesty me. Call me 'Ka'ahu,' you hear?"

Kaumuali'i bowed. "Can someone bring me and my son new slippers and lead us to a nearby stream? We want to soak our feet," he said.

They spent the next hour splashing stream water with blistered feet.

Father and son went to her cottage before sunset. There was no crowd, no party ready.

"Mabo come in," she greeted, and emptied her cottage of servants. She cuddled to him and whispered, "Mabo, you know my situation. I am alone. Will you marry me and help me run my government?"

Kaumuali'i cleared his throat twice. *What?* he wanted to scream. "Ka'ahu, I am sick. I go in and out of a funny world, and I know nothing about running a government. But if you want me . . ." He feared a spear if he refused.

"Thank you, Mabo. Yes I want you."

His father's answer shocked Keali'i'ahonui. Turning now to him, Ka'ahu continued, "I want to marry you too."

Keali'i'ahonui, seventeen, developed a bloody nose.

"Me?" he asked, stultified.

"Yes, you."

The father never saw his son with larger eyes.

"I never marry before and I don't know government. But if you want me, Your Majesty . . ."

"You, too, call me 'Ka'ahu,' understand?"

"Not easy but I will try."

"You two make me so happy for accepting . . ."

That was that. No wedding ceremonies, just instant husbands. She had just swallowed Liholiho's rising *mana*.

"When is your party?" Kaumuali'i asked.

"What party?"

Kaumuali'i mumbled something that only his son understood.

"Yes, far advanced," Keali'iahonui said.

Ka'ahu's double wedding shocked her *haole* friends. "Drop Keali'i'ahonui. Jehovah will find your marriage to father and son abominable," they said.

But not yet baptized, she just returned a stare.

Despite her illness, Ka'ahu, forty five, was still sex driven. That night, she untied Kaumuali'i's *malo*. He was shocked. *First time anybody did it,* he croaked. After an hour she left him spent, then rolled over to Keali'i'ahonui like a seal and untied his *malo*. He couldn't get excited. "Come on," she urged. He only thought of escape while supporting dead weight.

After the sessions, Ka'ahumanu slowly sank into her abyss. Delighted, father and son grabbed their *malo* and slipped back to Lahaina. She emerged from her depth weeks later looking fresh, lively. But she had no memory of ever marrying the two.

Neither reminded her.

§

Meanwhile, the missionaries' zeal intensified. The Kahu told Ka'ahumanu, "Visit the outer islands, tell your people about the joys of Christian life, have them destroy their pagan customs and memorabilia and give them the chance to be reborn in Christ. Tell them to start learning English so they can study the Bible. We are here to teach them. And tell them to give up on their old pagan customs like wailing, giving first fruits to ugly god idols and dancing the *hula*. Jehovah hates *hula*, its movements are lascivious, incompatible with Christian decency," he told her. "And remind them to stop speaking Hawaiian, learn to speak only English. The Hawaiian language is the language of the devil."

"Kahu, you give me so much to remember," she said, "but I will try."

Kainoa realized that the missionaries aimed to convert Hawaiians void of gods and scared of *po* into Bible-reading, god-fearing Christians, not to save sickly lives.

Ka'ahumanu started a craze that pleased the Kahu. She told her people, "Bring your *haka, ahu'ula, aumakua* altar, god idols, *kapu* sticks, *kāhili,* and things like your *lei niho, malo* and *pā'ū* to my *kauhale* by next week Monday. Let's make a big fire, watch all the symbols of paganism burn while we sing *himeni* (hymns) and praise the Lord."

"*Ae,*" they said.

Singing Christian hymns around pagan bon fires became fashionable.

"The Kahu needs Ka'ahumanu's power," Mākaha said. "If we can stop her, we can stop the Kahu from destroying what's left."

Kainoa shook his head. "No *kanaka* can. She won't listen to us because she thinks we're all dumb. Unless we go abroad to study and return home as educated *kānaka,* she won't even notice us."

"But we need money and connections to go abroad and study, and we have neither," Mākaha mourned.

Money. Kainoa remembered something half forgotten.

21

Dwight Noble, captain of the brig *Cape Cod*, paid a surprise visit to the Alapa'i *kauhale* on a November morning in 1821.

"Hello, Kainoa!" he yelled, startling him at the *papalā'au* (*poi* board) when he arrived. "I want to see you before I leave. Is Pualani home?"

"Yes, she is."

"Please take this to her." He handed to Kainoa about a fifteen-pound fish just caught at the pier.

"Whii" Kainoa yelled. *"Ulua! Mahalo*! It will go good with this *poi* I'm pounding. I'll take it to her now."

"From Captain Noble?" Pualani asked. "He's here?"

"Yes, he's outside."

She rushed out holding the fish by its tail. "Captain Noble, welcome back, and thank you for this *ulua!*"

"I thought of you when my deckhand caught it. Kainoa said the fish will go good with *poi*."

"You don't know how good. Please stay for dinner."

"Sorry, I can't. After I have a talk with Kainoa, I must get back."

"All right. Please come back again, next time for dinner. Bring another *ulua.*"

She laughed and waved him good bye.

Why he wants to talk to me? Kainoa wondered.

"Kainoa, I heard in the village that you wanted to go abroad to study. True?"

"True, sir, who told you? Nobody knows except Mākaha."

"He didn't tell me, but words move. You youngsters should go abroad, get educated and return home to help save Hawai'i before she runs aground on the reef."

"Aground!" He grabbed Kainoa's attention.

"I am a Christian. I have no problem seeing the missionaries spread the Gospel in Hawai'i," Dwight Noble said. "I believe in their god. But I see them moving into your government to run your lives in their best interest. That's scary. They can eventually steal your land."

Steal! The captain sees into my heart, he thought.

"Kainoa, would you work for me for about six months so you earn enough money to go abroad to study?" he asked.

"Captain, please wait here. I want to go home and bring back something to show you."

He was curious. "Sure, I'll be visiting Pualani."

Kainoa returned puffing and gave to the captain a pigskin pouch. He stood back and said, "Look inside."

Noble saw bluish-gray balls. He rolled some into his hand and gaped. "They—they look like pearls! So huge and iridescent. Are these real?"

"Yes. Real!"

"You have a treasure, Kainoa!" He felt their weight. "Where did you find them?"

"I found a bed, saved the biggest and sold the rest to pay off my father's debts. Can you buy them, so I'll have money to go abroad now?"

"I have a better idea," the captain said, rolling out more into his hand. "In exchange for these pearls you can live in my home for two years while you study. You like that?"

"You mean it, sir?" Kainoa asked.

"Yes, I do."

This is a miracle, Kainoa thought.

"Captain Noble, sir, I accept. Keep the bag, twelve pearls inside."

A suddenly wealthy Noble told Kainoa, "Meet me at the harbor in the morning around ten. Let's draw up a plan."

Kainoa rushed home to tell 'Eme.

"You really gave him all your pearls?"

"I did, for the future of our *'āina.*"

"So it's decided?"

"Yes, but if you say no, I won't go."

"Kai, go. That's what you want," she said with a strong chin and moist eyes. "I will wait, but you must return as someone special."

Kainoa looked at 'Eme without blinking. "I promise you I will return as someone special. I love you 'Eme."

She nodded with her eyes closed.

"'Eme, let's go to *Hale'ano'i*. I must finish my *honu* (turtle) engraving."

A lifeless 'Eme went and watched Kainoa take his blue-rock graver and finish a foot-long *honu* on *Hale'ano'i's* volcanic-ash wall.

"He is Kekai," he told 'Eme, holding her hand. "Kekai will protect you while I am gone."

They spent the next hour in transcendental embrace.

"Kainoa!" Captain Noble yelled when he arrived next morning at the harbor. "Come meet Peter London, the captain of that ship *Lynn*," he pointed to a schooner offshore. "He is leaving for Boston tomorrow. I know it's sudden, but you can work your way to Boston as one of his deckhands. I got your identification paper from His Majesty earlier. You'll need it in Boston."

"I heard so many good things about ya," London said, giving Kainoa a hard hand squeeze. "Welcome onboard. Be here by noon tomorrow with things you wanna take."

Tomorrow? Too little time with 'Eme, he moaned. But he recovered to say, "I will be here before noon."

"Here, take some of my old clothes. Don't wear that *malo* in Boston," Noble joked.

News of Kainoa's departure spread. Hundreds, including Liholiho and Crown Prince Kauikeaouli, seven, were at the wharf next day to bid him *aloha*. "Here, something for you," the Crown Prince said and gave to Kainoa a book, *Early American History* by Douglas Sheer that he happened to have.

"Your Highness, what a valuable present. I will read every page of it."

Kainoa's royalty friends impressed Captain London.

"'Eme, I can't believe I am leaving," he said. "In spirit I will always be with you."

'Eme, wearing a green wraparound skirt of hand-printed Chinese silk flowing to her ankles, said, "Me, too." She gave to Kainoa a bunch of her hair tied with *olona* string. "This is me, please keep it."

Dwight Noble gave to Kainoa a hundred dollars, a large sum, and a small wooden box with the cover nailed shut. "Please give this box to my wife Dian when you meet her."

"Yes, sir, thank you, sir," he said, embracing Captain Noble.

The shoreboat began to move. Well into a panic state, Kainoa told Mākaha, "Sorry we both can't go. When I return let's crisscross the land and spread our message."

"Kainoa, I will be ready. This is war!"

He boarded the *Lynn* and rushed to aft and continued his goodbye to 'Eme. The schooner began to leave the harbor. Suddenly, as if pushed by divine hands, Kainoa and 'Eme dove into the harbor at the same time and swam into each other's arms.

Captain Peter London was forced to make a wide turn to pick up a man overboard. The pigtailed oriental passengers onboard the ship laughed.

Before Kainoa passed Lē'ahi on November 24, 1821, he was already brushing his lips with 'Eme's jet-black hair. *Wait for me,* he whispered into the wind and began his long journey.

With the passing of months, Peter London and Kainoa became close. Kainoa worked the sails by day, and received intensive English and arithmetic lessons at night. By the time *Lynn* approached Boston Harbor, Kainoa was past sixth grade.

Through the morning mist he saw the city of Boston loom ahead. "So big the harbor, so many big boats, tall buildings. Pinch me, captain!" He had seen nothing bigger than Honolulu Harbor and missionary churches.

London smiled. He felt happy for Kainoa, who was dressed tightly in Captain Noble's castoff suit.

"Thank you for your lessons and the chance to be your shiphand, Captain London, Sir."

"Thank you, Kainoa. You were wonderful, dependable. You will succeed in whatever you do. Here, take this," he said, and gave to him a fifty dollar bill.

"No, no, captain, I must pay you something."

"Keep it," the captain replied.

Kainoa bowed and hugged him.

Two boats came alongside. "Harbor inspectors, Kainoa. They will escort us to the foreign arrival pier." The *Lynn's* sailing master gave to them a salute.

"Get ready to disembark. Be close to me. I will help you get through."

Kainoa glanced at some unfinished work onboard.

"Don't worry. My crew knows what to do. Your time is over," London said.

Dripping with perspiration, Kainoa followed the captain down the gangplank and into the Federal Customs House, holding his wicker trunk.

"Please open," the inspector said. He stuck his hand inside, pulled out a bunch of things from the bottom and asked, "What are they?"

London couldn't help; he didn't know.

"This is the image of our God Lono. This is my loved one's hair clipping, and that's a wooden gecko, my personal god."

The inspector shook his head, charged Kainoa nothing.

The captain tipped his hat to the inspector and went to the immigration counter. An official stared at Kainoa and studied his identification paper.

"The Kingdom of Hawai'i is located in the middle of the Pacific Ocean, sir," London volunteered. "This man will be studying in Boston for a few years before returning to Hawai'i. He will live in Captain Dwight Noble's home."

The official knew Captain Noble. He gave to the native of this unknown Kingdom an extra stare, and stamped, "APPROVED FOR ENTRY" on the paper.

"Thank you, *Ho'omaika'i!*" a nervous, relieved Kainoa said to Captain London outside the Federal House.

"That was easy. Now comes the difficult part. We are going to Captain Noble's home. Mrs. Noble will be shocked to meet you, so let me do the explaining."

They clacked through the heart of Boston in a horse-drawn taxi. Kainoa was too tense to enjoy the spectacular sights on both sides of worn cobblestone roads. After thirty minutes they arrived at the Noble's home in the Beacon Hill district.

"Kainoa, be seated. I will check if Mrs. Noble is in."

London strode up and knocked on the door. Mrs. Noble answered the knock.

"Peter!" Dian exclaimed, opening the door. "So nice to see you. I thought you were in the Far East!"

"I was. Just returned an hour ago."

"Come in, let me fix you tea."

"Not . . . this morning," Peter stumbled. "I have a promising lad sitting in the carriage. He is a native of an island kingdom in the middle of the Pacific Ocean where Dwight temporarily lives. Dwight wants you to take him into your home while he gets an education in Boston."

"In my house?" She looked at the native sitting in the buggy. "You are joking," she laughed.

Peter shook his head. "Dwight knew you would be shocked. He asked for your forgiveness. Since the trip was decided in two days, he had no chance to get your approval. Dwight hopes the native lad can have the extra bedroom in your home while he studies.

"Kainoa, please come," the captain called.

He ran up the steps with his wicker trunk.

"Kainoa, meet Mrs. Dian Noble, Captain Noble's wife. Dian, this is Kainoa Kahemoku."

Mrs. Noble froze in fright.

"Hello, Mrs. Noble. I heard so much about you. And you must be Paul?"

The boy looked up, saw a tall bronze man and nodded.

"Your father told me how much he misses both of you."

Captain London interrupted. "I will leave now to surprise my family. If you need me Dian, just come."

"Thank you, Peter. I'm sure I will."

"Good bye, Kainoa. You're in good hands. Let's meet soon."

Kainoa smiled, just waved his hand, his throat too tight to utter a word.

Dian walked aimlessly around the living room, a frown on her face, picking up something here and straightening things there.

Kainoa opened his trunk and handed to Mrs. Noble a wooden box with a cover nailed shut. "Captain Noble asked me to give this to you."

She pried it open. A letter sat on top of something. She read it first.

November 24, 1821

    Beloved Dian, please forgive me for the shock I will give you. Kainoa's trip was decided so suddenly I had no chance to inform you earlier. I apologize.

I truly want to help him. I know you will too after you get to know him. Please welcome him to our house. He has paid me handsomely to go to Boston.

I will return soon as possible. Miss you and Paul.

Love, Dwight

Somewhat relieved, Dian told Kainoa, "Welcome to America."

"Welcome," Paul repeated, extending his soft right hand.

"How is Dwight?" she asked.

"He is fine, very active. He got from the king of Hawai'i an exclusive inter-island shipping contract. He must give him back half of his earnings, but it is still profitable. He plans to return home in a year. He wants to finish his contract and get a big bonus from the king."

"Thank you, Kana. It's so good to know first hand he's healthy and active."

"My name is Ka-i-no-a," he said, and they laughed together for the first time.

Dian took a double take on the tight suit he was wearing, Dwight's old. She held back a laugh. She at last noticed a non-threatening, broad-shouldered handsome youth over six feet tall with a deep, sonorous voice, his wide, upwardly bowing mouth and young wrinkles at both ends of his penetrating eyes when he smiled.

But Dian thought, *What will our friends and neighbors think?*

She asked Kainoa, "What are your plans in Boston and how long do you intend to stay?"

"I came to stay for around two years. Before returning to Hawai'i, I want to get an education and find temporary work to support it. Captain Noble said I may find a job at a shipbuilding company."

"Did he say at Kincaid Shipbuilding?"

"Yes, Kincaid!"

"I know Mr. Kincaid. I'll talk to him, but first please tell me more about your plans. What are you going to study?"

"First, I want to read and write better and . . ."

"You, you can't, yet?"

"Not well. When English Captain Cook discovered Hawai'i in 1778, we were still in the Stone Age without a written language. We learned to speak English by ear, listening to visiting sea captains, but we still cannot read or write. We have no schools in Hawai'i. That's why I came."

"Then what?"

"After I get an education, I want to return to home and help my Kingdom of Hawai'i. It has many problems."

"Like what?"

"Like saving our dying people. Captain Cook and his men, and foreign visitors after him brought to Hawai'i all kinds of dreadful diseases. Today, we have more deaths than births. I want to learn how we can reverse that."

Dian hoped Kainoa wasn't a carrier of something deadly.

"We have other problems. Missionaries from Boston are erasing our culture and forcing us to become Christians of the absolute kind. They convinced our chiefs that there is no higher good than the salvation of their souls in Christ. I think there is a more urgent good, the salvation of our land and people. I want to go back to Hawai'i and challenge them.

"We are weak and defenseless today. Anyone using force can swallow us in an hour. That's why I want to learn how we could establish an effective militia cheaply. I also want to find a way to mass-educate our people. If we remain illiterate and dumb, we die."

Dian's mind spun to keep up with the focused aborigine.

"What is your ancestry?" she asked, changing the subject.

"I am a Hawaiian. My Kingdom of Hawai'i is located in a vast area called Oceania in the Pacific Ocean.

Dian had heard enough. "I'll show you to your room," she said.

A long week went by. Whenever Kainoa spoke, Dian wondered, *Should I tell him?*

"Greetings, Mrs. Noble," Kainoa said. "I just took the Freedom Trail and visited the Old Meeting House, Faneuil Hall, Paul Revere's house, saw many historic places Captain London talked about. I spoke to many people and was happy they understood me."

Dian just looked at him.

"Anything wrong?" he asked.

"Promise you won't get mad?"

"Tell me anything, Mrs. Noble, I can't get mad."

"All right. It's about your breath. It smells so bad that I have to stand away from you when you talk to me."

Kainoa was embarrassed. "What causes it? How can I stop it?"

Dian stepped back again. "It is caused by foods putrefying between the teeth and deep down on your tongue."

"What is 'putrefying,' Mrs. Noble?"

"It means souring due to germs. Do Hawaiians brush their teeth?"

"Never, we have no brush. Sorry, I cannot smell my own bad breath. What can I do?"

She took Kainoa to the bathroom and gave to him a brush, some toothpicks, a cup of salty water and fresh mint leaves from her garden. "Brush your gums and teeth with salt water, front and back. Brush your tongue, go way down. Use these picks to poke between teeth. Push out old food, squish with salt water and spit it out into this pan. Repeat it three times, all right? When you are done just chew on these mint leaves, spit them out and drink water."

"Why the leaves?"

"They leave a fresh smell. We chew them all the time."

"Why drink water?"

"So you drink the germs in your mouth."

How did 'Eme stand me? Kainoa wondered and went to work. He brushed his gums, teeth and tongue, poked, rinsed, chewed leaves and drank germs.

"Done, Mrs. Noble," he proudly said emerging from the bathroom.

"Open your mouth. Hmmm . . . good job! Brush daily and your teeth won't rot and fall out. I see one molar already did."

"Mrs. Noble, mine didn't fall out. A *kahuna* pulled it out to stop my toothache."

"*Kahuna?*"

"*Kāhuna* are priests with specialties. Some are surgeons, others dentists, canoe builders, even navigators of the open seas. Only priests can do such specialty work."

Dian was curious, asked, "How did your *kahuna* pull it out?"

"He filed a groove around the *piko* (cusp) below the gum with a thin lava-stone blade while five big guys held me down. He then tied *olonā* string around the groove."

Dian shuddered. "He started to pull?"

"Not yet. With a flat wooden shovel he began to separate gum from tooth, and then he started to shake the tooth back and forth with his fingers until it started to move. I screamed insane. A big guy lifted my head and slammed it down shouting, 'Shut up, no move.'

"The *kahuna* began to jerk the string. I was numb. After a while I saw a tooth dangling at the end of the line."

"Oh my god!" a shocked Dian exclaimed.

"I continued to suffer because some tooth pieces remained deep down, all didn't come out. The *kahuna*, using a long pick, felt something hard inside the hole. He tried to flip it out. I felt something snap, and half of my mouth went numb, it still is."

"My gosh!" Dian exclaimed again.

"I bled heavily. The *kahuna* told me to go swimming, keep my body and face cool and squish my mouth with ocean water. I spit blood all the way to the beach, dove in and squished. Suddenly, I felt two small pieces of tooth in my mouth. I yelled, *'Kupanaha!'*"

Dian knew more about Hawai'i than she cared to know.

After three short weeks, the townfolks of Beacon Hill were no longer staring at Kainoa. They had melted to his wide, Polynesian smile, his ability to remember names, and his resonant, friendly, "Hello, Mrs. Riley, Good morning, Mr. Hutaff," always by their last names.

One morning, Mrs. Noble opened the door in answer to a knock. A cool autumn breeze floated in. "Mr. Kincaid!" she exclaimed. "So nice to see you."

"Good morning Dian. You told me about that lad from a faraway place. Is he still looking for a job?"

"Yes! His name is Kainoa Kahemoku from the Kingdom of Hawai'i.

"I came to tell you I have an opening. Have, er, Kalano come to the yard in the morning for an interview."

"His skin is dark. Is that all right?"

"Yes. I don't think my crew would mind."

"Thank you, Mr. Kincaid, he will be so glad."

Next morning Kainoa rose early, brushed his teeth and tongue, picked between his teeth, squished with salt water, chewed mint leaves, drank germs, and ran to Kincaid Shipyard for an interview, forgetting breakfast.

They talked for half an hour. Kincaid learned of Kainoa's canoe-building experience and asked him questions on lamination. Kainoa answered each in detail, often teaching Kincaid something new, like notching and tying laminates with cordage.

Kincaid found a jewel. "You're hired," he said. "I'm assigning you to the hull-framing detail. Your starting pay is twelve dollars a month. Report at seven tomorrow morning."

Kainoa screamed, *"Hulō!"* and rushed home to tell Dian.

She had been waiting for this moment. After dinner one night she told Kainoa, "You now have a job. Why don't you go find a place to live maybe near the Yard, and begin living your own life?"

Her words stung. *She hates me? My skin color? What about Captain Noble's promise in exchange for the pearls?*

For Dian it was color, her upbringing. She couldn't get comfortable sharing a home with a dark man.

"Of course it's about time," Kainoa said, forcing a smile. "I will start looking for a place right away. Can I use your home as my mailing address and may I occasionally visit?"

"Sure you can," she said, relieved Kainoa would be moving out.

With his meager belongings he left Beacon Hill to face a New World with his god idols and a bunch of 'Eme's hair tied with *olonā* string.

He found a place deep in the black slums of Boston, as nobody in the white slums would have him. His tiny room was windowless, doorless, stinking of urine and without furniture. He shared toilet with fifty others and sometimes paid his neighbors five cents for dinner. But not minding where he slept or ate, he studied hard under oil light while stroking his lips with 'Eme's hair.

He learned enough to read halfway through Sheer's *Early American History* and do ninth-grade geometry. By late fall, Kainoa had earned two raises, was now at a whopping eighteen dollars a month. He felt ready to live his dreams and meet people who could help Hawai'i nei.

Like John Quincy Adams.

Mr. Adams never forgot Mr. Kincaid's financial aid when, as a young man, he ran for a seat in the United States Senate and won. Whenever he was near the Shipyard, he would drop by to shake his hands.

"How are you, Mister Secretary," Kincaid said, greeting him on this day. They shared a warm handshake.

"Kainoa, come here. Mister Secretary, this is Kainoa Kahemoku, an outstanding member of my crew from the Kingdom of Hawai'i."

"How do you do, Kana?" Mr. Adams said, never hesitating to grab a dirty hand.

"Kainoa, the Honorable Mr. Adams is America's Secretary of State under President Monroe. His father, the Honorable John Adams, was America's second President."

"Oh, my, sir." Kainoa quickly wiped his gluey hands on the side of his pants. "What a great honor to meet you, sir."

"Where is Hawai'i?" Adams asked.

Kainoa glanced apologetically at Mr. Kincaid.

"It's all right, Kainoa. You don't have to work every moment. Go ahead, tell Mister Secretary Adams about you and Hawai'i. I want to listen too."

Kainoa was glad. "I was born on an island in Oceania, a place called Hawai'i, created by God Hawai'iloa. It was later our God Wākea's secret abode until Englishman Captain Cook exposed us to the world in 1778. Cook named our eight islands, 'Sandwich Islands,' but we do not use that name."

"God who?"

"Hawai'iloa, sir. We love him."

The Secretary of State had heard of the Sandwich Isles, but nothing more. "Did you know America was at war with Captain Cook's country in 1778?" Mr. Adams asked.

"Yes, I learned about your Revolutionary War. It happened not too long ago."

Mr. Adams was eager to learn more about an island chain created by a pagan god.

"Let's sit over there," Kincaid said, pointing to an old bench beneath a tree. "I'll have refreshments brought."

They walked over and sat.

"Who is the leader of Hawai'i?"

"He is King Liholiho, twenty-five years old. His stepmother, the Prime Minister Ka'ahumanu, controls him. Since she in turn is controlled by missionaries from Boston, Reverend Bingham, leader of the mission, is the real king of the kingdom, sir. He is trying to change us into people we are not for Christ's sake."

The Secretary shook his head, felt sorry for Kainoa and Hawai'i. "Whenever church controls government, you will have tyranny, proven over and over again through the ages. Our forefathers fled England, where church and government were one, and went to America in 1612 to escape tyranny. When their descendants enacted

America's highest law, the Constitution, they separated government from church."

"I won't forget that, sir." Kainoa said. *The Kahu would have never told me that,* he thought.

Adams lifted a chained clock from his vest. "I have an afternoon appointment nearing," he told Kainoa. "Let's continue this another time. I appreciate your lessons in geography and culture."

Me, giving Mr. Adams lessons? Kainoa was embarrassed.

"I have an office on the corner of State and Tremont Streets, not far from here," he said. "It used to be my father's. My aide there is Conrad Wellings. Go visit him. I will tell him to help you anyway he can."

Kainoa fell prostrate before John Quincy Adams.

An embarrassed Mr. Adams told Kainoa, "Now please get up, I'm an ordinary human." They laughed. He turned to Kincaid. "Goodbye, Fred. Thank you for the hospitality. It's always a pleasure visiting you." They shook hands. Adams gave to Kainoa a warm nod and boarded his waiting coach.

Despite Mr. Wellings' tight schedule, he opened doors for Kainoa, invited him to lunches at the State House and introduced him to other lawmakers. They too were eager to help Kainoa, knowing it would please Mr. Adams.

They found Kainoa likable. He laughed at their jokes, looked at them with magnetic pagan eyes, listened, took advice. He touched some State senators' hearts. What a politician he would make, they thought.

With the backing of his new, influential friends, Kainoa had instant credibility. Harvard Medical School gave to him medical texts and reams of papers dealing with treatment of sicknesses. The Boston Medical Hospital offered to send doctors to Hawai'i to help treat the sickly. Alan Saunders, President of a new school, Amherst College, promised grade-school scholarships to three Hawaiian students annually. Colonel George Pew, who led the forces trying to defend the White House during the War of 1812, offered to help organize a Company-size Hawaiian militia. Other offers poured in. America was indeed nice to Kainoa.

The fall season came to New England. Kainoa inhaled his first nippy autumn air and rejoiced. Mr. Kincaid had just promoted him to the elite keel-construction crew with more pay. He spent the night under a blanket with a worn dictionary at his side and finished reading *Early*

American History. In the hills and streets of Boston, a million leaves had turned from green to red, yellow, and everything in between at once. They sprinkled the rooftops and streets, decorated his slum and crackled under his feet. The *kanaka* boy would never forget the scenes and smell of fall 1822.

One December day, Kainoa caught his first throb of the holiday season. With pay in pocket, he visited an elegant gift shop on Stuart Street, purchased a woolen scarf for Dian Noble and a pair of leather gloves for Paul. He had them beautifully gift-wrapped. On Christmas Eve he knocked on the door. Dian answered.

"Kainoa!" she exclaimed, caught off guard. "Come in, come in. Paul and I have been thinking of you."

"Thank you. I won't stay long. I brought my Christmas presents. This is for you, Mrs. Noble, and Paul, this is for you," he said, with his broad smile.

Dian felt uneasy. "We deeply appreciate your kind thought, Kainoa. But we do not celebrate Christmas by giving or exchanging gifts."

"What? I thought all Christians did!"

"No, that's pagan. We Presbyterians keep our activities simple. You saw the Advent Wreath on the door?"

"Yes I did. It's beautiful," Kainoa said.

"We hang that wreath before Christmas, and on Christmas morning before we go to church, we drink spiced apple cider dipped from this Wassail Bowl. That's all we do to celebrate Christ's birth."

"Ahuh. What is 'Advent,' Mrs. Noble?"

"Advent is the start of our Christian season to prepare for the Nativity, the birth of Jesus on Christmas day. But thank you for the presents and thinking of us. We love you."

Those sweet words, "We love you," overwhelmed Kainoa.

They also surprised Dian by the ease she said it.

"Please accept my presents as . . . as my winter gifts," he said.

"No, Kainoa. Let us make believe we are pagans and celebrate Christmas like they do. Thank you, Kainoa, for your Christmas presents!

"Here, I have a . . . ah . . . Christmas gift for you too," Dian said, and gave him a box. It was her turn to be pagan.

He gingerly opened it, found a set of gold-tipped pen and personal stationery.

"That's for you to write to 'Eme!" she smiled.

"So beautiful. I am a real pagan so I accept!" he exclaimed, and embraced Mrs. Noble for the first time. Paul paid little attention; he was busy trying on his new mitts.

"Kainoa, I have something personal to tell you. Paul and I have been miserable since you left the house. You are always on our mind. Please accept this from us," she said, and handed to him a small envelope.

He opened it, found his familiar key to the house.

"Please return to your room," Dian said. She had been transformed by Kainoa's soul into a woman blind to humanity's colors.

Kainoa held the key tightly, looked deeply into Dian's eyes, and said, "Thank you, Mrs. Noble. I will be back."

Kainoa returned to his slumroom, packed his things in the old woven chest with a wooden gecko inside, bade goodbye to his new black slumfriends and headed for the Noble residence on Beacon Hill after leaving one dollar on top of his "table," a wooden box.

Dian and Paul were waiting when he returned on Christmas morning in 1822.

Paul ran to him. "Brother Kainoa, welcome back," he said with eyes bright with tears.

"You're just in time for a dip into the Wassail Bowl," Dian said, offering him a ladle.

22

An American sea captain would soon destroy Kainoa.

Michael Chaplain was born in 1798 in Salem, a settlement in the Massachusetts Bay Colony. His parents, father Leslie and mother Meriam, daughter of a Congregational minister, owned a sugar-maple farm with two hundred Narragansett and Massachusett indentured Indians working the land.

He and his sister, Deborah, four years younger, never went to school. Mother Meriam tutored them at home. She had Michael on a strict puritanical regimen for an ecclesiastical career, but Deborah fared better. She just wanted her daughter polished so she could marry well one day.

Meriam kept her family stiff. She frowned when Michael laughed aloud or uttered heathenish words like "Sunday" around the house; it had to be "the Sabbath," or else the stick. He never forgot some welts on his behind.

Morning Star, a Narragansett Indian manservant who had cared for Michael since his birth and called him, "Son," soothed the welts each time.

Since little, Michael loved the smell of bituminous coal from Liverpool permeating Salem harbor. He often went there with father, with fishing pole and worms, and watched big ships come and go. A seafaring career settled deep in young Michael's heart.

Michael stood over six feet tall by sixteen. His blond, tightly-pulled pony tail exposed his sharp facial features and deep-set blue eyes. He was handsome.

In 1816, with Leslie's blessing and under his mother's protest, Michael joined a shipping line and launched his nautical career as a deckhand onboard the *Cape Ann* plying the West Indies trade.

When Leslie was in Boston on business one fall day in 1820, he walked past the venerable Kincaid Shipyard. He back stepped, entered the Yard and saw several ships nearly ready for the ocean, including a seventy-foot schooner.

"May I see her?" he asked. Someone escorted him onboard. Leslie checked her tall, rigged mainmast and foremast, the rudder gear, the laminated floor, stateroom, working galley and the hold below. He called for Mr. Kincaid, asked him, "Is she available?"

"Yes! I received a rare cancellation."

Elated, Leslie closed the transaction in thirty minutes with a strong signature backed by his maple sugar.

Leslie surprised Michael on his twenty-second birthday. He took his deckhand son to the Kincaid Shipyard. "Our birthday present, she's yours," Leslie said, pointing to a sleek seventy footer.

"M . . . ine?" Michael held his hand at his mouth, then wept with joy. "I'm a captain?"

Leslie, watching his son, knew he had done the right thing.

On christening day, Michael invited Morning Star to Boston Harbor. *What for?* he thought. "Please wear your Narragansett tribal clothes, with fringed shirt and feathered headgear," he said.

The Indian bowed, but wondered why.

Michael's family and friends, including Morning Star, arrived early at Pier Sixteen. They saw moored a white-painted schooner gleaming under morning sun with a canvas sheet roped over her stem. It was flapping in the ocean breeze.

The moment had come.

With Reverend Wilmer Cushman at his side, Father Leslie untied the rope and gave its end to Deborah. Michael signaled.

Deborah smiled at Morning Star and pulled. The canvas sheet fluttered down to a wild cheer, revealing the name *Morning Star* on the bow.

It startled the faithful servant. Turning to Michael with outstretched arms in traditional style, he thanked him in his native language as tears ran down the sides of his high thin nose. "My son, thank you," he said in English at the end.

Reverend Cushman, his hand on the name, blessed the *Morning Star* and prayed she would take Michael through all the storms safely to destination.

§

Michael chose to ply the Boston-to-Baltimore trade route. Somewhere he heard old news that Sandwich Island chiefs paid handsomely for firearms, even relics. His business was slow. He decided to go to the Isles with muskets and stuffs and make quick money. He knew where to get the latest.

He sailed up the Delaware River and went to the Union Army's Philadelphia Quartermaster Depot where Isaac Davis had earlier been. His family friends, veterans of the Revolutionary War, gladly stuffed *Morning Star's* hold with surplus American muskets, bayonets, cannons and ammunition from the War of 1812, and charged Michael just a dollar.

Loaded down with booty, her hull low, the *Morning Star* headed for the Isles in June 1822 with a crew of five.

After seven salty months she arrived in Honolulu Harbor. Michael entered in his log, "December 26, 1822, 7:34 AM" and changed into his captain's blue uniform, eager to meet anyone important.

A canoe pulled alongside and three folks climbed on board. Michael's five crewmen took positions with fixed bayonets, but seeing a white cleric among them relieved Michael.

A big bronze man approached Michael and said, "I am the king's emissary at this harbor. Who are you? Where from? Why you here? And where you going?"

Not bad English for a bearded aborigine in loincloth. All legitimate questions, a surprised Michael thought.

The cleric, Asa Thurston from Boston, stood nearby to lend language help if needed.

"I am Captain Michael Chaplain from Salem, Massachusetts, in America. I came to meet your king and sell him western arms," he told the man in loincloth.

Kalanikua shook his head in disbelief. "Our old king, who died four years ago, disbanded our army years earlier. We no need arms, we are at peace."

"I think you better leave Hawai'i," Thurston said. "We cannot be around to protect you."

Michael wasn't intimidated. He suffered too long getting here and wasn't ready to leave on a cleric's advice.

The handsome young captain impressed Kalanikua, who stared at him with envy.

"Can you eat with us tonight?" he asked.

Michael smiled over the stupid question. "Ah, yes, I have no prior engagement. Where and when?" he asked, staring at Thurston.

"This afternoon, in Waikīkī."

"I thought you said tonight?"

"*Ae*, we start early, end late."

"Oh hoooo. How far to Waikīkī?"

"Half hour on my boat, depending on wind and wave conditions," Kalanikua said, pointing to his single-mast, double-hulled canoe with eight big men holding paddles.

Michael shook his head. "Let us go on my boat. You three be my guests."

"Nice!" Kalanikua said.

But Thurston declined. "I must return to Kona."

No loss, Michael thought.

On the way to Waikīkī a curious Michael asked Kalanikua, "What do you folks eat at dinner?"

"Many things, some roasted, most raw. You will see tonight."

Most raw? Michael rolled his eyes.

Kalanikua stood on the bridge of a *haole* boat and let the wind caress his face.

"Waikīkī portside" he said.

Michael began a lazy turn.

"The boy approaching in that canoe is our Crown Prince. I will introduce when he comes onboard."

Michael anchored offshore. "Lower ropes!" he yelled.

The Crown Prince pulled alongside and climbed onboard.

"Captain Chaplain, please meet our Crown Prince Kauikeaouli. He prefers being called just Kaui."

Michael took a step back, gave to him a snappy salute, and said "Pleased to meet you, Your Highness."

"I just met the captain in Honolulu with Kahu Thurston," Kalanikua said. "He came to sell us arms, but I told him we don't need them, we are at peace."

"Welcome to Hawai'i," Kaui said.

"Is this not the Sandwich Islands?"

"No, English say Sandwich. We call it by real name, 'Hawai'i.' Since 1810, our full name is The Kingdom of Hawai'i," Kaui said. "You came all the way here just to sell us arms that we don't need?"

"Every country I know keeps an army even in peacetime," Michael said. "It needs good equipment and I have the best." He then asked: "Don't you keep even a small defensive force?"

"No, captain, we don't have even that," Kaui said. "Nobody harms us."

You ignorant Hawaiians, Michael thought.

"Can I see your boat?" Kaui asked.

"Certainly, Your Highness." Still smarting, Michael led him below deck, first to his neat stateroom, then to the crew's quarters, all in ship shape.

Kaui liked the galley and dining room, went twice to the cookie jar. He stared at Michael from every angle, more interested in the tall captain with a ponytail than in his cargo.

"I hear Kalanikua invited you for dinner tonight?"

"Yes, Your Highness, I already accepted. Where?"

"Over there." Kaui pointed to a former *heiau* at the foothill of Lē'ahi.

"Shall I deliver something to the party, Your Highness?"

"No, no need . . . Yes! You have swell wine? You got some?"

"Yes, sir, a case of swell red. But you look too young to drink spirits, Your Highness."

"I drink rum all the time. That's bad?"

"Yes, spirits are not good for young, tender organs."

"Organs?"

"Like your heart and liver."

"Ah hah. My organs strong, not to worry. Captain, your crew members are also invited."

"Thank you, Your Highness, but they will remain onboard the ship."

"No fear. Your ship will be safe," Kaui assured.

"No doubt, but captain and crew keep a polite distance, we don't socialize."

"Oh hoo," the heir exhaled, impressed with his discipline. "Until recently, men and women ate separately in Hawai'i, too."

Michael wondered why.

They left for shore with Kalanikua. "Let's walk to the old *heiau* and see what they're cooking," Kaui said.

After walking thirty minutes, they arrived at a dilapidated stone structure standing on a dusty tract of land above a rocky shore. "It used to be one of my father's personal temples. Our *kāhuna* smashed it good a few years ago in a religious revolution." Michael saw crumbling stonewalls standing here and there, survivals of their attempt at total demolition. Inside he saw ruins of huts and defaced giant god idols lying face down near a fallen tower. Obviously, no cleanup attempt had been made.

Kaui took Michael to the far end of the *heiau* ground. Guests were already seated, eating, laughing and drinking around a long "table" of leaves on the ground, with *kāne* (male) *hula* dancers entertaining them.

Kaui approached the queens. "Captain . . . er, Chapin, please meet Queen Ka'ahumanu, Queen Keōpūolani, Queen Kamehamalu, Queen Kīna'u and Queen Liliha."

Each time the captain bowed stiffly and repeated, "This is an honor, Your Majesty," thinking, *My, so many queens and just one king?*

"Sit there." The Crown Prince pointed. "The lady across is 'Eme Alapa'i, Queen Kamehamalu's personal English interpreter." Michael bowed, dazzled by her beauty. He tried to avoid ogling at her exposed breasts.

"Welcome to Hawai'i, hope you had a nice trip," she said, smiling.

"Thank you Amy, you speak English without an accent. Who taught you?"

"My name is pronounced Eh-meh, spelled e-m-e."

"Yes, ma'am," he said, staring into her melancholic, haunting eyes. For him the party instantly became secondary.

"My English. Since I was small, many American and English seamen taught me," she said, parting her hair from one side of her breast to the other and thinking, *What a young, handsome captain!* For a moment, Kainoa was off her mind. From another angle, Lani, too, stared at Michael with wild fancy.

After seven months at sea, Michael's stomach began to churn and digest the aroma rising from the *imu*. Food kept coming to the "table" in large trays.

He cringed seeing shrimps and lobsters with busy antennae checking their surroundings.

A huge roasted pig was raised from the *imu*. *That I can eat!* Michael rejoiced.

"Just four years earlier men and women eating together in this sacred *heiau* meant prompt death to all," Kaui told Michael.

"Why? Was there a law against it?"

"No, not laws but *kapu*, *'Ai kapu*, proclaimed by our gods."

"Ah huh," Michael said, politely.

Lack of Michael's attention seethed Ka'ahumanu. She sucked a raw *'alamihi* (black rock crab) and threw up her hands, her signal that she wanted to leave.

Two swarthy men *hāpai* (lifted) her torso onto a litter. Michael stood, said "Good night Your Majesty." Other queens soon raised their hands.

Catching the moment, Kaui asked a servant, "Open swell wine," signaling the start of the real party.

Michael walked around the "table" and sat on a mat next to 'Eme. "Hello," he said, staring into her brown eyes. "What are the chanters saying?"

"They are giving praise to many things, to our *'āina*, to the gods for this lovely evening, the foods, the gentle winds, the stars above, the penis for procreation. We consider everything very sacred."

Penis? She said that? He was too shocked to ask.

After sundown, *kukui* torches lit the *heiau* floor. *Hula* dancers raised the tempo of the party as inhibitions dissolved. Michael never expected to see male *ali'i* fondling girls.

"Sorry, 'Eme, for just staring at you. You are the most beautiful girl I have ever met, white or native."

"What is native?"

Michael laughed, wished he had not said it.

"It has many meanings. In my family it means someone not white, but never mind," Michael said.

"Anything wrong by being a native?"

"No, no," he said, trying to cover.

"Can I call you 'Mikaele?' It's easier for me than 'Michael'."

"Of course. 'Eme, are you . . . married?" he asked.

"No, but I have someone dear in Boston studying. We will marry when he returns."

Michael became anxious. "Is he a Hawaiian?" he asked.

"Yes, a native."

"Can we talk about him, maybe at dinner on my boat tomorrow night?"

Ever since Kainoa left, loneliness had left 'Eme desolate, often times disoriented. As an unbalanced soul she accepted Michael's dinner invitation without considering the consequence.

Late next afternoon, wearing the same green silk *pā'ū* she wore when Kainoa left, 'Eme arrived at the shore. Michael was waiting.

"Welcome 'Eme! I have dinner ready onboard," Michael said. He sat her down on a boat and rowed to the *Morning Star* moored offshore.

They went onboard, strolled to the bow to watch the sun slowly set. He felt the stares from shore.

The crew got a leave.

"'Eme, I'll show you the boat."

'Eme smiled, nodded. Blinded by wild curiosity of being alone with a handsome *haole* captain, she didn't resist when Michael opened his stateroom door and gently nudged her onto his bed.

The crew returned later that evening and saw dinner still on the table and the stateroom door closed. They knew.

Morning was half gone when they awoke from an evening of white heat. "'Eme, are you ready for breakfast? I have salted pork and boiled potatoes."

"Yes, if you also have *poi*," she answered. They laughed and kissed.

"'Eme, let's go to the map room and talk about your dear friend."

'Eme wondered why, and followed Michael into the room. He lit an oil lamp hanging over a table that was fixed to the floor. Except for the table and nautical maps on the walls, 'Eme saw a bare room. They sat on the floor.

"I am jealous. Can you tell me more about your man in Boston?"

'Eme continued to wonder why. "All right. His name is Kainoa Kahemoku, maybe the most ambitious young man in Hawai'i."

After ten minutes Michael interrupted, asked, "Do you love him?"

"Yes, deeply. Since long time our souls have joined. One cannot exist without the other."

"Then why did you make love to me last night?"

"I don't know. I guess because I am so lonely."

"'Eme, I can become one with you too," he said, already falling in love.

"Thank you, Mikaele, but I will wait for him."

Mikaele's world crashed.

So did 'Eme's. Word spread of her overnight dalliance in Michael's roost. Adultery was one of only four crimes in Hawai'i, but it extended morally to betrothed couples. 'Eme became estranged from her friends and members of her incredulous family, even from her employer, Queen Kamehamalu. They had expected more of her.

Now without a home, 'Eme began spending her days and nights floating aimlessly on board the *Morning Star*. She decided to inform Kainoa about Mikaele before others did. After eight attempts 'Eme mailed her ninth draft:

February 15, 1823

Dearest Kai:

I wish I was in Boston helping you get organized. I miss you.

Here, so many of our friends are listening to Ka'ahumanu, Kalanimoku, that group, and joining the Christian church.

In Kahului, Auntie Ka'ilei and Uncle Kalama died from *haole* sickness. They suffered for long time.

Your parents, my family are healthy. But they are not happy with me because I spend time with Michael Chaplain, an American captain from Salem, onboard his boat. I make believe he is you.

I love only you. I wait for you.

Love, 'Eme

23

The cargo just sitting onboard the *Morning Star* had Michael concerned. He knew salt air could turn his ammunition and powder soggy and useless, and render his weapons worthless from rust. He had heard of the Chinese emissaries on the big island.

In early March 1823 he went to Kona in a rented *peleleu*. Michael stopped a *haole* and asked questions.

The man had answers. "The emissaries live over there," he pointed, opposite the Ahu'ena Heiau. "The head man is Chinn Sun."

Michael scribbled the name on a paper. After a short walk he came to an open gate and followed a winding, pebbled pathway that led to an open pavilion, just as the man said. He walked up several warped wooden steps and stood on an open wood floor about fifty by sixty feet, bare of any furniture. Michael noticed its high ceiling. A small brass bell hung above the steps. He rattled it. A burley native in loincloth appeared.

"Yes?" he asked.

"I am Captain Michael Chaplain, an American." He checked his scribble. "I came to see Emissary Chinn Sun on business. Is he available?"

"Chaplain. That's you? You have appointment?"

"No, but I have something important to ask Chinn Sun," Michael said, his body language heavy of urgency.

"You wait here," the native said, and disappeared behind the pavilion wall.

Michael fidgeted nearly an hour, standing, Chinese penalty for no appointment. *That's you? What is he saying?* he mumbled.

Around noon, a skinny, middle-aged Chinese man appeared. He was wearing loose-fitting, black, silk-like pants and shirt and white stockings.

"You Captain Michael Chaplain?"

"Yes, that's me."

"We feel solly for Kainoa. He a good boy. He helped us dig first sandalwood *puka.*"

What's going on around me? He shook his head.

"Chinn Sun Shian Sun asked me to inquire your business, why you came. I am Ah Fat."

A fat. I'll curse my father if I had that name. He's sorry for Kainoa? I must be a celebrity around here, Michael mused.

Ah Fat, fortyish, had black piercing eyes, black bushy eyebrows and drooping mustache that half covered his narrow chin. A black braided pigtail went down to his slender buttocks. The color black caught Michael's eyes.

"Why you came?" Ah Fat asked.

"Do we talk standing up?" Michael asked, sarcastically.

"Take off shoes. We can go alound the wall and sit down."

They came to a verandah facing a central courtyard. "Sit down," Ah Fat said, pointing to one of several tree stumps around a square wooden table. "You begin talk?"

"Yes. I'm Michael Chaplain from America, captain and owner of my ship *Morning Star,* docked in Honolulu. I have a stockpile of cannons and muskets and fresh ammunition. I learned there is no demand for them here. I want to go to China and sell them to one customer. Can you give me a lead? I'll pay."

"You have list of . . . what say, stockpile?" he asked, smiling.

"Yes, here it is."

Ah Fat, fluent in English, scanned it. He stopped smiling.

"You wait here," he said and disappeared with the list.

Shortly, the same native appeared said, "Chinn Sun Shian Sun and Ah Fat Shian Sun ask if you can join them for lunch."

Oh hooo. That list must be talking, he thought. "Yess."

"You wait here," he said and disappeared again.

The smell of food came wafting in. Ah Fat and another Chinese man wearing the same kind of loose-fitting black clothes came to the table.

"Solly making you wait, Captain Chaplain. This is Chinn Sun Shian Sun, head of our group."

Michael stood immediately. "Nice to meet you, Your Emissary," Michael said, not knowing how to address him.

Chinn Sun bowed. He kept both hands inside his wide-mouthed sleeves, obviously with no intent to shake Michael's hands. "We have lunch, then we talk. Hope you like our cooking," Chinn said.

Michael stretched his neck to see what two Hawaiian natives were setting on the table. "What are they?" he asked, pointing to a platter of shellfish, each about three inches across.

"Hawaiians call it 'opihi. Our cook Nijun steamed them with sea water."

"Good, I don't eat raw meat."

"We also don't," Chinn Sun said, pointing to another dish. "That is fish fried with stem of taro leaf. We have so little vegetables here. Hawaiians eat seaweed; we don't. Try."

"Thank you, I will." Michael still had not seen the man's hands, wondered how he was going to eat.

Michael downed his first 'opihi. His eyes widened. "This is more delicious than our abalone," he told Chinn Sun. He reached for another.

"We eat only big opihi, leave smaller two-inch kind alone."

Ah Fat interrupted. "Your weapons made in America?"

"Yes, one hundred percent."

Ah Fat frowned, indicating interest. "How much you asking whole thing?"

"Just two thousand dollars."

"You take Spanish silver?"

"Of course."

"You take cargo to China at no charge?"

"Er, yes."

"If you make sale through our contact, how much you pay us?"

"The usual ten percent of sale."

"Ten?" Ah Fat's mouth and mustache sagged. "Twenty-five percent normal. I was hoping you would pay us more."

Are you kidding? he thought.

"Can we shake hands at fifteen percent?"

Chinn Sun said few more words in Cantonese to Ah Fat.

"Captain, in China, we don't negotiate back, forth. You accept twenty-five percent, or you don't. If you don't, it is allight, we still continue lunch and we no eat you," Ah Fat said with a smile.

Not funny, Michael thought.

"That is roast wild pig," Ah Fat pointed.

It didn't interest Michael; he had lost his appetite. Michael kept figuring, thought the Chinese offer was slightly better than dumping his cargo in the ocean.

"All right, twenty-five percent," he said with a shrug.

"Good. After you make sale, how do we know you will come back and pay us?" Chinn Sun asked.

"There is a girl I want to marry."

"'Eme Alapa'i?"

You devils, he thought. Covering his shock, he asked, "Who do I see and where in China?"

"Captain, you know the penalty if you don't pay full amount?"

"No."

"We sink your ship," Chinn Sun said. "Come back in one hour. We will give you a letter and the information you need."

"Yes, allight, I mean all right," Michael said. *Sink my ship? No chance*, Michael laughed.

Ah Fat answered the bell when Michael returned from a walk. "Our contact lives in Portuguese Macao, not far from Canton," he said. "After you dock, walk to Chin Jin Pa Hotel. Manager is Kai Nan Shek, half Portuguese and half Chinese. Give him this letter. He will arrange a meeting with buyer not always in Macao. You may wait long time until he returns, allight?"

"All right," Michael said. He took the letter and jotted down "Chin Jin Pa" and "Kai Nan Shek" on the back in English, saluted Ah Fat and left.

"'Eme!" Michael yelled when he returned from Kona. "The Chinese emissaries gave me this letter of introduction to a likely Chinese buyer in Macao for my cargo. I'd like to go there, sell it, and spend the rest of my life with you."

"Please don't worry about me. Go," 'Eme said.

"I worry, you don't have a home, a place to live because of me. I arranged for you to stay in the old Kanahele compound with two servants to care for you. And please have this," he said. She opened a heavy pouch and saw many large gold coins inside. "Buy whatever you need," Michael said.

"Thank you, I will keep the coins but I will not be going to Kanahele's."

"Why? Where will you live?"

"The cave that Kainoa and I discovered, *Hale'ano'i*."

"No, not in a cave!"

"It is my personal home. Good luck with your sale."

Michael exhaled, shook his head and wrote a short letter to his father.

March 20, 1823

Dear Father, I am leaving shortly for Macao near Canton, China, to sell my cargo. I'll be back in Honolulu before June 1824. Can the whole family join me in Honolulu after that for a grand reunion? I miss all of you so much.

Love, Michael

Next morning Michael waited at the shore for visitors to arrive to bid him *aloha*. No one came. He saluted the gulls and left on a shoreboat for his ship.

From *Hale'ano'i*, 'Eme saw the *Morning Star* fade into a dot, not suspecting she was a month *hāpai* (pregnant).

After three months she began to show.

Mamo was devastated. "Tell Kainoa before others do," he advised 'Eme. 'Eme nodded with her eyes closed.

June 2, 1823

My dearest Kai, I miss you so much. Mikaele left for China, will be gone over a year. My folks are still mad at me so I now live in *Hale'ano'i*. My friends avoid me, but I have more time to dream about you. Mamo is staying close by, bringing me food, walking with me to the river where I bathe, anything, so thankful.

Kai, I ask for another forgiveness. I hāpai Mikaele's keiki. It will be born in about five, six months. I was going to ho'ohemo (abort). But when I felt the baby's first 'eku (kick) inside of me I was overcome. I couldn't.

I beg your forgiveness. I am to blame. I miss you.

Love, 'Eme

§

Michael's trip to Macao was smooth, uneventful. In October 1823, he raised a clenched fist when he saw Hong Kong at starboard. But the thought of 'Eme living in a cave doused his joy.

The *Morning Star* sailed past Canton and arrived at overcast Macao. Michael only knew that Macao was a Portuguese enclave grabbed from the Chinese in the 1550s.

He found the harbor jammed with Chinese junks and foreign brigs and schooners, many flying flags that he had not seen before. *Why no ships here flying the Stars and Stripes?* he wondered.

The shore bobbed with native headgear of Arabs, Indians, Punjabis, Chinese and others.

A flatboat with three European crewmen came alongside and escorted the *Morning Star* to a nearby landing for inspection of her hold. "You discharging cargo in Macao?" a man from the Portuguese Customs asked

"Yes, sir, if I find a buyer."

"What is your cargo?"

"Weaponry, arms. What is the duty?"

"For arms, ten percent of your sales. We accept only English or Spanish gold. Until you find a buyer, you can visit our town. We have no immigration procedure."

Ten percent! You bandits! Michael puffed, then jumped on the pier with Ah Fat's letter in his vest.

Michael hollered to his sailing master, Stan Grace, "I'll be gone for about two hours."

"Good luck," the master said with a neat salute.

His shaky legs on land felt good. Michael smelled food cooking from inside Chinese junks. *Kona pavilion with Chinn Sun,* he recalled. *Maybe 'opihi steamed with sea water? Mmmm.*

The third European he stopped for directions was a craggy seaman who spoke fluent Cockney. "Chin Jin Pa, a two-story 'otel, is thataway," he pointed. "'Bout ten minutes walk from 'ere, painted bright green, wid red trim. Name's on the door in tiny bloody English, so look 'ard. I sometimes takes me supper there."

"Thank you, sir," Michael said, and pointed his nose thataway. He took long steps along narrow cobblestone roads lined on both sides with outdoor shops. A fog of oriental smell permeated the air. He peeked, saw what looked like animal paws in thick glass jars, and crispy-looking locusts next to them. Baked cockroaches ended his curiosity. Heaven's right here for those flies, he thought.

He came upon a two-story building painted bright green with red trim. Walking closer he saw, in tiny bloody English, 'Chin Jin Pa' on the door.

"Destination!" he exclaimed.

Restraining his joy, Michael strode into a small darkish lobby laid with cobblestones, same as the streets. The material must be cheap, he guessed.

A man with an abacus was totaling something under an oil lamp, yesterday's sales maybe. "Excuse me, I'm looking for Mr. Kai Nan Shek," he told the man. "I understand he works here."

"Yes he does. He's me," the man replied in a high-pitched voice heavy with a foreign accent.

"Oh, I found you!"

Kai Nan was surprised. "Why me? I inherited something?"

Fortyish, Kai stood barely five feet tall. He appeared sinister with his drooping lips and large round eyes with lots of white showing.

"I am Captain Michael Chaplain, an American. We docked an hour ago."

"So?"

Michael reached into his vest and gave to him Ah Fat's letter. Kai opened it apprehensively, and began reading. Michael saw his eyes move from top to bottom, right to left. *He must be fluent in Chinese,* he thought.

Kai Nan lowered the letter and stared at Michael.

"Ah Fat asks I introduce you to Zhou En Lum. He was here last week. Will not return soon unless he makes big catch."

"Is he a fisherman?"

"No, he a pirate boss. Has sixteen boats all with cannons. His men use swords and muskets."

"I am here to sell arms, not to meet pirates, Mr. Kai."

"You came to right place. Zhou always lookin' for latest cannons, muskets. His business is to overwhelm others."

Of course, Michael sighed.

"You serve food in this 'otel, I mean hotel? Something smells good."

"Every hotel in Macao serves meals to its guests; it is Chinese custom."

"Ohoo! Wonderful! May I see your menu?"

"No hotel in Macao has menu like European hotels."

"Then how do your customers order?"

"Hotel guests tell us in morning what they want for lunch or dinner. Our cooks go buy materials and cook how guests like."

Like home, Michael thought.

"While you wait, you want women? Half Portuguese-Chinese, pure Chinese, I have from age ten and up, and a special room upstairs."

Michael's strict puritanical upbringing censored his flush. Changing the mood he asked, "What is Ah Fat's connection with Chin Jin Pa?"

"His father owned it before he died; he and Zhou's father were close friends," Kai said. "Zhou makes his home here when he is in port."

"I see. I'll go now and return for dinner. Please tell the cook that I want fried chicken with vegetables and rice. Some *'opihi* on the side."

"*'Opihi?*"

Michael smiled, tapped a one-dollar silver coin on the counter and gave it to Kai. It was worth two day's work for him.

Zhou's long absence taxed Michael's patience. After over a month, he had seen Macao's bright spots and noisy, seamy bars filled with prostitutes, and had enough of Chin Jin Pa's cooking.

In early December 1823, Kai Nan Shek jumped on board the *Morning Star* at daybreak and knocked hard on Michael's stateroom door.

"Yes" he growled, opening the door halfway.

"Zhou En Lum just returned. He made beeg catch. I gave him Ah Fat's letter. He read it, told me he wants see you. Now."

"Yes, sir!" Michael yelled, and closed the door. He emerged in his captain's blue uniform and headed for Chin Jin Pa, taking long steps that kept Kai Nan half running. When they arrived, some thirty people were in the dining room eating.

"That man in center waving at us is Zhou. He knows you are with me and wants you to join him for *chuk*, chicken-based rice porridge. It's insult if you lefuse," Kai Nan said.

Michael walked towards the pirate boss and stopped. "Good morning, sir, my name is Michael Chaplain, from America," he said, looking at Kai for language help. Zhou smiled and waved Michael over, pointing to a seat next to him.

"Go," Kai said.

Michael went and sat.

Late thirtyish, the pigtailed Zhou seemed like a village fisherman, hardly a swashbuckling, scar-faced picaroon. But Michael noticed his unusually large hands. *He must use them a lot,* he thought.

"Captain, tell Zhou why you are in Macao. I will translate your every word."

"All right." He turned his chair to face Zhou, talked for ten minutes, then said, "Ah Fat, an emissary in Hawai'i of the *taikuns* of Canton, recommended that I see you. Kai has his letter."

Zhou glanced at it again and said something to Kai Nan.

"Captain, Zhou is puzzled, asked if you came all the way to Macao on Ah Fat's word hoping to sell your cargo to him?"

Michael nodded.

Zhou and his men bellylaughed. He told Kai Nan more.

Kai smiled. "Zhou says he no need to buy your cargo. He can just take it, your boat and you too."

Michael paled.

"Have some *chuk*. Zhou insists."

"No thank you, I can't see food."

Zhou and his men cackled when they learned of his reply.

"No wolly, Zhou is only joking," Kai Nan said. Chinese pirates have strict code of ethics. They never take anything from anybody on land. It blings bad luck, so no wolly."

Michael sighed.

Zhou said something more to Kai Nan.

"Zhou wants to see your weapons."

"Let's go!" Michael said, "but give me a bowl of *chuk* first!" He swallowed the porridge, chicken livers and all.

Kai asked his hotel assistant, Wang Lo, "Watch the desk until I get back."

In ten minutes they were walking the deck of *Morning Star*. Michael led them below. Zhou saw the weaponry stored neatly in rows of open wooden crates. He grabbed a musket at random, wiped off the oil and looked into the bore. He loaded a round, went on the deck and fired into the water. Bore clean, ammunition dry, good recoil. He didn't smile.

Zhou's gunner, inspecting a Lopaka barrel, said something.

"What did he say?" Michael asked Kai.

"He tells Zhou no rust in bore."

"Zhou called Kai Nan and said something brief.

"What's your price for whole thing?"

"Tell him two-thousand dollars in gold, in cash."

There was a long pause. "He ask are you buying something with the money?"

"Yes. After I get paid I want to go to Canton or Shanghai and buy things like curios, spices, cloths, to take back to Hawai'i to sell."

Zhou smiled when he heard. He told Kai more.

"Zhou says you can't go to Canton. Long time ago Manchu emperors closed the city to foreigners who don't have a *taikun's* pass. But no need to go there. He has everything you want in Macao. Want to go see?"

"Are they pirated goods?" Michael asked.

"Not your business. They are now his."

"Tell Zhou I cannot pay him until he pays me for my cargo."

"Zhou understands. Please follow him."

They walked down cobblestone alleys and came to a large, windowless single-story wooden building with two iron gates. Zhou unbolted one. Michael stepped inside of a huge pirate's warehouse and saw two armed guards patrolling the cold interior. He walked the aisles and drooled. *Zhou is right! Forget Canton, everything I want is right here. Pirate goods must be cheaper too,* he thought.

Kai Nan got more instructions.

"Captain, Zhou says you can have anything in this warehouse, as much as you can take home in your boat. And he will pay you one thousand dollars in Spanish gold."

Michael frowned, Chinese style, suppressing his glee. "All right, I will make a pile of what I want." With coolie help he emptied his shipboard weaponry into Zhou's nearby warehouse and stuffed his pile into the void. "Here, one thousand dollars in Spanish gold coins from Zhou to complete the transaction," Kai said.

"Thank you, Kai. I am thankful for your help."

Michael loaded *Morning Star's* galley with provision and returned to the Chin Jin Pa. Kai Nan and Zhou greeted him. "I am leaving tomorrow. I came to say goodbye and to thank you and Zhou for everything," Michael told Kai. "And tell Zhou I hope I won't ever meet him on the high seas!"

They laughed. The fair play of merchants of Chinese ancestry impressed Michael. He dropped a ten-dollar gold coin into Kai Nan's pocket.

"No need to pay customs duty for your sale. Zhou already took care of that," Kai Nan said.

Michael shook his head. He dropped another coin into his pocket and gave to each a neat seaman's salute.

Walking back to the *Morning Star,* Michael stopped at a busy marketplace. He saw paws. "What kind?" he asked.

"Bear paws, delicious steamed," a man said.

Michael thought for a moment, then purchased one for dinner. I'm going to celebrate Chinese style! *Steam it? Hairs and all?*

One night during his return voyage, Michael awoke sweating. He dreamt he had become a father, a boy, by 'Eme! Momentous messages are often sent telepathically by God. "Oh no!" he screamed and stepped into the map room. Of puritan upbringing, he scribbled a note on his December 22, 1823 log: "Am I an illegitimate father? What would mother think?"

A day before, Mamo had rushed to see Pualani. "'Eme is having *kokohi* (labor pains) at *Hale'ano'i.* Please go, she needs you."

Pualani forgot they were estranged. She rushed with Mamo to her helpless side. Seeing 'Eme so emaciated unhinged her. She glanced at the interior of her primitive tabernacle with horror, hated herself for not asking 'Eme to come home sooner. Pualani bent down, hugged her daughter with teary eyes and said, "Hello, 'Eme," for the first time in a year.

"Thank you for coming, Mother!" She held her hand tightly and continued to push, finally giving birth to an active, healthy boy on December 21, 1823. Pualani cut off his umbilical cord, wiped his body with moist tapa and placed him in 'Eme's sweaty arms.

"Thank you, mother. He's beautiful!" she said touching his nose. She passed her fingers through her mother's hair and said, "I missed you so very much."

Eme lifted the baby to admire him. "I thought of his name. You like 'Kaikai?'" she asked.

Pualani just sobbed, too broken to see a baby not Kainoa's.

§

Earlier in Boston, Kainoa went to several upscale food shops to buy anything that looked *'ono* (delicious). Although his life was in turmoil, he wanted to surprise Dian. Smoked sausages from Germany, cheeses from Switzerland, beef from the Midwest plains, and fresh fruits from down south. All expensive, but he had pay in pocket.

He opened the front door and yelled, "Surprise!" carrying two large packages.

"Welcome back," Mrs. Noble said. "What are they?"

"Surprise," he said.

Dian looked troubled.

"Anything wrong Mrs. Noble?"

"Kainoa, you haven't spoken to me about 'Eme lately. Is anything wrong?"

Her suspicion shocked Kainoa. He walked to the kitchen, dropped his packages and told her, "Yes, Mrs. Noble, there is something painful. I got 'Eme's letter. She told me that in her loneliness, she was living with an American sea captain from Salem onboard his ship in Honolulu. How could she do that to me? She asks forgiveness but how can I, Mrs. Noble?"

"Salem. That's fourteen miles north. Who might he be?"

"Chaplain."

"That name is familiar, I think the family owns a big, maple-sugar farm. I thought there was something wrong when I saw you burn a letter recently, and someone told me you were at the harbor checking on boats leaving for Hawai'i."

"I did burn that letter and buried the ashes with my soul. I don't have one any more."

"You still do!" Dian shouted. She placed her two hands on Kainoa's shoulders and said, "I am sorry. I understand why you cannot forgive.

But remember that beautiful promise you made to 'Eme, that you will return home as someone special? I was so moved when you told me that. But if you quit now you'll go home a failure."

Kainoa's eyes welled. "Thank you, Mrs. Noble. I was going home to break that captain's neck, but you're right. I have a higher purpose than murder. I will finish what I came for."

24

In Salem, the excited Chaplains were counting the weeks before they would be leaving for a grand reunion with Michael in faraway Hawai'i. For Deborah, "Hawai'i" sounded primitive, exciting. She was eager to escape from her stiff puritanical surrounding.

Leslie invited Morning Star to the house.

He was in the kitchen preparing drinks when he heard his knock on the door. "Come in," he yelled. "How's the farm doing?"

"Can't be better, sir," he said. "Another bumper sap harvest coming spring."

"Wonderful. I'll be with you shortly." Leslie walked to the living room and laid on a table a tray with two cold drinks. *What's happening?* Morning Star wondered. He never had a private drink before with his Master.

He told Morning Star, "We're going soon to a faraway place, Hawai'i, for a reunion with Michael. We will be gone for a long time. Please continue to take good care of the farm. Our family is so grateful to you for your long, faithful service to our family. Before we leave, we are giving to you a portion of our farm. I have drawn the papers. Let's take a stroll around your farm tomorrow."

Morning Star stood stoically, his eyes closed.

With one hand on his shoulder, Leslie led him to the verandah railing for a drink in the Salem gloaming, beholding the sylvan scene of rows upon rows of sugar maple trees fading into the sunset. The autumn air was nippy, primordial. Except for few diehards, the red leaves were down, the buds awaiting rebirth in the spring.

"You've been a vital part of our family, Morning Star. Let's toast to our past, and to your future, may it continue to be blessed," Leslie said.

Morning Star clinked, laid down his glass and returned to his cottage.

Leslie wrote a letter to 'Eme, hoping she would eventually get it.

November 8, 1823

Dear Miss Alapa'i. Michael frequently mentioned your name in his letters, telling us how much he cares for you and your family. I am his father. My wife Meriam, daughter Deborah and I are arriving in Honolulu around June/July next year onboard the Nantucket Wind for a reunion with Michael.

If he returns from Macao before we arrive, please tell him we are on our way to Honolulu. We look forward to meeting you.

Thank you very much.

Sincerely,
Leslie Chaplain

§

On a November day in 1823, Dian Noble received a letter from her husband. "Kainoa, Paul, come!" Dian yelled. "I just got this letter. Paul, your father is returning soon!" For Dian the letter was a gift from God.

Kainoa began scanning the Boston *Gazette* daily for names of ships entering Boston Harbor. In its November 15, 1823 manifest, Kainoa spotted a tiny entry: "The trader *Cape Cod* sighted today off Long Island Sound heading north."

He ran home to show the manifest to Dian. She almost fainted seeing the ship's name in print. Paul grabbed Kainoa and dripped happy tears. They were soon dancing around the living room screaming, *Alleluia!* Kainoa knew Lono would forgive.

He rushed to the shipyard. "Mr. Kincaid, I think *Cape Cod* and Captain Noble returning today. Can I be excused from work so I can help Mrs. Noble?"

"Of course, Kainoa, go with full pay."

Kainoa tipped his cap and flew home.

"*Cape Cod* must be awfully close, Mrs. Noble."

"Let's go to the harbor and wait, no matter how long," Dian said. She went into her room, made up and changed to her prettiest ankle-length, high neckline dress. "Paul, comb your hair, wear your Sabbath clothes and the new gloves from Kainoa."

Kainoa dashed out and hired a horse-drawn carriage with a fringe on top. They were soon clack clacking, singing songs that came to mind. Seeing Dian deliriously happy shoved Michael off Kainoa's mind.

They arrived at the harbor. Mrs. Noble saw a dot on the horizon. "That's her!" she yelled.

A man sitting on the wharf with a fishing pole turned to her. "Your man comin' home?" he asked.

"Yes, yes."

"Wish I had someone happy when I come home."

"Paul, your father will be proud to see how tall you are."

"I am so glad having a father again."

The *Cape Cod* approached the North End of the harbor, her foresail fluttering. A sloop with red sails of a harbor official's boat, escorted her in.

When the *Cape* got closer, Dian recognized Dwight. She stood on the carriage and waved. He spotted Dian, Paul, and Kainoa from two hundred yards out, waved madly back from the bow.

He wondered, *How did they know I was returning today?* They spoiled his plan of sneaking to home and surprising everyone.

The carriage driver followed the boats to the Inner Harbor, where the *Cape* finally docked at Long Wharf. Dwight jumped off and rushed to Dian and Paul. All three just hugged, too overcome for words.

Kainoa watched them from a faraway corner. Dwight spotted him and yelled, "Hello Kainoa! Come!" He just waved back, wanting to leave the family alone.

Dwight told Peter Rice, the *Cape's* sailing master, "Take care of her. See you tomorrow."

"Yes, sir," Rice replied.

Dwight threw his luggages onto the carriage and yelled, "Kainoa, jump in."

He waved and disappeared.

On the way home Dwight asked, "Did Kainoa give you problems?"

"No, he is the finest young man I have ever met. I consider him a member of our family," Dian said. "I love him."

Dwight sighed, felt relieved. "Sorry for the initial shock I caused." They laughed together.

At full stride, Kainoa left the harbor, took shortcuts from State Street through grounds of the Old State House, the Court House and up Mt. Vernon Street to home. He beat the carriage by ten minutes, and greeted them with a wide smile when they pulled up.

How did he do it? Dwight thought.

Kainoa jumped into the carriage for a rolling, happy reunion.

That evening the Nobles asked Kainoa, "Join us for turkey dinner at the Lantern House on the banks of the Charles River. This is our family's Thanksgiving Day."

"Yes, sir, thank you," Kainoa said.

Before sunset they strolled to the Lantern House, sat down at a table, held hands while Dwight gave a prayer. Kainoa joined the family and said, *"Amen,"* at the end.

"How's home?" Kainoa asked.

"Ka'ahumanu and the missionaries are transforming the kingdom into a church. They are paying no attention to more important things."

"Like our people vanishing?"

"Yes, evanescence is out of control."

Kainoa dropped his fork. "There won't be Hawaiians left," he sighed, and finished dinner quietly.

Another black moment awaited Kainoa. After they returned from Lantern House, the Captain handed to Kainoa a bag. "Here's your sack of mail. Hope it's all good news inside."

"Thank you for dinner, and for this," Kainoa nervously said. Without bidding the family good night he went to his room, spread the letters on his bunk, and read 'Eme's letter of June 2, 1823, last. He vomited his entire dinner, bile and all.

Dian exclaimed next morning, "Kainoa, you look horrible! What's wrong? The food was bad?"

"No," he whispered. "I died when 'Eme informed me she is having a *keiki*, Chaplain's. Maybe, already born!"

Dian and Dwight stood appalled, helpless. Neither knew how to console a person destroyed.

The captain's return was signal for Kainoa to head for home. He would be returning as someone special, as 'Eme wished, but to a life no longer vital.

He went to the Harbor to check departures, noted the *Clementine* was leaving Boston on December 15, 1823, for Shanghai, China, with stops at Rio de Janeiro and Honolulu.

"Captain Noble, I made a reservation to return to Hawai'i on the *Clementine* in middle December."

"*Clem?* I know the ship's captain, Stan Coleman; he's a wonderful gruff, speaks with a hoarse. You want to work your way home?"

"Yes if I could," he said, almost in a whisper.

"I'll schedule an interview."

Coleman greeted Kainoa next day. "Forget the interview. Dwight told me that you were special. That's good enough for me. Welcome, mate!"

"Thank you, sir," Kainoa said with a ravaged heart.

He later strolled to the end of the wharf and leaned against a boulder. Memories of his treasured days in Boston wet his eyes. "Thank you," he mumbled to all those who had made them indelible.

Kainoa penned a note to Pualani, made sure it got on the *West Wind* sailing next day for Hawai'i and the Orient.

On his departure morning, Kainoa felt the pang of bidding Dian and Paul goodbye.

"You are a member of our family. We will miss you," Dwight Noble said. Kainoa saw Dian weeping.

"I have a farewell present for you," Dwight said, and reached into his pocket. He gave to Kainoa a pigskin pouch.

Kainoa was shocked. "That was mine!" he yelled.

"Yes, I want you to have it back, the pearls and all. I had so much pleasure just holding and admiring them."

Kainoa felt the power of a man's soul strike his. He realized how huge a *haole* heart can get.

He opened the pouch, picked the two largest and pressed them into Dian's wet hand. "Remember I'm a pagan?" he whispered. "Merry Christmas, Mrs. Noble." They shared a precious moment agonizing in farewell.

"Captain Noble, here are two for you, and brother Paul, this one is for you," he said, and held their hands tightly, not wanting to let go.

Kainoa gave to the Captain four more pearls. "Can you give one to Mr. Kincaid, Captain Peter London, Mr. Conrad Wellings and to Secretary John Quincy Adams for me? I owe them so much."

The Nobles felt how huge a *kanaka* heart can get.

Kainoa was finally ready for Hawai'i.

25

Three months earlier in Lahaina, Maui, Keōpūolani was at home breathing hard with a worried Hoapili at her side. She knew death was calling. Her friends and members of the missionary arrived.

"I think Keōpūolani is very ill. Go see her," Mamo suggested to Mākaha. "Return the kindness she showed to your family after your father disappeared. But she may not recognize you," he warned.

"Why?"

"Her mind may be gone. I saw the king take her to Maui last week. She boarded a canoe at Waikīkī for the ride to the *Ha'aheo*. Suddenly, she turned to shore with outstretched arms and greeted no one at the beach. She might have been reliving the time she arrived in Kona with her mother twenty-seven years ago."

"I will leave for Maui tonight," Mākaha said, shaken by Mamo's story.

He arrived in Lahaina just in time to witness a dramatic confrontation. Near death, Keōpūolani asked Kahu Bingham, "Save me from *po*. Baptize me! I want to enter your church, please!" she begged.

Being once a goddess, she knew how severe retribution of pagan gods could be.

Bingham walked away. Rev. William Richards, a recent arrival from Boston with the Second Missionary Company, grabbed him and pleaded, "That's her final wish. Please grant it." Bingham pushed his hand away and kept walking.

Another Kahu stepped forward. "I will," English Reverend William Ellis said. He blessed an *ipu* of water, sprinkled it over her forehead and baptized her in an Anglican Ceremony as she lay comatose. She passed away on September 16, 1823, holding a conch shell with fifty-two whorls, unaware if she had died a pagan or a Christian.

Hoapili, now a Congregationalist, arranged a Christian funeral for his wife, but it turned heavy with pagan overtones. A huge throng wailed at the graveyard. *Kāhili* standards of royalty covered the burial site like flowers in bloom. Christians recited the Verses, but they were drowned by the *kāhuna* who pleaded to her *'aumakua* gods to receive her spirit. The ritual stirred yesterday's memories. Bingham stood back, bit his lips and watched the priests plant *kapu* sticks around fresh dirt.

A heated exchange erupted between Ellis and Bingham after the funeral.

"Why did you refuse to give her our good Lord's blessing?" Ellis bitterly asked.

"Because it was useless. My dear Reverend Ellis, the Bible is clear. God predestines each of us for Heaven or Hell before we are born. No person can change what He had ordained."

"My dear Reverend Bingham, how do you know God ordained the queen to Hell?" Ellis asked, with scornful lips.

"Because she was born of sin, of incest. No baptism by me or you could erase original sin," he said. With an air of infallibility the man of Puritan root walked away, giving Ellis no chance to rebut.

§

Liholiho left Lahaina for Honolulu soon after the funeral to escape spiritual defilement. He learned at Waikīkī that his mother had willed all her land and possessions to Hoapili, leaving him nothing. He opened a cork and suffered alone. The thought of going somewhere beyond the reach of Ka'ahumanu, Hoapili, Bingham and their ilk, surfaced. His occasional drinking partner, English whaler Milton Ruddles, suggested London. "Go meet King George IV, shake my king's hands, get his highest *haole mana*."

London! The thought grew.

After a week of rum, Liholiho made a fateful decision. He called Ruddles, told him, "Take me, Queen Kamehamalu, Governor Boki, his wife Liliha, and six others on this list to London next month on your *L'Aigle*."

Me? Not on my stink whaler! he thought. Then he imagined receiving honors and invitations to royal receptions from his king, for taking a foreign king to England.

"Your Majesty, I will take you. Let me figure the cost."

"No need figure. I give you one thousand dollars in Spanish silver," Liholiho replied.

"Can I have the full amount now?"

"No, after we return."

Ruddles rolled his eyeballs.

The news of the journey spread. Mākaha shuddered. "Please, Your Majesty, don't go," he pleaded. "Ka'ahumanu and Bingham are waiting for you to leave so they can force the Ten Commandments on us as the law of the land and impose their will on us. We *kānaka* will lose our freedom."

Those words bounced off Liholiho's ears. Mākaha changed the subject.

"Your Majesty, if you must, please don't go to England on a whaler. It's embarrassing. *Ha'aheo* is more befitting a King."

Liholiho knew he was right, but he wanted to save his jewel from a grueling journey. Mākaha's advice just hung in the wind.

Liholiho's departure cast gloom over the village. "Why is he running away?" the dying asked.

"Maybe, we can stop the king," Mamo told Mākaha.

"How?"

"He won't go without Queen Kamehamalu."

Mākaha's eyes lit. "Let's go!"

They ran to the queen's royal compound on Beretania Street below Puowaina (Punchbowl). She recognized the two. "Hello Mākaha, Mamo. What a surprise," she said from the second-floor balcony.

"Your Majesty, may we talk to you about your trip to England? It's urgent," Mamo said.

"Come, come inside," the queen said, waving her hand.

Two ladies-in-waiting escorted the boys into the king's reception room.

The queen swished in and told the boys, "I am finishing a farewell chant. I don't have too much time." Wiping beads of sweat from her forehead, she asked, "Now, then, what's so urgent?"

"Your Majesty, we come to ask you not to let the king leave tomorrow."

"Why?"

"In his absence, Ka'ahumanu and Bingham will force on us the Ten Commandments as the law of our *'āina*. Please help us prevent it.

Besides, you are risking your life going on a long journey on a whaler, Your Majesty."

The queen stared at the boys, shocked.

"We are thinking about the same thing. How can I prevent it?"

"By refusing to join him, Your Majesty. He won't go if you won't. Getting George IV's *mana* is meaningless."

"My *'aumakua* told me that if we went to England we won't return alive. I told this to the king. He just laughed and said, 'Be ready to leave.' That is why I am finishing my farewell chant to my people and to Hawai'i nei. I will give it before the boat leaves the shore."

"Your Majesty, it's suicide to go on that small whaler!"

"The king's words are final, Mākaha. There is nothing a woman, even his queen, can do. I must obediently go if he says I must. That is my duty."

"Duty to him, maybe, but not to your people."

"That is his choice. I only . . . follow." Her voice trailed. Forgetting she was queen, Mākaha and Mamo hugged her tearfully. She too sobbed on their shoulders. *"Mahalo,"* the queen whispered to them.

The distraught youths staggered home to let the queen finish her death chant.

On November 27, 1823, a somber crowd was at the shore to wish the Majesties *aloha.* Mamo was bitter. "How can he leave on such a long trip while Hawai'i is sinking?" he asked Mākaha.

With departure imminent, Queen Kamehamalu went to the stern of the shoreboat, nodded to Mākaha and Mamo.

"Looks like she didn't sleep all night."

"The king looks worse," Mamo replied.

She began her farewell chant to her people.

The crowd responded, *"Aloha,"* in crushed tone.

A young Hawaiian scholar, David Malo, was in the crowd. He heard the chant, was so moved by it that he made a rough English translation of it for posterity.

The people loitered until the *L'Aigle,* her hold jammed with booze, became a foreboding dot on the horizon.

"The king is gone. The queen's chant will come true," Mamo mourned.

"And the Ten Commandments will be upon us," Mākaha grieved.

Mamo glanced at the dot, kicked dirt, and walked away with Mākaha to nowhere in particular.

The whaler was ahead of schedule even after a week's pause at Rio and losing a passenger there. She had encountered no storms so far, just monotonous gentle winds.

Just weeks from Portsmouth, the king was on the deck dozing when a rooster with outstretched neck crowed into his ear. He jumped, gave a feeble smile to Kamehamalu resting nearby and said, "I had a bad dream."

"That wasn't a dream, I heard it too!"

"What did you hear?"

"A rooster crowing in pain."

Crazed by her reply, the king called Boki. "There's a rooster onboard. Bring it to me. I want to wring his neck."

Boki was shocked. *There is no rooster onboard! He lost his mind?*

"I think something bad is happening in Hawai'i," the mystic queen said, shaking her head. She was touched by telepathy.

Liholiho's trusted friend, Captain Manu Kaleokawa, the caretaker of the *Ha'aheo* during his absence, had an urge to go to Kauai and receive Chief Kapena's legendary hospitality. He sent a messenger to alert him. Kaleokawa gathered his cronies and sailed for Kauai on board the *Ha'aheo* one morning in May 1824, arriving at Hanalei at dusk. After dropping a single anchor, they rushed to shore. For an inexplicable reason, the crew failed to drop the second anchor before starting on their booze party.

Late that moonlit evening, rising tides and high winds began pushing the *Ha'aheo* reefward. A rooster crowed in wild distress when the lone anchor line snapped.

Local folks, in panic, rushed to Kapena's *kauhale* and screamed, "*Ha'aheo* in trouble!"

They startled Kaleokawa and his bunch. Leaving their women, they rushed to the Bay and saw, by moonlight, His Majesty's ship listing on Hanalei reef receiving the onslaught of crashing waves. Even the paunchy Ali'i Koke'e turned nimble. He paddled out with his friends, climbed onboard the distressed ship to help the drunken crew members throw ballast rocks, anything heavy overboard to float *Ha'aheo* off the reef. Nothing worked. She was stuck, taking in more water, listing further.

"Abandon ship!" a hopeless voice yelled.

Queen Kamehamalu had predicted ill luck if Liholiho changed the *Barge's* name. By mid morning on May 15, *Ha'aheo o Hawai'i* had rolled over, dead. So were Kaleokawa, Koke'e and every member of their bunch. They had failed to abandon ship on time.

§

The *L'Aigle* sailed into Portsmouth, England, in mid May 1824.

Local officials were shocked to learn that a foreign monarch had arrived onboard a whaler, unannounced. They whisked Liholiho and his entourage in hired carriages to the St. Regis Hotel in London, and reported their arrival to the Home Office.

An Office official rushed to the Hotel. Liholiho brashly told him, "I am King Kamehameha II of the Kingdom of Hawai'i in the middle of the Pacific Ocean, and she is my Queen Kamehamalu. I want audience with my friend, King George IV. Please arrange it for me and my party."

A giant figure, without front teeth, wearing just a loincloth, intimidated the timid official. "Yes, Your Majesty," he said, and left hurriedly after turning his head around for a second look at the giant.

George IV procrastinated, finally decided to grant an audience to his "friend." He scheduled it for June 21, out of curiosity.

It had to be canceled.

Kamehamalu was composing another farewell chant to her people when an acute seizure ended her life suddenly on June 8, 1824. Clean of any disease, she had no warning of impending death. Days later a grieving Liholiho joined her, ending his pathetic life in a London hotel room with a spilled glass of rum nearby.

George IV offered the formal last rites of the Church to the royal couple, but he later withdrew it when he learned that they were pagans.

After The Majesties' passing, Governor Boki became the ranking chief of the Hawaiian legation in London. To his credit, he shocked the Home Office. "I am not leaving England until I receive an audience from George IV," he told an official. Weeks went by. Boki's funds dwindled. Impatient, Captain Ruddles was kicking air at Portsmouth onboard the *L'Aigle*.

A royal courier arrived at the St. Regis Hotel in early August 1824, bearing a scroll sealed with wax. Lālāmilo read the message to illiterate Boki.

"Hulō!" Boki screamed when he learned that George IV had invited him and members of his legation for lunch at Windsor Castle on September 12, 1824. "Please tell His Majesty we accept," he told the courier.

George IV had heard that Boki had no front teeth, was a rotund six-footer who couldn't rise from a sitting position without help, or walk with a normal stride because his two massive thighs blocked each other. Boki was a cripple except for his appetite.

The king was eager to meet such a royalty.

A tailor called on Boki to measure his dimensions. *How am I going to make his mannequin?* he thought. As the luncheon day neared, officials from the Home Office made frequent visits to the St. Regis to coach Boki on court etiquette, how to bow, table manners and endless other details.

September 12 finally came. The tailor arrived just in time with Boki's morning suit under his arm. Three royal horse-drawn coaches with drivers arrived at the St. Regis to take the legation to Windsor Castle twenty miles away. Boki's suit didn't fit, too tight at the underarm and too short at the crotch. It dug into his groin. He wanted his loincloth.

After clack clacking for over two hours, they arrived at the Castle, the horses with their tongues hanging. Boki's groin was raw from just bouncing off the bumps on the road. And, like others in the party, he had to *mimi* (urinate). Now!

The Hawaiians kept George IV and his ladies waiting in the reception hall for some time before they emerged from the toilets. *My pants so tight it's hard to close, and the toilet bowl so small, just a dot,* Boki grumbled, struggling to close his fly before the ladies.

The king in white regalia greeted members of the Hawaiian legation. "Welcome to England," George IV said to Boki. "Please accept our deepest condolences on the deaths of The Majesties, the King and Queen of Hawai'i. We are saddened and sorry."

Boki returned a perfunctory bow, an insult to the king. He was hungrier than a starving locust and wanted lunch without further ado.

"Please, through the door," the king gestured.

They entered an ornate room and gaped at its high gilded ceiling and the three huge chandeliers hanging in the king's private dining room. Boki had seen nothing more ornate than his hotel lobby. He peeked outside in wild curiosity, saw a brook running through a manicured garden and the Keep Tower beyond. Elegant lunch settings were on a large round dining table standing on green slate.

The king personally showed Boki to his stuffed chair. He quickly sat down and fixed his napkin while the ladies were still standing.

His Majesty's manservant goggled.

When the ladies were seated, the king, last to sit, winked to the head sommelier.

He opened a bottle of white wine from Penzance, a town in southern England, for the king's approval. With his nod the sommelier served the ladies and Boki. He thought his half-glass serving was too stingy. He clucked it down, wanted more before George IV could offer a toast.

Service began—ladies first. Boki turned left to inhale the steam rising from his wife Liliha's wild mushroom soup. When Boki was served he brought the bowl to his mouth, downed it without a spoon, and wiped both ends of his mouth before the king was served. He glanced across the table and saw people with raised eyebrows. *English ladies look funny,* he thought.

Next came a dish of poached Atlantic salmon topped with cream truffle sauce. Boki devoured it, burped, and waited for the next course. It never came—the salmon was it! No seconds either, by court etiquette. The king tried to start a conversation about their trip, anything. No luck. Boki was trying to catch any waiter's attention. The eyebrows across went higher.

Boki humiliated himself and Hawai'i. But George IV didn't mind. He thought the luncheon without conversation hilarious, the truffle delicious, and watching the hulk suck soup without front teeth unforgettable.

After lunch they adjourned to a nearby room for tea and pudding. A British naval captain was waiting. He stood, said "Your Majesty," and gave to his king and Boki a stiff salute when they came in.

"Please meet Captain George Lord Byron," the king gestured to Boki. "He will take the Royal biers, you and your party back to Hawai'i aboard the frigate, HMS *Blonde*."

Going home on a warship? Boki bowed deeply, knocked over a glass of water with his head, and said, with a lisp, "Thank you, Your Majesty, Hawai'i will be grateful. It is a pleasure to meet you, Captain Bron."

Since Kamehameha II and his queen were uninvited guests of the Crown, George IV wasn't obliged to return the biers to Hawai'i on a warship. But he wanted to pay respect to the dead king's father, who once offered to cede Hawai'i to England, though it was refused.

"What shall we do about our boat waiting at Portsmouth to take us back?" Boki asked.

"We have already met with Captain Ruddles," the king said suppressing a smile. "We will take care of the whaler."

"Ah, we owe Ruddles one thousand dollars," Boki said.

"We'll take care of that, too."

They all sat down for tea.

Boki became lively. "Your Majesty, have you a message for our people?" he asked, leaking tea between his lips.

"Yes. Please tell them England has no desire to take your kingdom or control your affairs, but if any country tries to, we will come to your aid."

Those words made Boki's long wait rewarding.

"Thank you, Your Majesty. I will take back your *mana* and your words to our people."

"You are welcome. What is *mana*?"

"It means awesome spiritual power to prevail, win, succeed. Only a chief with *mana* can rule in our land."

"I think I understand."

Members of Boki's group lifted him off his chair so he could bid George IV goodbye. He acknowledged the ladies' deeper curtsy with a quick wave of his hand and disappeared into the toilet.

After returning to his chamber, George IV laughed for nearly half an hour, letting the king of Monrovia pace the floor and wait for his moment with him.

Boki was a memorable hulk

26

On June 16, 1824, the schooner *Nantucket Wind* with Michael Chaplain's family on board was sighted off Lē'ahi. Deborah stood at the bridge enthralled. "Look, father, that bright rainbow," she said, pointing towards Nu'uanu Valley. "It's so stunning against that dark mountain range."

Meriam's eyes were on bare-breasted native women and on men in flimsy loincloths. "O Lord, have mercy on their souls," she begged, with the same contempt shared by the First Company of missionary ladies.

"Never mind," Leslie said. "We are safely in Hawai'i. Let us kneel and thank the good Lord." He recited something religious, which he seldom did.

The ship anchored offshore. The Chaplains stood at the bow and scanned the crowd for anyone waving, found no one. Mamo climbed onboard and saw three souls in distress. "Are you the Chaplains?" he asked.

"Yes!" Leslie said, fearing the worst.

"'Eme told me about you folks. Captain Chaplain, he no return from China yet. But no worry. He is good sailor, must be delayed somewhere," Mamo said.

Thank God, Leslie sighed, relieved. Meriam began to cry.

"You Mrs. Chaplain? No need cry, he is safe. I am Mamo. I look after Captain Michael's wife, 'Eme, and their six months-old baby boy, Kaikai. She not feeling well so she asked me to greet you."

Meriam stopped crying and stared at Mamo. "His wife? He has . . . a baby?"

Mamo nodded.

"Leslie, what shall we do? We have a native in our family!"

"Be patient," Leslie said, changing the subject. "Mamo is right; Michael must be delayed somewhere."

"Mother, I believe it too," Deborah said. "Let's get off this ship and explore Honolulu."

"You go, I'm staying back. I'm sick!" Meriam exploded.

"You must be the captain's sister, Deborah?"

"Yes!"

"He told us about you too."

Captain Nielson, standing nearby, caught the commotion and suggested to the Chaplains, "You can keep your *Nantucket* quarters for twenty-five cents a night while I am in port, meals extra."

"Thank you. Here's five dollars for the first twenty nights," Leslie said.

Pualani, Lani and Mākaha knew the Chaplains had arrived, but they stayed at home.

Morning Star was two hundred miles from Honolulu with her sails stretched making up time this June day in 1824. Next morning Michael had Wai'anae Range at portside, the Ko'olau beyond and Honolulu less than an hour away. The spiritual experience of returning restored his soul, but the awful dream of becoming a father lingered.

'Eme was still at *Hale'ano'i* nursing Kaikai despite Pualani's pleas to return to home. She had a need to remain near her wall friends. An object of public scorn, she had seldom ventured out, preferred caring for Kaikai in the company of her true friends, the engraved creatures on the cave wall, and Mamo.

"'Eme!" he yelled. "Someone just sighted *Morning Star!*"

"What?" she screamed in a whisper. They went to the edge of the cave to see. She recognized the speck. "That's her!" she choked.

"Please inform my folks and the Chaplains," 'Eme said. "I will take Kaikai to the pier and wait for him."

"I'm taking Kaikai," Mamo told 'Eme. "Let's go."

"Thank you, and for all these months."

Her tender words touched Mamo.

"I'm ready," she said, and began walking downhill filled with trepidation. *Will Michael accept a hapa haole (half white)? Will his parents?*

They arrived at the wharf. Mamo sat her down beneath a tree and passed Kaikai to her. "I am going to see your folks," he said.

He dashed to her *kauhale*. "Pualani!" he yelled.

She and Lani stuck their heads out from the *hale moe*.

"Pualani, someone sighted the *Morning Star*. Mikaele returning!"

"Big trouble begins," she told Lani. "I know he didn't want a baby."

"Mother, we have no control. Let everything just unfold."

"I am not going to the pier," Pualani said, shaking her head.

"Me neither. Let 'Eme and Kaikai be alone with him."

Mamo understood. "Goodbye," he said and dashed to the *Nantucket*. He climbed onboard and saw the Chaplains on deck reading, relaxing. "Captain Chaplain returning! *Morning Star* docking there soon," Mamo said, pointing to a spot in the harbor.

Leslie climbed *Nantucket's* mast, squinted. "It's her!" he yelled down. Meriam went on her knees and cried.

"Mamo, you were right. He is a good sailor!" Deborah said and hugged him.

"Will 'Eme be here?" Meriam asked.

"Yes, that's her over there with baby," he pointed, and rushed to her side.

The *Morning Star* was no longer just a silhouette against the horizon. 'Eme recognized her former home powered by new, yellow sails.

"Mother and Lani coming?" she asked Mamo.

"No," he whispered.

She understood.

"'Eme! The Chaplains are coming! I told them you were Michael's wife and he was Kaikai's father. Mrs. Chaplain was upset."

Leslie approached, took off his hat. "I presume you're 'Eme Alapa'i?"

"Yes."

"I am Leslie Chaplain, Michael's father. Please meet my wife Meriam and our daughter Deborah. We're here for a reunion with our son."

"Yes, I read your letter. Welcome to Hawai'i."

"We heard you were ill. Hope you're better."

"Thank you," 'Eme softly said.

Deborah never thought an aborigine could be so beautiful.

'Eme held out Kaikai to Meriam. "Meet our son, seven months old. He has Michael's eyes, doesn't he?"

She hoped Meriam would reach for him. But she just stood and stared, showing no feeling of love for the child. Deborah bent down, touched his nose and said, "Hello, Kaikai."

"Hello, Kaikai," Leslie repeated.

The *Morning Star* dropped anchor. Michael boarded a craft and made it to shore. His family ran to the boat and mobbed him. "So wonderful to see you. Thank you for coming. Sorry I got delayed in Macao," he said.

He wiped tears and sweat off his face and scanned the crowd for 'Eme. He saw her seated way back with Mamo, carrying a baby. *It must be mine! It says so in the log. What will mother think?*

"Father, I can't wait to tell you how I sold my cargo. I had an adventure . . . with . . . pirates." Michael's last words trailed as he started to walk toward 'Eme.

She saw him coming and waved. "Welcome back, Mikaele!"

Michael knelt and embraced 'Eme. "So glad to see you," he said. Finding 'Eme just half her former size shocked him.

Turning Kaikai around, she boasted, "You have a son. Isn't he cute? I named him Kaikai in your absence. Here, carry him."

This is for real, he cursed.

"'Eme, I got to settle my family. I'll be back soon," he said, and started to leave without reaching for Kaikai. He turned and asked, "Did Pualani meet my family?"

Mamo answered for her with a strong, "No!"

'Eme was devastated. *Not even a moment to hold his son? Must be his color!* "Not to worry," she whispered to Kaikai. "I will care for you, love you with all my heart."

With Kaikai in Mamo's arm, she headed for the *Morning Star* without saying goodbye to the Chaplains. 'Eme would have preferred *Hale'ano'i* if she had the strength.

Michael settled his family in deceased Ali'i Kanahele's *kauhale* and returned to his boat. He found Mamo standing outside the stateroom.

"I laid 'Eme and Kaikai down," Mamo said, "and I tried to make them comfortable. She is eating little, getting weaker. Please look after her closely." He started to leave.

"One moment, Mamo. I heard the emissaries returned to China. You know anything more?"

"Yes. They found *kaokao* (syphilitic) sores on their bodies. They left *wiki* (in hurry) for Canton on board the *Lē'ahi*, captained by my friend, Kalihi, to be on *weuweu* (herbal diet). After Kalihi returned, he told me

Ah Fat, Chinn Sun, Chun Ji and Mei Ling panicked when their sores spread. They were ashamed to land in Canton, wanted to die."

"They died?"

"Yes, five days before Canton."

"How?"

"Drank poison. Kalihi saw their bodies piled on each other holding hands. He buried them at sea."

"Thank you, Mamo," Michael said. His obligation to pay the emissaries five hundred dollars in commission had just vanished.

He opened the stateroom door. "I'm back," he told 'Eme.

He heard Kaikai bellowing. He shook his head, went to the deck and spent the balance of the humid night tossing on the lounger.

"Not to worry," she repeated after he left the room. "I will care for you, love you with all my heart."

A week later Michael staged a reunion party, inviting the members of the Alapa'i family and his *ali'i* and royalty friends. He especially wanted Pualani to meet his parents.

A sparse turnout embarrassed Michael. Pualani and Lani declined. 'Eme preferred the seclusion of her stateroom. Royalty stayed away, afraid to send a wrong message to Kainoa. The captain's *ali'i* friends had gone fishing.

Michael warmly greeted Mākaha when he arrived. "Thank you for coming," he said. "Father, mother, Debo, come meet Mākaha, 'Eme's older brother."

They met tentatively.

The arrival of a minor American official uplifted Michael.

"Mākaha, mother, father, Deborah, meet Mr. Ashley Cooper, the American Consular Agent in Hawai'i. We met yesterday."

"Good evening," Cooper said, glancing at Deborah twice. Her beauty dazzled him.

"Please sit down," Michael said.

"Thank you. We are kind of neighbors," he said to the Chaplains, eager to make a good impression. "I understand you're from Massachusetts. I'm from New York and returning soon. How long do you folks plan to stay?"

"Sir, we don't have a timetable," Leslie said.

"Sir? Just call me Ash. I am here to help protect the safety and interests of all Americans visiting or living in Hawai'i." he said. "May I show you folks Honolulu tomorrow?"

"No, Ash, we need to get settled," Deborah said.

"I understand, I will wait."

"Excuse me, I'm going to the entrance to greet my guests." Michael hurriedly left, not suspecting that Ash was his last.

Ashley, twenty-five, was born and raised in one of the largest Westchester County estates in New York. Pink cheeks *sans* beard, Ashley looked like a college freshman. His wealthy father had the exclusive right above the Mason and Dixon Line to market all the crops of Thomas Wellington O'Hara's huge Tara Plantation in Atlanta, including his cotton.

He attended King's College in New York City. After graduation, he joined the United States Consular Corps and volunteered to serve in remote posts, first in Jakarta in Java, and now in Honolulu.

Deborah's eyes had stopped on Mākaha, seated diagonally across. He was wearing just a *malo* that accentuated his lithe physique.

She found him attractive.

Meriam stood, told Mākaha and Ash, "Good night, I'm retiring."

"I'm leaving, too," Leslie said. "Good night, Mākaha, it was a pleasure meeting you."

Ash was delighted. He moved over and sat next to Deborah. She felt his sugary stare.

"Mākaha, what do you do every day?" she asked.

"Many things. Help my mother manage our *'ili*, try to save our dying as best as I can, promote the education of our youths, things our people need."

"You try to save the dying? How?"

"We give them loving care in our retreats. We have no government aid, no western medicines or doctors.

"That's so noble. Can I see how you give loving care?" She was more than just curious.

"It's better if you stayed away from our retreats," he said.

"Why?"

"The air inside the huts is bad, I still have trouble breathing in there. And what you will see is ugly."

"I still want to go," she said, being drawn to a person floating in air like a free element, what she couldn't be in Salem.

Ashley had heard enough. He stood and said, "Good night."

"Good night, Ash." She turned and rolled her eyes.

"All right, I'll be at your *kauhale* at nine in the morning," Mākaha said.

"Thank you. Before I leave tell me about 'Eme. She is so stunning. Her deep-set eyes are unbelievably beautiful. But she looks so weak. Is she ill?"

"Yes, her heart is pumping grief, not blood."

"Why?"

"Trouble started after your brother arrived in Honolulu. For reasons we still don't know, my sister left our world and entered Michael's, became his common-law wife. She destroyed her lover Kainoa, who is in Boston, studying. We painfully cut our ties with her.

"Then came the worst news. After Michael left for Macao, Mamo told us that 'Eme was *hāpai*, pregnant, with his baby. We are still in shock. That's when her health began to deteriorate. Mamo told us she hardly ate and had trouble sleeping in *Hale'ano'i*, her private mountainside cavehouse."

"Maybe she was torn by guilt, felt anguish for failing Kainoa. I suspect 'Eme's body and mind split, became two people. Her body shared Michael's bed as an unbalanced soul. Her mind must have realized that only in death could their souls unite again."

Her insight, so close to home, shocked Mākaha.

"'Eme gave birth to a boy eight months after Michael left for Macao. She named him Kaikai and nursed him inside the cavehouse with Mamo's help.

"When Michael returned, he ignored Kaikai at the shore. Maybe he was ashamed of his dark skin color. Mamo said 'Eme was devastated."

"Thank you for sharing that with me." She paused and asked, "How can we help her?"

"Only Kainoa can, by forgiving her. But he won't, so we are helpless."

Michael came by and told Deborah, "I'm returning to the *Morning Star*. Good night Mākaha, see you in the morning, Debo."

Lacking energy, the party closed early with a heap of untouched food in the back.

Deborah stood and said, "I'm leaving, too. I'll be ready around nine. Call me Debo from now on, my parents call me that. It's easier. Good night."

"Yes Debo. Good night," he said and wondered, *What's happening?*

Mākaha arrived at Deborah's next morning with a tapa cloth over his head to soak up rain. "Let's wait for it to stop," he suggested.

Debo nodded. Her mind was swirling around Mākaha. "About the retreats. You built them?" she asked.

"Twelve of us did at our expense because our government offered no help. We had a desperate need to separate our sick and dying relatives and friends from the healthy. So we built two retreats along the shore, one at Kewalo, the other at Kaka'ako, each with a Camp One of six huts for treatable patients, and a Camp Two of eight huts for the hopeless. At Camp One, we try to help the patients recover so they can go home. At Camp Two, we cook their last meals and prepare them for their 'aumakua.

"The two retreats quickly filled. We couldn't refuse the strangers who came. We got forty more people together and built four more retreats. They, too, quickly overflowed. But it was beyond our poor power to build more."

"Never mind the rain, let's go," Debo said. "I may want to become the fifty-third person in your group."

Mākaha's eyes enlarged.

Patients in Kewalo Camp One cheered when a *haole* girl swished in with a smile. *Maybe we're not that sick,* some thought.

Caretaker Kaloko ran to Mākaha. "We sent Mary Kalele home, no more bloody *kūkae*, stomach pain gone. Hot tea and boiled food worked!"

"What kind of tea?" Debo asked.

"For dysentery patients we boil a roast of *kiawe* (algaroba) beans and *pia* (arrowroot) and serve the tea strong. We also feed them cooked fish and *poi* and a mixed drink of guava and *'ōhelo* berry juice. The drink seems to ease their pain and harden watery shit," Mākaha said, not knowing that word is not spoken in polite company.

Deborah entered a hut in Camp Two and heaved into her handkerchief. She rushed outside to suck fresh rain air. *Mākaha is right about the air,* she thought.

"Sorry, we clean our huts twice a day, but they get filthy quickly with *kūkaemaku'u* (uncontrollable excreta)," Mākaha lamented.

"What was the chanter inside the hut saying?" Debo asked.

"The chanter, a *kahuna*, was reassuring Kimo that his gods and ancestral deities are waiting for him in the realm of his *'aumakua*."

"Mākaha, I wish I had an *'aumakua*."

"Not possible, you're a Christian."

"I can become a pagan so easily."

She stunned Mākaha.

Debo asked, "Do women have goddesses besides their ancestral deities?"

"Yes. In the 1819 Revolution, Ka'ahumanu destroyed the gods but left goddesses alone."

"Whiii! Who are the important ones?"

"Haumea, Goddess Pele and her twelve Hi'iaka sisters. The most famous is Hi'iaka Pele, a sorceress. She is not just the goddess of the volcano, but is volcano itself, now making her home inside Halema'uma'u pit in the Kīlauea volcanic crater. She can erupt at will, or remain dormant for the people's benefit.

"The missionaries are now trying to exterminate Haumea, Pele and her sisters to finish the revolution that Ka'ahumanu started. They want to make way for Mother Mary," Mākaha said.

"That's murder!" she cried.

"Not to worry. The goddesses exist as spirits in our souls. They will survive Kahu Bingham's wrath so long as there is one *kanaka* soul left in our universe.

"I pay homage to Hi'iaka Laka, the goddess of our *hula* spiritual world. She is Pele's sister," Mākaha said.

"*Hula*, that's your pagan dance, no?"

"That is."

"Can I see a performance?"

"I can arrange it, secretly."

"Why secretly?"

"Ka'ahumanu outlawed *hula* at the request of Kahu Bingham."

"Why?" Debo asked, appalled.

"The Kahu told her that the *hula* hip movements are sinful, too sexual, outside of Christian morality. He doesn't know that *hula* is spiritual. A chanter tells a story in praise of many things, our gods, our *ali'i*, our *'āina*, things we cherish. The dancer interprets the story in the chant with his whole body, to the beat of *pūniu* and drums. The movements draw us spiritually."

"That's how our Narragansett Indians dance too, to a chant and beat of drums made of wood and buffalo skin in praise of their gods and nature during festival days," Deborah said.

"*Hula* will also survive Bingham's wrath," Mākaha assured. "It's locked into our pagan spirit. Can you imagine dancing the *hula* in praise of Jehovah? All movements will stop because *hula* cannot connect with Him."

"So sorry you must dance your dance in hiding. It's not right." Debo thought for a moment. "Someone must challenge Bingham. Can I?"

"How?"

"With your help let this *haole* Christian stage a *hula* festival in public, invite Bingham and Ka'ahumanu, and see what they'll do to me."

"I like it!" Mākaha said. "I'll round up the performers and crowd. Every festival has a guest of honor. Why not invite the patients in Camp One strong enough to go as your honored guests?"

She whispered into his ear, "I will."

He felt her warmth. *She is getting too close*, he feared.

Deborah called on Bingham next day. Ka'ahumanu was at his side taking lessons. "I am staging a *hula* festival tomorrow night opposite Kewalo Camp One. Please come," she said and left before he could scold her.

On festival day, the participants decorated the stark ground with mounds of cut leaves, vines and flowers picked from the mountains, turning it into a lush garden, and placed Laka's altar on the "stage."

"Debo, just a few years back this whole place would have been under Laka's strict *kapu*."

"Let's make believe it still is," Debo said.

An early crowd swelled the *hula* ground.

The performance began at twilight with a ritual honoring Goddess Hi'iaka Laka. Wearing colorful *malo*, over a hundred *kāne* (male) *hula* dancers entered the ground to the rhythm of chants and beat of *ipu hula* and *pahu* drums, holding offerings of *lei*. With exquisite grace they placed them on Laka's central altar.

"This is magical! The men, so graceful!" Debo said.

"Yes, they are performing elevated *hula*," Mākaha explained. "Their special moves are reserved for making offerings to Laka."

"Why are the dancers all men?"

"Since ancient time our gods gave to *kāne* the dominant role in Hawai'i. But you'll see tonight that's changing. *Wāhine* (women) are getting involved."

"The *lei* of vine they are wearing around their heads and ankles are so beautiful," she marveled.

"*Lei* are worn only during special occasions. They personify the body of Laka," Mākaha said. "At the end of the occasion the wearers would cast them to sea, tie them around trees or around rocks, with prayers that they wither, return to earth and bless our *'āina*. *Lei* are never just thrown away."

"What is *'āina?*"

"It is not just land, but the spirit of all the people who lived on the land since creation. For us, the *'āina* is sacred." Debo was getting lessons in local culture that no *haole* would get.

Hundreds of torches lit the festival ground at sunset. A squall passed and a half-moon and million stars created a mood of pagan splendor.

"Can I learn to *hula?*" Deborah whispered. "I'd rather do that and work in your camps than return to Salem." She drew closer.

He backed away. "My *Kumu hula* friends would be happy to teach you, but I know what they'll tell you. 'Learn the Hawaiian language first, so you can express the symbolic and double meanings in the chants.' Otherwise you'd only be going through memorized *hula* motions lacking feeling."

"That's so true. Where do they teach the *hula?*"

"No set place, sometimes along the beach, on mountain tops, next to waterfalls, in the valleys, close to the open *'āina* against the sounds of nature under Laka's strict *kapu*. But many *kumu hula* teach the *hula* these days in protected *hālau* (long house)."

"I will start learning Hawaiian from tomorrow," she promised, moving her arms, hands and fingers effortlessly, mimicking the *wāhine* dancers.

A mass finale of a hundred *kāne* and *wāhine* dancers closed the spectacular evening. Camp One hutmates made it back laughing, chatting, as if vastly improved.

Debo felt the power of pagan spirituality touch her soul. She knelt and thanked the Kahu and Ka'ahumanu for not halting the performance.

A week after the *hula* festival, Debo and Mākaha were deep in Manoa Valley picking mountain apples for the patients. All alone in the company of Nature, their passions, fueled by suppressed desires, merged. They let it run wild. Not even Hi'iaka Pele's eruption could have stopped them. "Debo, let's purify our bodies with water and offer thanks to our gods for this wondrous moment. There's a stream over there, let's go."

"Let's!" she yelled, already nude. They jumped in, purified their bodies with mountain water, and spent the next hours unaware of the stream chattering at their feet.

Mākaha awoke after a brief slumber. He regretted letting passion overcome him. "Debo, please get up, I must get back to the Kaka'ako Retreat. Let's leave, I'll take you back to the Kanahele's."

Debo wanted to linger, spend the evening there, have another go.

She was hopelessly in love, wanted to accept Mākaha's gods. She tried to make him see a Hawaiian girl, not a *haole*.

Mākaha realized she had marital desire.

Meriam was upset seeing her daughter emotionally involved with a Polynesian. Pualani was also worried. "Lani, you think your brother might marry a *haole?*"

"He might. She is becoming a local *wahine.*"

But Mākaha had been moving away from Debo. Each time she hinted marriage, he shrank.

They were at Le'ahi beach one afternoon. It was gray, drizzling, a favorite time for sharks. Mākaha decided to end it now. He dreaded the next ten minutes. He held Debo's wet face with his two hands, looked into her eyes and said, "I must end our relationship. We should go our separate ways, not see each other any more."

Debo felt a recent change in Mākaha, but was shocked. She softly asked, "Why?"

"I promised my gods I would get back to my patients. That is more important to me than marriage and settling down. Besides, I would be embarrassed making you live in a hut, under my conditions, eating and sleeping off the floor as my *haole wahine*, and receiving the stares from my people. We would both be unhappy. Debo, I don't want to lead you on, give you a false hope of marriage. Let's bid each other goodbye now."

In the most desolate moment of her young life she asked, *"Hau'oli'ole? Pehea 'oe e 'ike ai?* (How do you know I'll be unhappy?)."

Mākaha made no attempt to reply.

"All right," she said with mouth trembling. "I will do anything you say. What you say is final. I only follow. But before we part, tell me from your heart, do you love me?"

Mākaha melted. He hugged Debo and said, "I do, I want to walk my last mile with you, but I can't . . ."

Debo sealed his mouth with her finger. "Say no more. I will remember your words and look elsewhere." She then whispered into his ear, *"Aloha, a hui hou kākou.* Farewell, Mākaha."

The words from her soul overwhelmed him.

Dazed, she walked to the beach and swam out, not caring where she went.

Mākaha spotted two fins. *"Manō!* Sharks!" he screamed.

Debo kept swimming out. The killers began to circle her. Mākaha dove in and swam as fast as he could. He reached Debo, grabbed her hair and, with his powerful legs, kicked hard to chase the monsters away. A huge jaw surfaced, just missing his head. Mākaha kicked harder. Just as he reached shore with Debo in tow, a shark lunged at her feet, missed, turned, and headed back to the deep.

They stumbled onto red bloody sand.

"Your right arm, Mākaha, it's gone!"

Debo pulled him to higher beach, unaware that she too was bleeding from gashes on both her legs.

Debo saw marrow oozing from his bone. In panic she tore her skirt, tied a tourniquet at the elbow, and dashed to find a medical *kahuna.*

She found two.

In six months, skin began to cover Mākaha's ugly cutoff. He wasn't bitter. *The loss of my hand means little compared to having Debo whole,* he thanked his gods.

27

The trader *West Wind* sailed into Honolulu harbor in mid-June 1824 with cargo and mail.

"Mākaha, Lani, Mamo, I got a letter from Kainoa!" Pualani shouted. She read it slowly as Lani looked over her shoulder.

November 23, 1823

Dear Mother Pualani—I am arriving Honolulu around end June 1824 on brig Clementine. I can't wait to see all of you and go to work with Mākaha. I learned so much in my short time in Boston. I think I can serve Hawai'i nei better now.

I am bringing back lots of medicines. Hope I can help cure many.

Please tell my parents about my returning. I didn't write to them because they still can't read.

Love, Kainoa

"Kainoa is returning!" Pualani moaned. She passed the letter to Lani. "Last week it was Mikaele, now Kainoa! How can 'Eme take it?"

"It will kill sister just to see Kainoa after failing him. I know he won't forgive her or look at Kaikai," Mākaha said.

"Who will inform 'Eme?" Pualani asked.

"Let me inform her in front of Mikaele," Mamo offered. "He knows about Kainoa."

"*Mahalo,* thank you," Pualani said.

Mamo rushed to the *Morning Star*. From outside the stateroom he heard Kaikai crying, the loudest yet, and 'Eme soothing him with soft words.

"'Eme," Mamo yelled, hoping Michael was inside.

She opened the door. "Mamo!"

"Hello, 'Eme. Mother Pualani just got a letter from Kainoa. He is returning end of this month, or early next, on *Clementine!*"

'Eme gulped.

"Is Michael in?"

"No, but he'll be back shortly. I'll tell him."

"Show me the letter!" she asked, anxious to see if she was mentioned.

"Lani has it."

Mamo tickled Kaikai's nose, saw his face turning red. "I think he is making *kūkae.*"

"Yes, because you came!"

They had a rare laugh together.

"Kainoa will be shocked to learn his mother collapsed and died two months ago, and his father died last month." Mamo said.

"Yes, I heard about his father. What really happened?"

"He and his workers were cutting down the oldest *'iliahi* growing on his *'ili*, maybe five hundred years old, over four feet across. He was saving it to make a fortune, but he waited too long."

"Then what happened?" 'Eme asked.

"After the tree fell, they were cutting off the branches when it started to roll down. His legs got caught. He screamed but his workers could do nothing except watch the log roll over him."

'Eme sat with her mouth open.

"Please bring me the letter tomorrow," she pleaded.

While on a lookout in late June 1824, Mamo stretched his telescope and spotted off Lē'ahi the name *Clementine* on the bow of a ship sailing towards Honolulu.

He shut it and dashed to the Alapa'i *kauhale*. "Pualani, Mākaha, Lani, Kainoa is back! See you at the harbor, I'm going to inform 'Eme," he said. He ran to the harbor, jumped onboard the *Morning Star* and knocked on the stateroom door. Michael opened.

"Good morning, Captain. Is 'Eme in?" Mamo asked. His body language begged of urgency.

Michael closed the door without uttering a word. Shortly, 'Eme opened the door.

"'Eme, the *Clementine* will be docking soon. Do you want to go and greet Kainoa?"

'Eme's eyes brightened.

"I'll ask Mikaele. Please wait," she said. He heard her talking to Mikaele. The moment was too personal. He ambled to the foredeck to wait. Shortly, 'Eme emerged with Kaikai. Mamo rushed to her side and took him. "Thank you, let's go," she said.

Mamo walked down the gangplank behind 'Eme and mourned to see her unsure steps. *Where flew her earlier self?* he lamented, and hoped Kainoa would forgive a withered 'Eme.

Members of the Chaplain family stayed away. The *Clementine* arrived and dropped anchor.

'Eme saw Kainoa and nearly fainted. Her guilty heart began to fibrillate. He hugged the captain and jumped onto a craft and reached shore. He kissed the wet sands. The members of the Alapa'i family and Mamo mobbed him. "I missed all of you," a teary Kainoa said.

He saw Mākaha's right arm heavily bandaged at the elbow. "What happened?" he screamed, touching his handless stump.

"Sharks. I'll tell you later. Just know, I don't miss my hand."

The Crown Prince, already nine, was in the crowd. *"Aloha,* welcome home," he said. "You brought me something from Boston?"

"Yes, Your Highness." Kainoa reached into his pocket, opened a pigskin pouch and pressed a dark-blue ball into his hand.

"What is it?"

"Momi, a valuable pearl, took an *'ōlepe* over thirty years to make it. It was mine. I got it back in Boston."

"Thank you," the Crown Prince said and hugged Kainoa.

He scanned the shore and recognized a different 'Eme sitting under a tree with a baby. He walked towards her with steps of an infant. "Hello," he said when he got closer. They exchanged deep gazes. He saw a depleted 'Eme carrying a baby. The two embodied his shattered dream.

Visitors got the cue and left quickly.

He extended his arm, but only to return a clipping of her hair still tied with *olonā* string. "I worshipped it. *Aloha 'oe,* 'Eme," he said, his eyes never wandering to the baby.

"Please don't stay mad at me. I have so short time," 'Eme pleaded. It stunned Kainoa to hear, "short time." He wanted to grab her, but he stepped back, shaking.

"Mākaha, please ask Mamo to unload my stuffs," he said, and ran from the scene.

'Eme wished for death. Holding Kaikai in his arm, Mamo helped her to her feet. With her slim legs stiffly supporting a body now on a free fall, she walked to a nearby shoreboat clinging to Mamo's arm.

Kainoa ran to *Hale'ano'i*, paused at the entrance and looked down in a daze. He saw the same Honolulu, changed little except for more white-painted Christian churches and larger trading vessels in the harbor.

He stepped inside the only private home he ever had. It was clean. The many new engravings on the wall, all unmistakably of 'Eme's hand, surprised him. A *honu* was besides his Kekai that he engraved before he left for Boston. He knew the pair was intended to be symbolic of the two. Below the *honu* two red *lehua* blossoms floated on water in a *hau* bowl. He knelt and inhaled the smell of yesterday's first love.

The creatures on the walls told him in concert, *'Eme needs you. Go, Kai, only you can save her.*

Now all alone, he wailed and told them, *How can I save her when I cannot forgive?*

'Eme willed herself back to the *Morning Star*. Mamo tried to pass Kaikai to her at the stateroom door, but Michael, who was waiting, reached for his child and tearfully welcomed 'Eme back. For the first time he cradled Kaikai and kissed him all over. Kaikai laughed and said, "Papa."

Michael thought he had lost 'Eme. Kaikai suddenly became her successor.

"'Eme, goodbye," Mamo whispered and left.

"Please forgive my disgraceful past," Michael begged 'Eme. "Why didn't I see Kaikai before? He is beautiful!"

Michael's change startled 'Eme.

"Of course I forgive. Thank you Mikaele for all you have done for me."

Transformed by her redeeming power of love, the ponytailed Michael went on his knees and bawled. That evening he abandoned the deck lounger and returned to his bed in the stateroom, not minding if Kaikai was at his ear every two hours.

'Eme lay on her side, smoothed Kaikai's hair and let her spirit take flight. *"Catch it,"* she asked Kainoa. Neither could exist without the other, and her time was up.

Tormented by 'Eme, and by what he saw in the village after returning, Kainoa lost his will to plunge into his life's work.

He told Mākaha, "Remember, we talked about the need to go abroad, get educated and return to lead, not follow?"

"Yes, Kainoa, many times."

"I lost my desire to challenge anyone," Kainoa said. "None of the reasons I went to Boston for now matters."

"Why?"

"When I toured the village with you, I saw with fresh eyes how little our chiefs were doing to rescue our *lāhui kānaka*. While our race is going extinct, they are spending their time in church studying the Bible and trying to gain salvation of their souls in Christ. We have no rescue power for a calamity this size," Kainoa moaned. "The only thing we can do is to watch it run its course."

At its end there'll be no Kingdom, lāhui kānaka or independence. The realization jolted Mākaha.

"Before I also give up, can you visit the Kuhina nui, give her one last chance to change her course?"

"It's useless. Her fear of *po* is too deep. But since it's your wish I will," Kainoa said. "Before I go, help me dispense the medicines I brought back."

"Let's go, Mamo is at the Kaka'ako retreat with all the medicines."

Not a doctor, Kainoa was unsure what medicine was indicated for whom.

With so many devastated humans needing prompt care, Kainoa dispensed his supply too thinly. In the end he had nothing to show.

"I needed a thousand times more," Kainoa sobbed.

"No you don't. Before too long there won't be any *kanaka* left to treat. Tell that to Ka'ahumanu."

Kainoa looked into Mākaha's eyes and nodded.

He called on the queen at her home. "Good morning, Your Majesty," Kainoa said. She was at her porch fanning her face on a rocker.

"Yes? What's on your mind, son?" she said, staring at his *haole* shoes.

"I came to plead, Your Majesty. Our kingdom desperately needs your help before it's too late."

"Too late? For what?"

"To save our *lāhui kānaka*, it is dying, can't you see? We need urgent foreign aid. We'll soon have too few people left to defend our *'aina*. That's why we should have even a small self-defense force—just three hundred trained men maybe—to defend it."

The queen felt offended. She thought he was criticizing her rule.

"*Akamai 'oe.* You're so smart," she said, fanning harder. He caught her sarcasm.

Since Kainoa's pleadings didn't relate to Jehovah, she told him, "Go get the Kahu's and Kalanimoku's opinions," to rid him.

Appalled, Kainoa farted and left.

He called on Bingham as he was told. He was working in the mission yard vegetable patch. "Good morning, Kahu, sir," Kainoa said. "I just met the Kuhina nui. She suggested that I discuss a project with you. It's urgent."

"Another time. I have work to finish." He guessed Kainoa wanted to talk about a militia. He loathed it, for fear the troops might turn on him one day.

"Reverend, sir, I will be brief."

"Next time," the Kahu repeated, narrowing his eyes.

Kainoa shook his head, farted and vowed never to return to the mission house again.

Against his common sense, he called on Billy Pitt Kalanimoku, not expecting to find a miracle at rope's end.

"Good morning, sir," he yelled.

Kalanimoku stuck his head out from his hut. "Yes?"

He listened to Kainoa for half minute and scolded him. "You heathens, go embrace Jesus. There is nothing more sacred you can do."

"Sir, I think the salvation of our Kingdom is more . . ."

"You boys know nothing," he snapped. "All our problems will blow away with time. Now go!" he said and stuck his head inside the hut.

Kainoa left his biggest fart and walked away.

He met Mākaha and stared silently into his eyes. He understood.

Kainoa whispered to his beloved land, *Aloha no, Goodbye. I failed Captain Noble and dear Dian.*

At night the thought of 'Eme sleeping with another man wrenched Kainoa's soul and sapped his will to live. With his projects terminal and 'Eme lost, Kainoa left his world and entered Mākaha's, to help palliate the sickly and cook their last suppers.

His too.

28

One late afternoon just fourteen days after his return from Boston, Kainoa, the chef of Kewalo Camp Two, left for *Hale'ano'i* to breathe fresh air and reminisce. From a distance he saw 'Eme sitting alone on a rock near the cave. He ran to her. "'Eme, who brought you here?" he yelled.

"Nobody. I wanted to go chicken-egg hunting so I came alone. I also wanted to visit *Hale'ano'i* to breathe the fresh air inside and reminisce." With only one heart between them, they shared the same thought.

Overwhelmed, Kainoa knelt, came face to face with a pair of pleading eyes. Forgetting the past he lifted her skeletal body off the rock and embraced her. "'Eme!" he cried. They drained on each other all the tears they had saved.

"Kai, please tell me you forgive me, so I can wait for you in peace."

"You asked me to return as someone special. I kept my promise. Why didn't . . ." She put her finger against his mouth, not wanting to hear more.

"Kai, I was lost, went astray without you and lived aimlessly as Mikaele's mistress, even having his baby. Please forgive me."

When he heard the word "mistress," Kainoa raised his arms in despair. He grazed her. She lost balance and fell. He heard a strange pop. Blood began to gush in spurts from her forehead. In panic Kainoa removed his shirt and pressed it hard against the wound, hoping to stop the flow. Nothing worked. "I'm sorry, I'm sorry," Kainoa repeated, and kissed her for the first time in two years.

"Please forgive me."

"Of course, Kai, there is nothing you do that I cannot forgive," she said, with a serene smile. "Remember, I promised you 'forever' in

Hale'ano'i? Kai, I have a headache. Take me inside quickly, and then take me home."

Kainoa cradled a weightless 'Eme into *Hale'ano'i*, a few steps away. "Thank you, Kai." She livened, grabbed some cinder soil and brought it to her nose. "This smell of ancient earth is precious. At last, just you, our friends on the wall, and me. I've been waiting for this moment from the day you left . . . It's even better than . . . than what I had imagined it . . . would be, like . . . old times. This is worth the wait. Tell me that you love me, again and again."

"I love you, I love you, I love you. I must die without your love."

"Thank you Kai. I can now hold your hands every day while I wait for you," she whispered, her cold hands gliding over Kainoa's eyebrows, nose and mouth, as if to take the touch to eternity.

She began to bleed less.

"Kai, here," she said, handing to him a clipping of her jet-black hair tied with *olonā* string. "Please take it back. Knowing you once . . . held it kept me going the past few days."

"Of course, 'Eme, it's my dearest possession. My life ended when I returned it to you . . . at the pier. 'Eme, please marry me. I promise to care for Kaikai like my own!"

"Yes, Kai, I am yours," she said with a final glow. "Thank you . . . for taking my soiled . . . body."

'Eme's bleeding stopped. Kainoa was delighted. Then he saw her arms slump to her side. "'Eme!" he yelled hysterically, "Don't go!" She barely opened her eyes. Kainoa realized her bleeding had stopped because her poor heart had nothing more to pump. With deep remorse he closed her eyes for the ages with his finger, and stared at a green, iridescent sunset that closed 'Eme's brief sojourn on earth. He at last found the forgiveness in his soul that had remained hidden.

Kainoa started downhill early next morning carrying a limp, gore-smeared 'Eme to her *'ili*. He crossed paths with Kalanimoku. "You did it?" he asked.

Kainoa nodded.

Kalanimoku glared at him and continued walking without offering help. He rushed to Ka'ahumanu's *kauhale*. "Get up," he said. "Kainoa killed 'Eme! He was walking down the Puowaina trail carrying a bloody, dead 'Eme. We crossed paths. I asked him, 'You did it?' He nodded."

The village of Honolulu burst with a sensational rumor. "Did you hear?" the people whispered. "Kainoa, out of jealousy, murdered 'Eme!"

"That's impossible," most said. Different versions of the ugly news spread.

Ka'ahumanu told Kalanimoku, "Open a trial, bring a murder charge against him, find him guilty and flog him to death in public. The Kahu will give us high marks for getting rid of even one pagan. Maybe, he'll baptize us sooner."

Kalanimoku smiled. "I'll ask Paul Rimick to be the judge. That American sea captain owes me a lot. I gave him so much inter-island shipping business. He'll favor us."

Though hardly a lawyer, Captain Rimick relented to Kalanimoku's pressure. "All right, I will take the case. Find me any book on procedural rules of law for a murder case, please."

Tall and slender, Rimick had a kindly face. His receding forehead and shaggy complexion, rusted by salt sprays, made him appear older than his fifty-one years.

He was born and raised in Medford, near Boston, by his mother. Paul Rimick never knew his father Sam, a corporal in the Federalist army. He was only two when the English redcoats shot him dead during his retreat with Washington's forces after the failed Battle of Brandywine.

His mother Betsy didn't remarry. She stuck to corn farming, and earned barely enough to put bread on the table for her family of two children.

From his youth, Paul longed for a seafaring career. Through years of faithful service to the Baileys of Boston, owners of several brigs and schooners, Rimick received command of their one hundred twelve-foot trader, *Shenandoah,* now in Hawaiian waters with a crew of ten.

After looking for two days, Kalanimoku told Rimick, "Foreign sea captains tell me they neva heard rules of law."

"Then can I try this case based on what I know about the American legal system, and on common sense and fair play?"

"I guess, but this case is simple, you no need to read rules. Kainoa killed 'Eme. He admitted it to me. He's guilty of murder and must die."

"He must first get a fair trial," Rimick replied. "Sir, one more thing. Will the kingdom accept my verdict as being final?"

"Of course, Captain. And after the verdict I promise you more inter-island shipping contracts."

"Thank you," Rimick replied. He caught the bribery attempt.

For his court, Ka'ahumanu picked a spot beneath the sprawling branches of a banyan tree standing on her Honolulu *kauhale*. She handled business of the kingdom wherever she happened to be.

"I need two wooden tables and twelve stools for me and my witness, and two long benches, one for the defense, the other for the prosecution," Rimick asked Kalanimoku.

He had them hacked and delivered.

The trial opened just three weeks after 'Eme's death. A constable led Kainoa, hands in rope, to the left-side bench. His supporters, over three hundred, gathered behind him on dirt. They called the trial, "Kū vs. Jehovah."

Morning sunbeams leaking through banyan branches cast shifting light on Kainoa sitting pathetically alone on the long bench. He seemed doped with melancholy. The smell of *lehua* blossoms from a nearby patch aroused him. "'Eme!" he yelled.

A constable escorted Reverend Bingham and Kalanimoku to the right bench. Ka'ahumanu arrived to join them in Honolulu's first court murder trial. It took her attendants all of ten minutes to get her off the litter and seated. The bench creaked. Naihe, who had gained notoriety for slipping poison into Davis's *'ōkolehao*, and hefty Kuakini joined the Kuhina nui on the same bench. It bowed to the brink. Only few *kānaka* missionary supporters sat behind them.

Judge Rimick arrived in his captain's uniform and glanced to see if all the participants were present.

Satisfied, he sat down, pounded his gavel awkwardly and announced, "This court is now in session. Kainoa Kahemoku, please rise. You are the Defendant in this case and the Government of the Kingdom of Hawai'i is the Plaintiff." Looking into Kainoa's eyes, Rimick said, "You are being charged by the Government with murder in the first degree of 'Eme Alapa'i. Do you plead innocent or guilty?"

"Captain, sir, what is first degree murder?"

"Defendant Kainoa, and every participant in this trial, address me only as, 'Your Honor' in this court. Is that clear?"

"Yes, sir, captain, Your Honor," Kainoa stumbled.

"Now to your earlier question. Murder in the first degree means murder planned beforehand and carried out willfully, not by accident."

"Not guilty, Your Honor."

Kalanimoku shook his head, told the Kuhina nui, "What a liar."

"Defendant Kainoa, who do you wish to represent you?"

"I don't need anyone, Your Honor."

"So noted. Is two weeks enough time to prepare for your defense?"

"Your Honor, I can start now. I won't need time to make up a story."

Rimick hinted a smile. "Very well, you may sit."

"Captain Michael Chaplain, please rise."

"Yes, sir, Your Honor."

"Please tell this court who you are and what was your relationship with the decedent 'Eme Alapa'i."

"My name is Michael Chaplain, an American trader born and raised in Salem, Massachusetts. I am captain of my ship, *Morning Star*, docked in Honolulu Harbor.

"I loved decedent 'Eme Alapa'i. She was my common-law wife."

"For how long?"

"About two years. I proposed marriage, maybe six times, but she didn't respond, Your Honor."

"As her common law husband, you have certain rights. Do you wish to join the Government as plaintiff against the defendant in this case?"

The question surprised him. "I decline, Your Honor."

"Please tell this court why."

"I will hurt the prosecution, Your Honor."

"Request granted."

The judge addressed Ka'ahumanu. "Your Majesty, you may remain seated. Please tell this court who will represent the Plaintiff, the Government?"

She ad-libbed, "Naihe Kalanikoa, Your Honor," pointing to the man seated at the end of her bench. Naihe was shocked. She had never asked him before.

"Naihe Kalanikoa, please rise."

Two men lifted him. It was not easy for a short four hundred-pound man to rise without a struggle. "You have been appointed to represent the Plaintiff. Do you accept?"

"I guess, Your Honor."

"Yes or no?"

"I guess, yes."

"How much preparation time will you need?"

"I know little about this case, Your Honor. Since Defendant is ready, can you let him start, we listen, then we prepare our case?"

"Very well. Defendant Kainoa, please rise. You have been asked to start first. You don't have to. Do you accept?"

"Yes, I have no problem."

"All right. You are innocent of the charge unless I find you guilty beyond a doubt. I am the sole judge. My verdict is final. There is no appeal. If I find you guilty, your penalty is immediate death by flogging. Is that very clear?"

"Yes, Your Honor."

"Defendant Kainoa, please come to this chair. Stand and face me." Kainoa obeyed. "Raise your right hand and repeat after me: 'I swear to tell this court all the truth and nothing but the truth, so help me, God.'"

Kainoa hesitated. "Your Honor, I will tell the truth, I don't need god's help."

"All right, but giving false testimony is like hiding guilt. Penalty for it can also be immediate death by flogging. Is that clear?"

"Clear, Your Honor."

"Please sit. Tell this court who you are, about your world, about decedent 'Eme Alapa'i, and how she died. You may take as long as you wish."

Kainoa glanced at Pualani, Lani and Mākaha. After a pause he began to speak for his life.

"I am Kainoa Kahemoku, born in 1797 in our Makiki, O'ahu 'ili that our last Mō'ī gave to my father as a reward for his bravery at 'Iao and Nu'uanu. He recently died. My mother Kapua, a former kapu chiefess, also died several months ago.

"We lived next to the Alapa'i kauhale. Mākaha Alapa'i, seated there, became my best friend. When my father went into hiding from his creditors in 1810, the Alapa'i family took care of me like family. I became like big brother to Mākaha and his sisters, 'Eme and Lani.

"As time went by 'Eme and I became close. We didn't know at that time that love, nature's most powerful force, was bringing us together.

"A very important day in our lives happened several years later. We were hunting for chicken eggs along the slopes of Puowaina (Punchbowl) in Honolulu when I saw a half-moon-shaped opening behind some trees on the western slope. I told her, 'Let's go see.'

"I scratched a path to it. We came to a cave and went inside. It just had a feel of a place that Time forgot. We made it our secret hide-away. 'Eme named it, *'Hale'ano'i,'* the house of love.

"That is where we first expressed our eternal love for each other, and where our souls joined, became one. We just sat with eyes closed, promised each other, 'Forever.'

"We had lots of free time growing up. I frequently went to the 'Iliwaina Stream where it meets the Waimalu Creek at the border of Pu'uloa, to catch huge *'ōpae* (freshwater shrimps). Once I followed the Waimalu to Pu'uloa Loko (Lake) Pa'akea and dove down just for fun. I saw at the bottom of sand and mud from the river large shellfish five to six inches across that looked like *'ōlepe* (mussels). I brought back a few to *Hale'ano'i.* 'Eme and I opened the shell lids with rock chisel and tried to eat them raw, but they were inedible, hard smell, tough. One had a swollen body. I squeezed it. I was shocked when a deep blue-colored *momi* (pearl) about half-inch in diameter came out. It reflected many colors.

"I didn't know the value of *momi.* I showed it to a captain at the wharf. He gave me five dollars in gold for it. Five dollars! And he wanted more.

"I found something that I could sell!

"I sneaked back regularly after that to Pu'uloa Loko Pa'akea. I kept the big *momi* and sold the rest to sea captains. They liked the lustrous, deep-blue inner surface of the shells and wanted them, too. I began paying off father's debts with *momi* and shell money. By the end of 1818, we were clean. We could once again walk in daylight. A big family burden was off my back.

"My *haole* customers eventually learned where I went for the *'ōlepe.* They nicknamed the Waimalu, 'Pearl River,' and Pu'uloa, 'Pearl Harbor,' because of me."

Kainoa took a deep breath and continued.

"Your Honor, in 1819, Queen Ka'ahumanu and her group of *ali'i* and *kāhuna* staged a spiritual revolution that lasted almost a year. It ended with our King Kamehameha dead, our religion and *heiau* crushed and our gods and our fundamental *kapu, 'Aikapu,* toppled.

"That *kapu,* against men eating with women to avoid getting polluted, had bound us Hawaiians for a millennium. When it vanished with our gods, we lost our identity. From the king down, we became just a group of Polynesians living on islands north of the equator."

"You have proof we did it?" the Kuhina nui screamed at Kainoa.

"Order, order. Your Majesty, do not interrupt. You will get your chance to respond without interruption. And speak only to me, not to the Defendant."

Ka'ahumanu showed the white of her eyes to Kainoa.

"Continue, Defendant Kainoa."

"Without our gods and religion, the King lost his omniscience, his divine right to rule and became a commoner. The *ali'i* could no longer claim genealogical lineage to their gods and they became commoners. Our three-tiered caste system vanished. Suddenly, the untouchable *kauā* slaves became commoners in our classless, godless new society."

Commoner Ka'ahumanu wiggled her rump and kept quiet. She knew he was right.

"A dramatic thing then happened. At every *heiau*, the mangled *ki'i akua* (god idols) that Ka'ahumanu and her chiefs had left for dead rose from the ruins. Moments before they died, the idols promised the *ali'i* perpetrators retribution of eternal life without food in *po* for their atrocities.

"The chiefs cracked from fright and lost their minds.

"In 1820 Christians from Boston arrived. They were on a mission to destroy our religion and turn us heathens into Bible-reading Christians of the absolute kind, or die trying. There was no middle ground.

"They learned that our chiefs had recently stamped out our pagan religion, but were now paranoid with fear of going to *po* for the atrocities they had committed against the gods. The missionaries seized the opportunity, soothed them with promise of the salvation of their *'unihipili* (spirit) in Christ.

"Our crazed chiefs and chiefesses reached for Jehovah in order to escape from *po*. Nothing else mattered with them. They paid little attention to the Kingdom's desperate needs for survival.

"In November 1821, I accepted the chance to go to Boston to study. I wanted to return home better equipped to change our course from doom. In Boston I received 'Eme's letter informing me that, in her loneliness, she was living with a Michael Chaplain onboard his boat. I wanted to hurry back and wring his neck.

"Then I got another letter informing me that she was pregnant with his baby. My life ceased to be vital.

"I returned to Honolulu three weeks ago and toured our village with Mākaha. With fresh eyes I saw the hopeless devastation of our sickly people. The *ali'i* were deeper into Jehovah, the survival needs of our Kingdom straggling and Kahu Bingham still dictating our lives, assuring the destruction of our pagan past and present. I pleaded with our Kuhina nui to establish a militia of just three hundred men to defend our depopulating *'āina*, and mount a gigantic effort to help save our *lāhui kānaka*. Since my pleadings didn't relate to Jehovah, she dismissed me.

"Your Honor, I had a rare chance to meet John Quincy Adams in Boston. He told me that if church and government became one, the cruel side of religion would suppress freedom and torment the people.

"Mr. Adams is right. With the Kahu's control over Her Majesty's mind, he is imposing his will on us. Your Honor, Jehovah is making us *kānaka* lose our freedom and go extinct."

The Kahu stood. "Your Honor, why do you let the Defendant waste our time listening to his groundless assertions?"

"Kahu Bingham, it's because I gave him a chance to speak for his life without interruption."

The Kahu's neck turned red, the color of the sacred *'ōhelo* berry, the body of Goddess Ka'ōhelo, Laka's sister. He waved a threatening finger at Kainoa and stalked out. Ka'ahumanu would have followed, but gravity kept her seated.

After taking a breath of air, the Kahu returned meekly to his bench. He didn't want to miss any of Kainoa's stinging testimony.

"Defendant Kainoa, I have a question," the judge said. "This John Quincy Adams you speak of, is he the present Secretary of State of America?"

"Yes, Your Honor."

"That's impossible," Bingham whispered to Ka'ahumanu.

Judge Rimick interrupted. "Defendant Kainoa, I think I know enough about you and your earlier relationship with the decedent. Can you tell this court what happened on the day she died?"

"Yes, Your Honor, I was getting to it."

"Last week, I left for *Hale'ano'i* and found 'Eme sitting on a rock near the cave. I melted seeing her forlorn eyes. Forgetting the past, I picked her up. Without spoken words, we embraced and shed our tears on each other for a very long time.

"She begged, 'Please forgive me, without you I went astray, lived aimlessly as the captain's mistress.'

"When I heard her say 'mistress,' I threw up my arms in despair. I must have grazed her. She lost her balance, fell and hit her forehead on a jagged rock. She started to bleed in spurts. I couldn't stop the flow. I asked her in panic, 'Please forgive me.'

"She smiled, gave me a soft nod and said, 'Take me to *Hale'ano'i*, then to home.'

"She died in *Hale'ano'i*. I won't describe our last private moments.

"We were again one in our cave that smelled of ancient earth. I was awake, unable to cope with the reality that 'Eme was dead. Suddenly, I had company. All the creatures that 'Eme and I carved—dog Laleo, gecko Le'i, fish Ama-ama, pig Momona, *honu* Kekai, fifteen in all, came off the cave wall and wailed with me, and returned at dawn to their places on the wall."

The Kahu whispered to Ka'ahumanu, "Now I'm sure he lost his mind." Strangely, she didn't agree.

"In the morning, I took her in my arms and started down the trail to take her home as she wished. I crossed paths with Kalanimoku. He stared at a limp 'Eme. 'You did it?' he asked. I nodded. He continued to walk, offered no help.

"Pualani, Lani and Mākaha were shocked when I entered their *kauhale* carrying a limp 'Eme with a large forehead wound. I tearfully laid her down, told them what had happened, and begged for their forgiveness.

"Mother Pualani reached for 'Eme's cold wrist, maybe for a hint of pulse. Two constables arrived. They tied rope around my arms and told me, 'Come to the fort.'

"Horrified, I told them, 'Let me go, I must prepare for a funeral.'

"When they refused I went berserk. But they had the clubs. I can show you the marks I still have on my body.

"I later learned that Mākaha went to see the Crown Prince. By his order, I was released. I ran back to the Alapa'i compound, found 'Eme dressed beautifully by Lani in her favorite green *pā'ū*, wearing a *lei haku* that hid her forehead gash.

"In a far away corner, I saw a *haole* weeping. I learned he was Michael Chaplain. I went over, extended my hand, not thinking of wringing his neck. We shook hands, but he avoided making eye contact.

"After 'Eme's funeral, I let the marshals take me back to prison, peacefully this time.

"Your Honor, that is my story. I am ready to answer any question."

Judge Rimick listened with stoic countenance, appearing unmoved. "Defendant Kainoa, I have a question. Where is 'Eme?"

"Your Honor, is it important?"

"Yes, I need closure."

"All right.

"With the consent of the Alapa'i family, I went to *Hale'ano'i* and dug two holes, one for me. Mākaha helped me. Michael Chaplain joined with a shovel without being asked.

"I then returned to the Alapa'i compound, took 'Eme in my arms and headed for *Hale'ano'i* the last time together. Her family, friends, and Michael followed behind. She was so light I never had to rest. No one had the chance to carry her. She was all mine.

"I laid her down on the floor of the hole covered with banana leaves and hundreds of white *lehua* blossoms of the sacred *'ōhi'a* tree that the Alapa'i family brought. While my old *kāhuna* friends offered prayers, I filled 'Eme's navel with salt, placed in her hands a pouch with two dark pearls, and covered her with red *lehua* blossoms until she disappeared. The *kāhuna* began filling the hole with cinder soil. The finality of it left me crazed.

"I saw Mrs. Chaplain sobbing nearby. She surprised me.

"I placed over the cinder mound a *hau* bowl with two red *lehua* blossoms floating on fresh water, like what I found at *Hale'ano'i* on the day I returned from Boston.

"She is resting at *Hale'ano'i*. I know she is happier there than anywhere else.

"That is it, Your Honor."

"Thank you, Defendant Kainoa. Before I ask Chief Naihe to cross-examine you, would anyone here wish to be Defendant Kainoa's character witness? If so, please stand."

Nearly three hundred stood. "Wait a moment," Rimick said. I don't have to hear from everybody. Let me select a few.

"Mrs. Pualani Alapa'i, I recognize you. Please stand." She rose, holding on to Mākaha's arm. "Defendant Kainoa admits doing something that caused your daughter to fall, strike her forehead on a rock, and bleed to death. What do you say?"

Pualani struggled to establish her composure. "Your Honor, Kainoa is a kind man, a hero of the kingdom. He was a faithful lover of my dear daughter. I believe his spoken words. My daughter died in an accident. Kainoa had no intent to kill her, Your Honor."

The Judge caught Mākaha nodding.

"Thank you. You both may sit.

"I recognize Kauikeaouli, the Crown Prince. Your Highness, I saw you standing. Please tell this court what you think of the Defendant."

The child tried to stand tall. "Your Honor, my brother Liholiho, King Kamehameha the Second, told me before he left for London that there were only five persons in our entire kingdom I can completely trust. Kainoa was one of them. I love him. I just want you to know that."

The court erupted with sobbing applause.

"Thank you, Your Highness. I am calling just one more person." The crowd wondered whom. "Captain Michael Chaplain, I recognize you. Have you anything to say about the Defendant and his earlier testimony?"

"Yes, Your Honor." Michael glanced at Pualani and said, "I am a trader but I remained in Hawai'i because I loved decedent 'Eme Alapa'i. I fathered our son Kaikai seated with me. I proposed marriage many times to her but she didn't respond.

"On the day she died, she asked me, 'Can I go to *Hale'ano'i?*' I read in her eyes that she hoped to meet Kainoa there. When I agreed, her face lit with joy. It was a face . . ." Mikaele paused, "a face I had not seen for a long time, serenely happy. She asked me to care for Kaikai, kissed us both, and left. Her steps were livelier. I told myself, if she did not return she was never mine.

"I became frantic seeing her leave my life. My love for Kaikai welled as if he was replacing 'Eme.

"I met the Defendant for the first time on the day we buried 'Eme. When I entered *Hale'ano'i* with my shovel to help dig 'Eme's grave, it felt like a *kapu* place where I did not belong. I realized then that she was always Kainoa's. He won, but in the end we both lost.

"After 'Eme's service, I threw some cinder soil into the grave and crawled out. I had no strength left."

Kainoa listened, head down.

"Now about the Defendant's testimony. I heard him speak for the first time today. As captain of a ship, I'm always managing people; most times I know when a man is lying. I can say that Defendant Kainoa was telling the whole truth about how 'Eme died. I believe he had no intent to kill 'Eme."

"Thank you, captain. I say there is no further need for character witnesses. Counselor Naihe Kalanikoa, you may now cross-examine Defendant Kainoa."

Naihe's attendants again helped him to his feet; he remained silent for a minute then stunned the court.

"After hearing what our Crown Prince and others said about Defendant Kainoa, I heard the voice of the people that is the voice of God. I will not cross-examine the Defendant. The kingdom rests, Your Honor."

"Thank you. You may sit," the Judge said. Strangely, Reverend Bingham and Ka'ahumanu remained calm, their earlier arrogance gone.

Naihe told the Judge, "Before I sit, may I question the Defendant about his earlier statement that a militia of three hundred men can defend our *'āina?*"

"Your question is irrelevant to this case. You may go ahead and ask, but be brief."

Turning his full weight at Kainoa, he said, "I fought with your father at 'Īao and Nu'uanu. You were never in the army. From my experience, I can tell you that a militia of three hundred men can never win a war. Would you like to comment?"

"May I, Your Honor?" Kainoa asked.

"Go ahead. Whatever you say is also irrelevant to this case."

"Understood." Kainoa faced Naihe.

"At 'Īao and Nu'uanu, the army on either side could have crushed Napoleon's best. The warriors were strong, fast and unafraid to die for their Ali'i Kāne." Naihe smiled broadly. "In such battles, both sides need big armies to overcome the other.

"But look at our opposition today. The *haole* off the ships have nothing to die for in Hawai'i. So if just fifty of our well-trained warriors charged them with the latest equipment, they will turn and run."

"*Ae, ae!*" the *kānaka* in court bellowed.

"Order!" the judge demanded for the third time.

"Defendant Kainoa, we got the gist. Save further explanation for another time. Counselor Naihe, please sit, I want to conclude this case."

"Yes, Your Honor, thank you for the chance to question the Defendant. I say I agree with him."

Kainoa was proud of his militia comments before Ka'ahumanu, Bingham and other Christian *ali'i* who were against him.

Judge Rimick leaned forward from his stool and looked straight at Kainoa with his mind made. The outdoor court hushed.

"Defendant Kainoa, based on your earlier testimony that the Government has not challenged, I agree with Captain Chaplain and Mrs. Alapa'i that you had no intent to kill the decedent, 'Eme Alapa'i."

The audience erupted again. The judge rapped his gavel.

"Kainoa, you could be charged with manslaughter in America. But in Hawai'i, there is no law against it. The Kingdom recognizes only four crimes, premeditated murder, burglary, dancing the *hula*, and adultery. I therefore rule that you are innocent of the Government's only charge of premeditated murder in the first degree."

Ka'ahumanu stood without help and asked, "Your Honor, can I add manslaughter now?"

"Yes, you can. But it will apply only to future cases, not to this one. It's over. Guards, untie Defendant Kainoa's hands. Set him free. This case is closed, the court is adjourned."

A wild celebration by Kainoa sympathizers erupted. Many danced illegal *hula* to the beat of clapping hands.

The decision failed to cheer Kainoa. His thoughts were too deeply immersed below a layer of red *lehua* blossoms. Michael, of puritanical upbringing, was in deep remorse. He cursed himself for living in sin after he learned from 'Eme about Kainoa inside his ship's map room.

Michael remained in Hawai'i long after the trial to expiate his troubled soul, if he could. He sold the stuffs from Zhou still jammed in his ship's hold and donated the entire proceeds to Mākaha for his retreats. He spent time in Kaka'ako Camp Two and helped prepare last suppers for many.

29

"It's time we go home," Michael suggested to his family months after the trial. Meriam, who had thinned noticeably, for once made it unanimous. While Michael was preparing for the journey home, Deborah often went to a *hula* festival site near Kewalo Camp One, and to Manoa valley to pick mountain apples near a stream, to recall her treasured moments in Hawai'i.

She was still suffering from Mākaha's rejection. On a rebound, Deborah accepted Ashley Cooper's persistent letter-proposal of marriage in New York.

Mākaha heard and languished. *I wish you happiness,* he whispered.

In December 1824, Michael, joined by Kaikai and his parents, called on the Alapa'i family. Debo remained onboard the *Morning Star*, unable to bear another painful moment with Mākaha if he were at home.

"*E komo mai,* welcome. What a surprise," Pualani said when they arrived.

"We came to say goodbye, Mother Pualani. We are leaving for Salem in the morning. I am very sorry, Mother Pualani, I feel responsible for all this." Gripping her hand, Michael repeated, "I am sorry."

Even Meriam shed a drop.

Pualani and Lani accepted Michael's plaintive cry with a nod.

"Mikaele, I've been wanting to ask you," Pualani said. "Can I *makua hānai* Kaikai? Adopt him? I will raise him like my child, give him all my love. And one day, when you return to Hawai'i, a proud Hawaiian boy will be waiting for you. He is 'Eme!"

She shocked Michael. "Yes, he is 'Eme. That is why I am taking Kaikai back to Salem. I love him. I am changing his name to Kainoa, Kainoa Chaplain."

"You're taking Kaikai? I will lose another?"

Mākaha interrupted her.

"Mother, the captain is his father. Let him take his son. I hope Kainoa and I will become best friends after he grows up."

"That's beautiful, Michael. I know 'Eme will approve," Lani said, and embraced Michael for the first time. With her head at his heart she whispered, "We'll see you in the morning."

Leslie whispered something to Pualani.

"Thank you, *aloha*," she said.

Mamo watched the drama unfold. Now forty-nine, he was aging beautifully, his hair more white than black. And he was in distress. He asked, "Captain, can I go with you to Salem, work on your farm, help you raise Kaikai, be his friend, talk stories of Hawai'i and the warm family he left behind, captain?"

Michael dropped his hat. The unexpected surprised him. "Of . . . course, Mamo. You may . . . if Pualani agrees," he said.

"Lose you, too?" Pualani asked, looking distressfully into Mamo's eyes.

"You're not losing anyone," Lani said. "No one can take away your memories of Kaikai and Mamo. 'Eme will be so happy if Mamo went and continued to watch over Kaikai."

Pualani regained her poise. "Yes, thank you, Mamo!" she cried.

On boat day, Mamo embraced Pualani and Mākaha with his eyes shut, knowing it would be for the ages. Usually unemotional, Mamo's face contorted. He tried to utter something, but the mumble remained in his throat.

Pualani heard every word.

Lani whispered to Michael, "Goodbye, take good care of Kaikai, I love him. I love you, too."

Love me? Michael choked.

Naihe appeared at the shore with four *maile lei*. He draped them over departing shoulders and left without a spoken word.

Morning Star began to pull away. Kaikai waved as if he was going on a short joyride. Michael saw Lani weaving through the crowd. He gave her a teary wave in slow motion when their eyes met. Lani waved back, her elegant face wet.

Pualani collapsed, then got up and waved to a distant ship. After passing the breakers, Michael and Mamo pitched their *lei* overboard, knowing they would float to shore to nourish the *'āina*.

"Look, Mamo, the rainbow over Nu'uanu Valley," Michael said.

"Yes Captain, Hawai'i nei is bidding us *aloha.*"

§

In Summer of 1825, *Morning Star* slipped into Salem harbor after a smooth, unexciting journey. Leslie and Deborah, gripped with nostalgia for the Isles, thought of turning back several times.

Just weeks after returning, Meriam suddenly passed away. At her burial, pagan Deborah draped on her shoulders Naihe's long-withered *maile lei* and chanted a tearful *aloha*.

Leslie, 57, was lost in Salem. He walked his family fields brooding over the land he left behind and recalling his times with Pualani. He missed her face, her smell, her voice. He missed Pualaninoe.

Deborah was busy packing for her impending move to Dobbs Ferry to become Mrs. Ashley Cooper.

In September 1825, Leslie received a letter from Lani.

March 25, 1825

My dear Chaplains:

Mother and I are hoping all of you are safely back. Fall must be beautiful. Kainoa often told us about your colorful autumn leaves, how they would fall and cover the walkways and crunch under the feet.

I have a sad message. Kainoa passed away last week of heartache. He knew he was dying. He asked Mākaha to take him to *Hale'ano'i*. He wanted to finish a wall engraving of 'Eme's other *'aumakua*, an owl. Lola. Mākaha said Kainoa finished the engraving with aid of a divine hand just before he dropped the rock graver.

It was impossible for him to live on without 'Eme. They are now one.

We experienced two miracles during his burial at *Hale'ano'i*. Kahu Bingham and Ka'ahumanu came with white *lehua*-blossom *lei* in hand and dropped them into Kainoa's grave, pagan style. The people saw love and compassion override hate. At that instant the creatures, led by Lola, came off the wall to comfort us. They stunned Bingham. He saw pagan power rising to its pinnacle. The Queen didn't appear shocked. I guess she knew the awesome power of pagan spirit, for deep down she was still a *kanaka queen*.

Please inform Mr. Kincaid and the Nobles of Kainoa's passing. Kai always felt indebted and close to them.

Aloha nui loa, Lani

Leslie just folded the letter and grieved. Some weeks later he called Michael. "Son," he said, "there is nothing I want to do in Salem. I am thinking of returning to Hawai'i after Deborah's wedding. Would you approve?"

"Pualani?"

"Yes, son. I've thought of marrying her if she would have me."

"Father, yes! I wanted to return to Hawai'i, too, with Kainoa and Mamo. I still can't get Lani off my mind, but for Kainoa's sake I've decided to stay in Salem, raise him here and put him through Yale. Go Dad. I know you'll be happier there. It won't be a final farewell, we'll meet again."

Father and son hugged, became closer than ever.

Leslie called Deborah. "Debo, I just made a big decision. After your wedding, I am returning to Hawai'i, hope to marry Pualani and live there."

Deborah jumped. "Father, please excuse me. I am about to do something . . . something horrible."

"Horrible?"

"Father, I am writing to Ashley that I can't marry him. I don't love him. I thought I would change, but I have not. Can I join you?"

"Mākaha?" he asked.

Deborah nodded. "I am ready to die if he won't have me."
Father understood. "Of course you can."

And then,

Michael never remarried, became a dedicated father, defended Kainoa from anyone critical of his color. He plied his trade as a sea captain. He let Morning Star and his two sons run the farm and Mamo care for Kainoa during his absence.

By 14, with his active Polynesian genes, Kainoa was a big boy, brilliant in his studies. But Mamo, 59, never let him forget his heritage, the language of his birth, and the time he waved to Pualani onboard the *Morning Star* when he was going for a short joyride. Alas, fighting goiter, Mamo was at peace in the twilight zone when his end came, knowing he had served the Alapa'i family well during his borrowed time on earth.

In Hawai'i, Mrs. Pualani Chaplain began a new life with her loving, *malo*-wearing husband who was fast developing a *poi* belly.

Lani, deluged by marriage offers, accepted the proposal of Mahi Kalihi, her shy, long-time admirer. Michael faded into antiquity.

Mākaha, brooding over the loss of Debo to Ash, saw a Hawaiian, not a *haole* when she returned to Hawai'i.

Mrs. Kepola (Deborah) Alapa'i, still scorned by the missionaries, eventually could commune with Laka in over a hundred *mele* (chants) on private stages. Dancing or watching the *hula* was still a crime. With the Goddess at her side, she became one of the great *hula* performers of her time and was unequaled with the *kālā'au* (sticks) that she made from dried *kauila* wood. She proved to her peers that a *haole* could spiritually connect with native deities and move the earth.

During the day pagan Debo toiled as one of her husband's dwindling volunteers in his retreats in a hopeless struggle. Hawai'i nei was sinking with the weight of her dead.

In 1832, Ka'ahumanu was on her death bed repeating, "O Jesus, here I am." Suddenly, the attendants heard her plead, "Oh please . . . !" as if He had turned away.

After her passing, powerful Hawaiian folks like Queen Kīna'u and Kalanimoku moved to the Kahu's side. With their support, the Christian religion continued to surge while the fortunes of Hawai'i sank.

But Hawai'i was too beautiful and young to die.

§

A brief sixty years later, in 1893, a clique of entrenched alien planters, sons of missionaries and assorted riffraff sniffed opportunity, staged a major *coup*. They booted out the Hawaiian Queen with Uncle Sam's aid, abolished the Monarchy as Alapa'i and Kainoa feared, and took legal reins of government. *Haole ali'i* became the new ruling class; *kānaka* became alien peasants in their native soil.

The Queen's loyalists fought back to restore her reign. But the ineffective band soon gave up, leaving the clique in absolute control of their newly created Provisional Republic of Hawai'i.

The clique handed the sovereignty of Hawai'i to a willing United States in 1898. "Manifest Destiny," someone whispered.

In the Annexation Ceremony at the Palace, a Portuguese trumpeter from the Royal Hawaiian Band, standing on the second floor of the Palace near Queen Liliuokalani's room, played, with moist eyes, *Hawai'i Pono'ī*, Hawai'i's national anthem, as Uncle Sam lowered the flag created by Kamehameha. No Hawaiian wanted the tune to end. When the flag reached bottom, a United States marine sounded Taps, accompanied by a ruffle of drums while a marine crew folded the Hawaiian flag.

Wākea stared accusingly at Kamehameha and Ka'ahumanu who were watching the event from a c: *Lani e*.

A United States marine then began to raise the 46-star Stars and Stripes to the tune of *The Stars Spangled Banner* played by the navy band from the USS *Mohican* at a fast tempo. Exuding compassion, Uncle Sam whispered to god Wākea, "I'm sorry."

A momentous thud shook the Isles when the American flag reached the top of the Palace pole. The Kingdom on free fall hit bottom with such a transcendent force that it ruptured *Lani e*, spilling the *'uhane* of over five million *kānaka* since the discovery of Hawai'i by the Marquesans in 775 AD, to wander in an alien land.

Mākaha's homeless *'uhane* shrieked. *Father, how could this happen to our land created and blessed by God Hawai'iloa?*

Father remained silent.

The Kingdom could have survived, Kainoa cried. *A force of only three hundred willing to die for our 'āina could have whipped those aliens and Uncle Sam's marines combined, and saved our Kingdom. Shame on us, don't blame the clique or Uncle Sam for our tragedy, blame our ali'i for oiling their way.*

Mākaha agreed.

Can we ever return to Lani e? 'Eme asked her father in panic.

No, 'Eme. There are too few kānaka left to confront Uncle Sam. Hawai'i nei, Lani e and pono are now legend!

Holding 'Eme tightly, Kainoa added, *But our 'āina will never fade away and die. It will rise daily forever somewhere in the Isles as a bright rainbow, to remind the living that a Kingdom and people too young and beautiful to die once thrived on this land.*